HYPNOSIS ON TRIAL

HYPNOSIS ON TRIAL

Anatomy
of a
Murder Case

A novel by

STEPHEN HRONES

SMALL BATCH BOOKS
AMHERST, MASSACHUSETTS

Printed in the United States of America

Cover and interior design by Susan Turner

ISBN: 978-1-951568-45-0
Library of Congress Control Number: 2024908380

SMALL
BATCH
BOOKS

493 South Pleasant Street
Amherst, Massachusetts 01002
413.230.3943
smallbatchbooks.com

To all criminal defense lawyers, whose client is the U.S. Constitution.

CONTENTS

CONTENTS

HYPNOSIS ON TRIAL

1

The Crime

"WITH EVERY BREATH, YOUR HEAD WILL BECOME HEAVY AND HEAVIER, so heavy, so relaxed, so heavy and so relaxed. And now, if you would, I'd like you, Julie, to see yourself in a beautiful, luxurious hotel on the twentieth floor. You're feeling so good, so comfortable. And you're walking across a lush carpet, and we're getting into the elevator. Inside this elevator, you will find yourself going deeper and deeper than you are now. This, then, is your elevator of relaxation. The doors are closing . . . twenty, nineteen . . . this elevator is descending . . . eighteen, seventeen . . . deeper still . . . sixteen, fifteen, fourteen . . . deeper and deeper . . . thirteen, twelve, eleven, ten, nine, eight, seven, six, five . . . so deep, lower, lower . . . four, three, two, one. You're doing so good, Julie, so good and you're so comfortable."

Detective Ben Ripley, the police hypnotist, was slowly hypnotizing Julie Connors, the key prosecution witness, in an effort to help her better "recall" what she had seen the night of the murder. He wanted to get this right. The words of Gus Grazzi, the crusty veteran homicide detective who led the case, echoed in his head: "This is one of the most vicious killings I have ever seen. We have a real psycho on the loose."

ON THE MORNING OF OCTOBER 30, 1979, Doug O'Brian, an employee of the Atlas Brothers, the construction company doing renovation work on 283 Beacon Street for James Realty Trust, unlocked the front door of the stately, four-story brick structure on fashionable Beacon Street, near the Boston Commons in the Back Bay area of Boston, to begin the day's work. Upon entering the building, at the bottom of the flight of stairs leading to the second floor, he spotted a navy-blue cape, with the number 624 on its collar, splattered with blood. Halfway up the stairway, there was blood splatter and brain matter, and on the third and fourth steps from the top, was a large pool of blood, a pair of eyeglasses, and a Marlboro cigarette pack. He hesitated to continue on, but his curiosity got the better of him.

He cautiously entered the gutted second-floor front room, which was being renovated. The floor was torn up, and plastic sheeting blocked off the other rooms. He stopped short as his eyes focused on a body ten feet from the entrance. She lay on her back with her feet toward the front of the building. Her head, covered in blood, was angled slightly to the left. Her only clothing was a lavender sweater pulled up over her left breast, which bore a one-inch red-rose tattoo. The end of a broomstick protruded from between her legs. Doug didn't need to see anymore. He turned and fled the building, frantically searching for a pay phone.

———

DETECTIVE GUS GRAZZI HAD BEEN a Boston police officer for twenty-eight years, most of those in the homicide unit. He was best known for his big cigars, which he was virtually never without. They had turned his teeth yellow. He always appeared to be on the last inch or two. Short and fat, he had grown up in the rough-and-tumble Italian neighborhood of Boston's North End, where there were only good guys and bad guys. They were either with you or against you.

The detective hated defendants almost as much as he adored his Garcia y Vega cigars. As he arrived at the murder scene, Gus caught a quick glimpse of the sign on the front of the under-construction house: "Spacious 2 to 3 Bedroom Units With Balconies, Totally New Renovation. Parking Available. From $175,000."

He entered the building and mounted the half-finished stairway. Puddles of blood stained the splintered furring strips, as well as the crumbled plaster, sawdust, and rusty pipes. The early morning sun broke sharply through the windows of the second-floor apartment onto the plywood flooring. The handsome brick fireplace with solid oak mantel and Victorian mirror caught the detective's attention, for a split second, before he focused on the body.

Gus observed a few coins scattered about, but there was no wallet or woman's purse in the area that he could see. He found a shopping list near the body with this notation on it: "Pick up cape at 7:20 a.m. at Jonathan's." He had noted a cape on the first floor when he entered.

Gus called in the identification section to take photos and search for fingerprints. He notified the crime lab and the medical examiner's office.

The victim was pronounced dead at 7:43 a.m.

The fingerprint man dusted the blood-smeared ankle of the victim, plus the surrounding area, for latent prints. He later attempted to develop prints on the broom found in the victim's vagina with the ninhydrin and silver nitrate method.

Gus conferred with the other officers who had arrived at the scene. "What do you have, Bill?"

"Nothing yet, Gus. We've searched the building and area and turned up no suspects. There are all kinds of potential murder weapons—bricks, pipes, assorted tools. But we've found nothing that appears to be the weapon."

"Have you checked the alleyway yet?"

"Not yet."

Gus and the officers went to the alley in the rear of the building to search through the rubble, piled there as a result of the renovation work, for the murder weapon and any other evidence.

"Check out this here dumpster," ordered Gus. It was six feet high. An officer went in search of a ladder.

"It appears that the murderer and victim gained access to the building from this alley," observed Gus. There were three punched-out windows and an entrance without a door. "I bet she knew the guy. I don't see evidence of a struggle until you get to the stairway. She must have entered the building with him voluntarily." The other officers agreed.

An elderly man was rummaging through the rubble. He was dressed in a trench coat, polished shoes, creased blue trousers, and a white pressed shirt.

"You can't take things from around here," bellowed Gus. "We're investigating a murder." The detective stared menacingly at the old man as he dropped a piece of BX cable and walked away, down the alley. Gus signaled by a nod of the head to one of the officers to follow the old man. The officer caught up to him and demanded, "What were you looking for?"

"A souvenir," replied the old man.

"What kind of souvenir?"

"I don't know. I've never seen the scene of a murder before. The word in the neighborhood is someone was murdered here. I'd like to go inside. Maybe find a shoe. Yeah, a shoe."

"What would you do with the shoe?" asked the officer, rolling his eyes.

"Put it in a box," answered the old man.

A blond woman who looked to be in her thirties stood on the balcony of the house next to the murder scene, her arms folded across a white sweater.

"Can I ask you a question?" the woman yelled.

The cop didn't respond.

"Are you investigating a murder?"

"I can't tell you that, ma'am."

"You know what I think?" the woman exclaimed. "I think this whole neighborhood is making me nauseous. Two weeks ago, I was asleep and I heard someone trying to break open my front door. I ran out my back door and went into my next-door neighbor's house and called the police. They came and caught these bums. One of the robbers had a huge knife. I've lived here six years, and it is getting terrible. How did the girl get killed?"

"I can't tell you that," responded the cop.

"If they catch the guy who did it, they should castrate him," said the woman as she withdrew from the balcony.

After supervising the futile search of the alleyway, Gus interviewed Ginger Dodds, a nurse in her late twenties who lived on Marlborough Street, a block from where the murder took place.

"I never park my car in the alley, even though I have a spot. I park on the street, illegally if I have to. I'll gladly pay the ticket, as long as I live to pay it. One of the things you're aware of here is the police. They patrol often. They're very good. But they can't be there all the time. I keep in mind, also, that although there are expensive condos here, they are often right next door to a twenty-five-dollars-a-week boardinghouse that attracts a lot of transients. You see many strange faces.

"But you learn to do things. When you park in the street, you wait until a group of cars is coming down the street before you get out. Most nights, I'll circle the block a few times before I'll park."

While on their way back to District Four from interviewing neighbors near the murder, Gus and his partner, Lou Levitt, received word over the radio that the victim was identified as Sasha Lewis of 559 Dartmouth Street. Gus immediately headed for that address. The victim's name on the directory listed her as living in the basement apartment. The building itself was a handsome one, constructed in brick and not unlike many others in the area, having been built in the nineteenth century. Solid-stone steps led up to a covered entryway. Although the basement apartment could be entered from the front, there was also a back door that exited into a small courtyard, enclosed by a brick wall. An alleyway separated 559 Dartmouth Street from the adjacent building. The murder site was some one hundred yards down the alleyway on the right from the victim's apartment.

Gus and Lou went in through the main door of the building and found the front door to the victim's apartment slightly ajar. They proceeded to enter the one-bedroom unit. It was untidy, but there did not appear to have been a struggle. Gus was overwhelmed by the stink of the place. Several cats were wandering about. While the detectives were in the process of searching the apartment, the telephone rang. Gus answered it, and the caller asked for Sasha. After a brief conversation, during which Gus determined the caller was a friend of the victim's, the man identified himself as Richard Raymond and agreed to come to the address immediately.

Fifteen minutes later, a tall, dark-haired man in his early twenties arrived at the front door wearing jeans and a white T-shirt. Gus invited him in and asked him to be seated in the small living room. His eyes darted around the room. He fidgeted up and down on the couch.

Gus produced a tape recorder from his rear pocket and placed it between himself and Richard. He looked at his watch and saw that it was 12:04 p.m. He asked: "Do you mind answering a few questions for us? My name is Detective Gus Grazzi of the homicide unit. With me is Detective Lou Levitt."

"Why, what happened to Sasha?"

"She's been murdered," answered Gus matter-of-factly.

"I knew she was in trouble from what you said on the phone, but I didn't want to think of that," Richard responded calmly.

"Do you mind talking to us about what you know about her?" repeated Gus.

After a short pause, Richard replied, "No, I'm a little shook up, but I guess not."

STATEMENT OF RICHARD RAYMOND

Q. Now, Richard, when did you last see Sasha?

A. Last evening.

Q. What time did you meet her?

A. I met her at about 10:30 at the Beacon Hill Pub on Charles Street.

Q. What happened?

A. We just had some drinks and played some video game machines.

Q. When did you leave?

A. About one o'clock this morning.

Q. When did she leave?

A. I don't know. She said she was going to stay for a little while longer and then go home.

Q. Why did you call her this morning?

A. She asked me to call and wake her up so she could go downtown.

Q. Had you been seeing her?

A. Well, we were getting a little bit steady, you know.

Q. You know what I am getting at, Richard? I want to try to fill this gap of when she was last seen alive and later found dead.

A. Right. I understand.

Q. Can you remember anything else that occurred at the Beacon Hill Pub last night?

A. The only strange thing that happened was there was a fairly large guy who asked me, "Hey, what's that girl's name?" I said, "Well, why don't you ask her yourself?" He said, "Well, I know it's Sasha." Then I forget exactly what the conversation was, but he said something like, "I'm just trying to bust your balls. Don't worry about it. Here, we're friends." He stayed for a little while longer, and I asked Sasha, "Do you know that guy?" She said, "Oh, don't you remember? He was the guy who tried to break my door down."

Q. Is it your practice for you and Sasha to go home separately?

A. Well, usually, yes. She generally would take a cab home.

Q. Did she drink a lot?

A. Sometimes she drank heavily, but that night maybe two drinks.

Q. Okay. Is that all, Richard?

A. I think so.

Q. Would you mind going to the morgue with one of my officers to identify the body? We can't locate her parents.

A. No, I'll do it.

Gus called Station Four and requested a squad car. It arrived in short order, and Richard Raymond was taken to the morgue. The search of the apartment continued. Gus went back into the bedroom. It was as much of a pigpen as the rest of the apartment. Clothes were strewn everywhere. The double bed was unmade, and the sole sheet on it was soiled and dusty. A plain orange bedspread lay half on the bed and half on the floor. The only other piece of furniture in the small room was a pine dresser. Gus opened the top drawer. He found a miscellany of little odds and ends but nothing of interest. He opened the second drawer. It contained underwear. Upon rummaging briefly through the clothing, his hand struck something solid. He pulled the object out. It was an old, battered green address book filled with names and addresses. Gus felt uplifted. Now they had something to go on. This would provide the basis for tracing Sasha's life through her acquaintances.

Finding nothing else of evidentiary interest, Gus and Lou left the building by the rear door, which had been locked. They surveyed the little courtyard and unlatched the wooden door leading to the alleyway. As they gazed down it, they could see, about one hundred yards down on the right, the building where the murder took place.

"Let's check out the other residents of the building," suggested Lou.

They re-entered the building and began knocking on the doors of other apartments. They received no responses until they reached the last apartment on the third floor. A redheaded woman who appeared to be in her midthirties opened the door a crack. Gus showed her his Boston Police detective identification card and identified himself. The door did not open any further. Gus continued: "Sorry to bother you, ma'am, but did you hear anything unusual last night?"

"No, nothing at all. If there was a fight or screams, we would have heard something. We always know when someone comes through the back alleys. I'm sure if anyone heard or saw anything unusual, they would have called the police first and then asked questions. Why, are you investigating the murder?"

"That's right, ma'am."

The woman talked about her fears and the high crime rates in the neighborhood, but it was apparent to Gus that she could not provide any meaningful information, so he and Lou politely said goodbye and left.

On the way down the stairs, the officers ran into another woman coming up. Gus asked whether she had heard anything unusual the prior night. She responded: "How horrible and tragic that killing was! What's this city coming to?" She added: "You know, a woman can't be on the streets at night. And it's terribly dangerous for women with cars who park in the alley. I have several locks on my door."

Gus attempted to move on, as he saw once again that no productive information was forthcoming, but the loquacious tenant kept talking. "I'd really be nervous if this were a random killing, because I could be a target. I fit the profile woman, thirty, living in the city, and often coming home late. I understand this is the seventy-third murder this year. It's not safe for a woman."

The officers finally pulled away and returned to their office at police headquarters. The homicide unit was on the second floor, down the end of a long, dark hallway. Gus's office was barely bigger than a cubicle, but he nevertheless had to share it with Lou. The only furniture in the room consisted of two battered old wooden desks and chairs. There was an old-fashioned Underwood typewriter on Gus's desk. Files were strewn everywhere.

Gus slumped into his chair and threw his feet up on his desk. He was exhausted. After lighting up a cigar, he checked his messages. There were two, one from his wife and one from Faye Whitehead.

He called his wife. "I won't be home till late tonight, Lucille. I got a new case today."

"Oh, did they give you that horrendous murder of the girl on Beacon Street?"

"Yes, that's the one."

"How terrible. Well, okay. Good luck on it, Gus. Don't be too late!"

Gus dialed the number on the other message slip. The phone rang several times. He was about to hang up when someone answered.

"Hello?"

"Hello, is this Faye Whitehead?"

"Yes."

"I'm Detective Gus Grazzi."

"Oh, thank you for calling, Detective. Have you found the guy who did it yet?"

"No, unfortunately. Not yet."

"I thought I could perhaps be of aid in some small way. I knew Sasha quite well."

The detective chewed on his cigar. Tobacco juice collected at the corners of his mouth. "We can use all the help we can get. Would you mind coming down to my office at the police headquarters?"

"No, not at all. Isn't it on Berkley Street?"

"Yes, that's it. Ask for me, Gus Grazzi. See you soon."

Twenty-five minutes later, Gus received word from the front desk that Faye Whitehead was in the lobby. He had her sent to his office.

Faye Whitehead could only be described as plain. She was flat-chested with a few extra pounds on her derriere. Her hair was dirty blond and stringy. She was tall, at five feet, ten inches, and she had an oval head with a ski-jump nose. She was dressed in baggy jeans and a men's blue dress shirt, rolled up at the sleeves. Gus got up from his chair as Faye entered his office.

"Take a seat, Miss Whitehead. I appreciate you coming down on such short notice."

Gus sat down again.

"I only want to ask you a few questions about Sasha so we can get a few leads to work on, if possible."

"I understand," responded Faye.

Gus noted her eyes were bloodshot. It appeared to him that she had been crying. "I'll try to make this as easy as possible. How well did you know Sasha?"

"For the last two years, pretty well," she replied as she wiped a tear from her cheek.

"How did you know her?"

"We would go drinking together."

"Where would you go drinking?"

"The Beacon Hill Pub on Charles Street. It used to be called the Father's Three."

"Did Sasha have a lot of friends there?"

"Yes, mostly male friends."

"Do you know the names of any of them?"

"Let me see. There was one guy she was involved with for a while. She called him Gray Hair. Let me see. I can't think of his name."

Gus leaned forward and asked, "What does he look like?"

"He was tall with gray hair. He was a construction worker," Faye calmly responded.

"Did his friends work in construction too?"

"Yeah, they were in construction."

"Please speak up, Faye, I can hardly hear you. Do you know where they worked in construction?"

"In the local Beacon Hill area. Most of the time they would come in with paint all over them."

"Are there any other male companions that you know of who Sasha kept company with?"

Faye asked Gus for a cigarette. He yelled for Lou, who offered his pack of Marlboros to choose from. "I know a lot of them by face, some of them by first name, but Sasha and I were not friends because of her male friends. We had other things in common that made us friends. Her male friends were a different part of her personality that she kept to herself in a little phone book, and she would call them periodically and go and visit them."

"Do you know anybody by the name of Richard Raymond?"

"That was a new friend of hers, but I've never met him."

"Do you know a Jonathan who was a friend of hers?"

"Yes, I do. He is a friend of hers through a working situation she had, down near the State Street area of Boston."

"Have you ever seen her with Jonathan?"

"No, I haven't."

"What other male companions did she have, if you know?"

"Oh, there was one guy she went with from the Coast Guard base for a while. I think his name is Jim. She went out with him for a while until he started getting violent with her."

Gus sat up in his chair and took the cigar out of his mouth. "What do you mean?"

"When they were alone together, he would do strange things."

"Like what?"

"He handcuffed her to the bed one time and wouldn't let her out of the handcuffs. She woke up one morning and found her panties all ripped up."

Gus continued his questioning, trying not to show emotion. "Did Sasha have any other male companions that you knew of?"

"Sasha has worked in a lot of temporary agencies and picked up friends through these types of circumstances."

Because there was no evidence of a struggle outside the building where Sasha was found, Gus wanted an opinion from Faye. "Do you know why Sasha would go into a vacant building?"

Faye did not hesitate in response. "If she met someone who was into construction, she would be very curious. She was into things like that. If she met someone who said, 'Come here, I want to show you what I've done,' Sasha would be the type to follow. She was very carefree and would do just about anything, especially if she knew the man."

"Are you saying she would go into that building just for the sake of looking it over?"

"I don't think she would do it with a stranger off the street, but if she knew him, she would. When she was out one night partying, she woke up the next day in the old burying ground on Tremont Street, not remembering why she was there. So it is very possible she would do something like that."

"So she could have met somebody doing construction work in that building during the day?"

"She could have. But she had a very spunky personality, and I don't think she would take any grief without a struggle."

Gus leaned back in his chair and took a puff of his cigar. "Getting back to yesterday, Faye, Monday, October 29, did you have an occasion to meet Sasha at any time during the day?"

"Well, not during the day, but I did that night."

"What time was it?"

"Approximately quarter of eleven. Mary and I went to the drive-in."

"What's Mary's last name?"

"Lane. We left after the second feature and went down to the Beacon Hill Pub. As I was parking the car, Sasha was walking out of the bar on her way to Phillips, the corner pharmacy there, to get cigarettes or what have you. She said there was something important she wanted to tell me, so I said I would talk to her later. Mary and I went into the bar, and when Sasha came back from whatever she went for, she sat on the other side of the bar by herself. We never did get a chance to talk. I just went on with my business and decided to leave and completely forgot about the conversation we were supposed to have."

Gus flicked his cigar into the wastepaper basket by his desk. "What time did you leave?"

"I left about quarter to one."

"Sasha was still there?"

"Yes."

"Did she drink a lot?"

"Very much."

"Would you say she was an alcoholic?"

Faye hesitated, then sighed. "Well, I guess all of us are alcoholics, but Sasha pushed it. Every night she would come into the bar at four in the afternoon and be there till two in the morning. She was on drugs once in a while, but nothing hard. She didn't shoot up drugs, although she did try once."

"She tried to shoot heroin?"

"Once—a half tablet or some kind of synthetic heroin that she got very sick on. She said she would never do it again, and I think she sold the other half to somebody. She had acid on her, and sometimes cocaine. She took a lot of speed. She was always going to doctors who would see her for five minutes and send her away with prescriptions. She would stay up all day on the speed and then go out at night and get stone drunk. But she told me that she used to drink more a few years ago and was drinking a lot less these days."

"Do you know if she worked?"

"She worked part-time. Most recently for a temporary secretary agency a few days a week. Before that it was for the phone company. She could get a good job. She had a good mind on her, but she couldn't hold it because the alcohol and the nightlife would get to her. She was a very fancy dresser. She would buy the most expensive new disco rage, one-hundred-dollar blouses and outfits."

"Where would she get her money?"

"Her parents. She had a hundred dollars on her last night when she went out."

"They just automatically sent her money?" asked Gus.

"When she asked for it. I don't think they know much about the situation. They sent her to Massachusetts to go to college and get away from small-town life. But it was still too mellow for her. Eventually, the thing inside of her that made her Sasha came back, and she started to go back out. She started failing in school and dropped out. She started hanging out at the Beacon Hill Pub."

Gus's inclination for the morbid was getting the best of him: "Is there anything else strange about her you can mention?"

Again, Faye did not hesitate. "Last Halloween, she wanted to wear leather. She asked me to go down to the Combat Zone with her to buy a whip, and I agreed. So we went down there, but she wanted a specialized leather whip with leather this and that and they were running hundreds of dollars, but she bought it anyway. She also purchased handcuffs. She said men handcuffed her to the bed and she in turn handcuffed people to the bed. She claimed it turned her on to be whipped. I guess you would call her a masochist."

Gus almost choked on his cigar. "Didn't you say Jim did that to her?"

"Yes, she said he handcuffed her to the bed one time and wouldn't unhandcuff her. Of course, she couldn't reach the keys, but he finally did. This is not my style. I would rather not hear about her sex life. When Sasha did these things, it was in times of depression, so I would listen as a friend, but I definitely wouldn't pull it apart to give her a solution."

"So when you left last night, to your knowledge, she wasn't talking to anybody and you didn't hear from her after that?"

"Right."

"Thank you, Faye. I think that's everything. We appreciate your coming down. We'll be in touch if we need you further."

"Wait, one more thing."

"Sure, what is it?"

"Sasha was a lonely person who would go out looking for someone to comfort her. The people she would go out with when she was drunk were entirely different than the type she would go with when sober. She was definitely schizo."

"Thank you again, Faye."

After completing the interview, Gus leaned back in his chair and put his feet on his desk. He started paging through Sasha's address book. His initial impression had been correct. It contained only names, addresses, and telephone numbers. But he was too tired to examine it further, so he decided to call it a day.

When he got home, Gus took an ice-cold bottle of Michelob out of the refrigerator and slumped into a chair at the kitchen table. He put his head in his hands and thought, "I'll get that maniac if it's the last thing I do." Gus finished the bottle and then slowly dragged himself upstairs. Lucille was already asleep. He slipped in beside her and was soon asleep himself.

2

The Lawyer

RED CZEK LEARNED OF THE MURDER WHEN HE OPENED HIS MORNING *Globe* as the 7:15 train pulled out of Concord on its daily run to Boston. His law firm represented corporations, and he couldn't imagine how any lawyer could represent a defendant in that case. It all seemed so removed from Thoreau's bucolic Concord, where he lived a quiet life with his wife, three children, and their Saint Bernard, Brandy. He made the commute to his firm in Boston every day, leaving the city and its problems behind when he returned in the evening.

The murder was a prime topic of conversation at the coffee machine and during hallway encounters at Red's law firm that day. The firm of Reynolds, McGuire & Jones was located at the newly renovated Faneuil Hall Marketplace in the heart of the downtown business district of Boston. Until recently, the old marketplace had been allowed to get run-down, but the renovations of the old granite and brick structures had made the area the most sought-after space, both for retail and office use.

Red Czek was an imposing figure, at six feet, four inches, with a full but trim red beard, a head of equally red curly hair, and rich blue eyes. He hardly looked his fifty years. Near the top of his class in the Boston public schools, he received a scholarship to Harvard College, where he graduated with honors in economics. He went to Harvard Law School, where he also did well. He assumed the next step for him was a job with a respected Boston law firm, and Reynolds, McGuire & Jones was happy to have him. He advanced rapidly in the firm, often working until 11:00 p.m. on weekdays and weekends. He soon became a partner. However, there was something about Red that separated him from the other partners, besides the fact that his ancestors didn't come over on the *Mayflower*, and he didn't grow up in Wellesley or attend Andover or Exeter.

Red's grandfather had come to this county as a small boy from a farm village in what is now Czechoslovakia. He was a tailor by trade and settled in Boston. Times were difficult, but he eked out a living by dint of hard work and long hours. He had cautioned Red many times as he grew up that life was "survival of the fittest" and that no one was going to give him anything in life. It was continuously brought home to the youngster that he had to confront his adversaries aggressively if he wanted to make anything of himself. The lesson was well learned, as Red grew up with little respect for authority and a reverence for hard work. His grandfather had never lost the idealistic vision that America was different, because the little man, through the righteousness of his cause, would eventually triumph. His idealism rubbed off on his grandson too.

Red divided his spare time between charitable work, such as the Community Chest drive and fundraising for Harvard, and church activities. The law firm was a sturdy, moneymaking operation run like a business. Red had never challenged that approach to the practice of law and, in fact, had profited richly from the success of the firm. Yet he was never completely comfortable with only representing corporations or the well possessed.

Red reread the *Globe* article on the broomstick murder on the train ride home. The following day, Red could not get the murder out of his head as the B&M commuter train raced past the lush fields and Victorian mansions of Lincoln. Red settled into his seat next to the window. Most of his fellow passengers had their noses attentively buried in their morning *Globe*. Those who did not were slumped in their seats, ties loosened, with heads occasionally nodding forward as they uneasily snoozed in rhythm with the sway of the train. A sprinkling of Concord bankers stood out from the rest of the passengers. They sat erect in their pinstripe suits and Harvard ties, reading their folded-in-half *Wall Street Journals*. Their too-short pants rode high on their legs. Occasionally, one would lean over to a colleague with a frivolous comment, such as, "Nice day yesterday at the club, wasn't it, Roger?"

The B&M conductors made their regular passes down the aisles after each stop. Formally suited up, all in black, their outfits topped off with the traditional visored caps, they were for the most part a friendly group who knew many of the passengers on a first-name basis. The popping of their ticket punchers complemented the steady hum of the rail as the train sped its way from station to station.

This morning, Red couldn't bring himself to read his *Globe* or open his briefcase and take out some work. He stared out the window the whole forty-five-minute trip into Boston. He couldn't get his mind off the broomstick murder.

Who was that poor girl? How did she come to be murdered? What kind of monster could commit a crime like that? He longed to explore the answers to these questions, but by the time the old, filthy train limped into North Station, he had resigned himself to another lucrative but uninteresting day at the office.

3

The Police Investigation Continues

GUS ARRIVED LATE AT WORK THE FOLLOWING DAY. LYING ON HIS DESK was the statement of a Donna Cressey. There was a note attached to it from Lou that said, "Gus—this girl called about the Lewis murder. I took down her statement."

INTERVIEW WITH DONNA CRESSEY
RE: SASHA LEWIS HOMICIDE

Donna met Sasha at Beacon Hill Pub two years ago. They would see each other about three times a week. Sasha and Donna stayed together at Donna's house at 39 Dale Street from Monday, October 15, until Friday,

October 19. Sasha was afraid of staying at her own place, as someone was peering through the window. On the nineteenth, they went to the Windsor Gate in Cambridge and met some men friends of Donna's. About 11:00 p.m., Sasha suddenly got up and walked out.

Donna stated that Sasha liked Richard Raymond a lot and would meet him at the pub at about 11:30 p.m. The night of the murder, Richard wanted to go home, but Sasha wanted to stay, so Richard left and Sasha stayed. Sasha told Donna about the bunny costume she rented for the Halloween party. Donna said Sasha told her, about two weeks prior to the murder, she could not open the door to the apartment, as the key seemed to stick. The fellow down the hall offered to help her, and as a result she stayed the night with him. Sasha would not leave the house until making sure the door was locked, as she was afraid that her cats would get out. Sasha would always use the front door, as the back door was tough to open. Donna stated that a few days after the murder, Richard Raymond called her and accused her of trying to get him in trouble. Donna was disturbed that Richard knew her number, as Sasha was the only one who knew it. She said Raymond said to her, "Leave my name out of it. I don't know anything about it." She interpreted it as a threat and is very much afraid of him. His call came about 1:30 a.m., and he appeared flaky.

Donna heard from Sasha about 11:00 p.m. on October 29. She called from Beacon Hill Pub and said she was going over to Jonathan's to pick up a cape for the Halloween party. She sounded drunk.

As Gus finished reading the statement and started for the coffee machine, Lou arrived.

"Hey, Gus, did you get my note and statement?"

"Yeah, thanks."

"I got another call too. It was from one of the astrologer quacks. She thinks she can help us," said Lou sarcastically.

"Don't knock her. We need all the help we can get in this case. I don't believe in them, either, but maybe we should let her have a crack at it. What harm will it do? I've heard stories about successes they've had. I don't know whether to believe any of that or not."

"Well, do you want her Goddamn number or not?"

"Okay, give it to me. I'll think it over." Gus poured a cup of coffee for him and Lou and returned to his desk. "Unless we get a lucky break, this case is going to be a long haul. This girl certainly was fucked up, according to her friends. We already have several possible suspects. I suppose we should give top priority to finding this guy she went to get the cape from shortly before her death. Maybe he's in the address book. Let me take a look."

"What about the family of the girl?" asked Lou as he put down his coffee cup. Lou had been in the homicide division almost as long as Gus. He was tall, about six feet, two inches, and thin. He was bald, with a few strands of hair he combed straight back. He complemented Gus, as he was a man of few words.

"Thanks for reminding me. I arranged to meet the girl's family at the airport today. I guess I'll have to do it. I don't relish meeting a mother under these circumstances. This mission is no fucking good."

Mrs. Lewis was a slight, nervous woman with short blond hair. Gus thought to himself how fortunate he was that she did not ask too many questions about the state her daughter was in when she was found. On the way to the morgue, the detective discussed with the mother her knowledge of her daughter's Boston life.

Mrs. Lewis explained that Sasha had been sent to Boston to go to college and escape the doldrums of small city life. And, yes, she had heard from Sasha about Richard Raymond. He had wanted her to go with him to Alaska. "But I discouraged her from going. I told her that sometimes young fellows take you places and just leave you there." The only other helpful information she had was that an Italian girl named June had called her. She mentioned having been with Sasha most of the day preceding the murder and referred to an argument between Sasha and the Raymond guy.

As Mrs. Lewis appeared very tired and volunteered little, Gus felt he had imposed on her enough under the circumstances. After the unpleasant viewing at the morgue, Gus drove her to her hotel. He then dropped back at police headquarters to pick up Lou. When he arrived at his office, he found Lou with his nose in the address book found in Sasha's apartment.

"Any luck on finding this Jonathan in there?" inquired Gus.

Lou motioned Gus over to his desk: "I've found two. Look at this." He pointed to an entry that read, "Jonathan Williams, 397 Marlborough Street, Boston."

"What about the other one?"

"There's a Jonathan in New York. That Marlborough address is near the murder scene, so let's give it a shot now."

"But this is just the beginning, Lou," remarked Gus with determination. "I want every Goddamn name in that book checked out!"

"But there's seventy-five names, Gus," protested Lou.

"I don't give a fuck. It has to be done."

"Oh, another thing. I found this message on your desk when I came back from lunch. Jonesie took it down. It's from the medical examiner."

Gus read to himself the typed one-page memorandum from Detective Jones:

At 1:30 p.m., Dr. Richmond called with the result of the autopsy performed on Sasha Lewis, the victim of yesterday's homicide. He stated that she had received multiple blows to the head (eight in all), seven on the rear left side, and on the right side toward the back of the head. Bone in head cracked. Lacerations of the brain and fracture of the skull. Time of death approximately sometime after 1:30 a.m. and no later than 4:00 a.m. Sperm in vagina. Sperm in rectum. Mouth negative. Cause of death multiple blows to head, lacerations of brain and skull.

"That fucking maniac bastard not only bashed her good, but apparently raped her, too, and up the ass at that."

Gus bitterly placed the memo back on his desk.

"I'm not surprised at the report," responded Lou calmly. "That broomstick suggests that we have one sick puppy on our hands."

Gus lifted another cigar. "Let's move our asses out of here, Lou."

The partners grabbed their worn and stained coats, as the weather had turned a bit cool, and left the office. It was now late afternoon, and they hoped to catch Jonathan, the cape man, the last known person to see Sasha alive, around dinnertime.

As Gus took the wheel of the unmarked police vehicle, he addressed his partner. "Hey, Lou, let's pass by the victim's apartment again. I want to get a good picture of where it is relative to the murder scene and this guy's apartment on Marlborough Street." As they passed the apartment at 559 Dartmouth Street, Gus saw a mailman come out of the building. They stopped the car and asked if he had seen Sasha recently.

"I haven't seen her recently, but she did approach me on Marlborough Street a couple of weeks ago. She was scared to death." The mailman hesitated at that point.

"Please, continue," said Gus.

"She asked me for help," continued the heavyset postman. "She told me some guy was following her in a car. I told her to call the police, but the car was gone. About a half hour later, I saw her going back into her apartment building."

"Have you seen this guy since?"

"I couldn't identify him if I saw him. Never got a good look."

"Thanks anyway, pal. So long." Gus pulled away and took a right on Beacon Street, going away from Boston Commons. They traveled some five or six blocks up, then took a left turn and left again onto Marlborough Street.

"There's Father's Five, the bar where the victim occasionally went." Lou pointed to the other side of Massachusetts Avenue at the corner of Marlborough.

"But she apparently hung out more regularly at the former Father's Three, or the Beacon Hill Pub. Where's that, Lou?"

"Oh, that's a real dive over on Charles Street near the Charles Street Jail."

Gus pulled into an open space one hundred yards down Marlborough Street in front of a fire hydrant. He flicked the ashes of his cigar out the window while pointing to a three-story brick townhouse numbered 397. A sign indicating conversion to condominiums in progress sat in front. Dense viburnum bushes nearly hid the first-floor window.

Lou and Gus approached the front door and Gus knocked loudly. No one came. He knocked again. Still no one answered. The officers were about to leave when a young man in his twenties with shoulder-length hair approached the steps. Gus said, "Excuse me, we're police officers. Could you tell us if Jonathan Williams lives here?"

"I just moved in, but I think there's a guy named Jonathan on the second floor."

"Would you mind letting us in?"

"No, of course not."

The young man opened the door to let himself in, and the officers followed. He pointed out the door on the second floor where he believed a Jonathan lived. Gus knocked. Immediately, the officers heard movement inside. The door was opened by a man in a brown pinstripe suit who appeared to be in his late thirties. His yellow tie was loosened. His blond hair was cut short.

Gus showed his Boston Police identification card and inquired as to the man's name. Upon being informed that this individual was, indeed, Jonathan Williams, Gus said, "Do you mind talking to us?"

Jonathan responded, "I suppose it's about Sasha Lewis."

"That's right. Do you mind if we come in?"

"No, come right ahead." The officers were ushered into the living room. They sank several inches as they sat on the only sofa in the small room. Jonathan took a seat on a revolving stool on the other side of a square oak coffee table.

"Did you date Sasha?" asked Gus.

"No. I didn't date her at all. When we worked together, I didn't know her very well, but after she left, I received a call from her one night at 2:30 a.m. She asked if she could come by, and I said all right."

"When was this?" Gus leaned forward.

"It was probably six months ago, I would say."

"Was that the last time you saw her?"

"No, that probably happened on four different occasions."

"She would call you up at 2:30 in the morning and ask if she could come over?"

"Right, or sometimes—once, she showed up without a call."

Gus paused before the next question. "When she came over, did you have sexual relations with her?"

"Yes," responded Jonathan without hesitation.

Gus decided to backtrack a bit before he keyed in on the critical questions. "How did you happen to meet Sasha, if you remember?"

"I met her at work."

"Do you know what bars she frequents?"

"I know that at times she's come to my place when she'd been out drinking. I know she has mentioned a few of them—I only remember the Beacon Hill Pub on Charles Street now. That's what she does often at night."

"Do you know if she drinks a lot?"

"My opinion is yes. She drinks a lot."

Lou cut in, as he wanted them to get what they came for while the guy was still talking: "Directing your attention to last night, Monday, October 29, did you have occasion to meet her?"

"Yes."

Lou and Gus straightened up. "Where was this?"

"Well, I talked to her first at approximately 9:00 p.m., when she called my apartment."

"How do you know about the time, Jonathan?"

"I had been sort of half asleep. In fact, I was watching the football game."

"That was just about starting?"

"Yes."

"This is the Monday night football game?"

"Right."

"What did she say to you?"

"The usual hello and how are you. Then she told me that June Andrews told her I had this cape I wore to the office Halloween party last year. She wanted to know if she could borrow it. I said yes. Then she asked when she could come pick it up. I told her probably the best time to get me home would be in the morning, before I went to work. She said she needed it for Wednesday."

"Okay. Was that the extent of your conversation?"

"Yes."

"Did she sound like she had been drinking?"

"At that time, she sounded like she had not been drinking, at least not heavily. There was a definite difference in Sasha from the times that I had seen her at 2:30 in the morning and when she appeared at work. It was like two different people altogether. At that time, she sounded more normal, so to speak."

"When was the next time you heard from her?"

"Between 2:00 and 2:30."

Gus and Lou's eyes met. There was a pause before Gus continued the questioning. "Is there any reason why you can remember the time?"

"Well, she woke me up, and I looked at the clock."

"You mean she called on the phone again?"

"Right."

"What did she say then?"

"She asked if she could come by and get the cape now."

"What did you say?"

"I said all right."

"Now, how soon after did she arrive?"

"Probably about fifteen minutes after the phone call. I had turned on the television. I remember channel five was still on. There was some sitcom rerun that was just ending when she got there."

"When she arrived at your apartment, how was she dressed?"

"She had on a sweater and a pair of slacks, and she was carrying a coat. Hey, you guys must think I did it, the way you're throwing questions at me."

"Now, Jonathan, you're the last one to see her alive. You're an important witness, that's all."

"I hope so!" exclaimed Jonathan as he threw up his hands in exasperation.

"Did you say she arrived around 2:30?"

"Yes."

"How long did she stay?"

"Approximately two hours."

"So that would mean it was about 4:30 when she left?"

"Around that, probably a little less than two hours."

"Could she have left before 4:00 a.m.?" cut in Lou. He remembered the medical examiner's report.

"I doubt it. I looked at the digital clock next to my bed before she left, and it was after four."

"While she was here did you have sexual relations with her?"

"Yes. I did."

"Did you use any protection?"

"You mean like a rubber? No."

"Did you ejaculate?"

"Yes, I believe so."

"Did you have anal relations with her?"

"No, I did not."

"Are you absolutely sure of that?"

"Yes."

"Can you tell us anything else that might help our investigation?"

"Well, yes, I found her panties this morning."

"Her panties?" exclaimed both cops at once.

"Yes."

"Where did you find them?"

"Beside my bed."

"You mean to say she left without her panties?" broke in Lou.

"Yes, apparently."

"Where are they?"

"They're around here someplace."

"We'll take them with us."

"Yes, sir."

"You say she left probably sometime after 4:00?"

"I am unsure about the exact time."

"How did she leave?"

"Well, I was still lying in bed and sort of dozing off and had been doing that for a while. I assumed she was going to go to sleep, and the next thing I knew, she was getting up and starting to get dressed. I asked her what she was doing. On other occasions, when she had come over, she had spent the night, and I had dropped her off near her apartment on my way to work the next day. She was not at all tired. She said she was going home and then said, 'Maybe I will go to a party.'"

"What party was that?"

"I don't know. She said she was invited to a party, and she said maybe she would go to it. I knew it was after four, so I thought that was a little ridiculous. She got on the phone and said she was calling a cab. She finished getting dressed, and I said I'd let her out. I could hear the door shut. But I never heard the cab arrive, the beep of the horn, or anything."

"How far is your apartment from hers?"

"Oh, it's probably a ten-minute walk—four or five blocks away. I've never been to her apartment."

"During the two hours, or the approximate two hours that she was there, what did you talk about?"

When he didn't answer right away, Lou took over the questioning: "Was she drinking?"

"No. She had been drinking before she got here, but she wasn't drinking here."

"Was she drunk or just feeling good?"

"Sasha always appeared to be feeling good. She could handle a lot of alcohol and not fall down drunk."

"When were you first made aware of anything that may have happened to Sasha?"

"When I woke up, I turned on the radio. I had the WEEI news station on, and I heard about a homicide in the Back Bay. Well, I can't say I didn't associate it, because that question flashed in my mind that it might be Sasha. I was sort of concerned how she was going to get home. So I put the two together and just had this bad feeling about it when I heard it. The news story I heard said it had just happened a few hours ago. I didn't think much more about it during the day. I heard the same story again on the way home from work last night, again with no name. I didn't actually hear it was Sasha until late yesterday when somebody from work called me. Within fifteen minutes of that, the story had come on the air with the same name."

"Are you sure she took a cab?"

"Well, she told me she was going to take a cab. She called a cab, or I believe she called a cab, and so I assumed she was taking a cab. I asked her how she was getting home. If she'd told me she was walking, I don't believe I would have let her."

"I guess that's all we have, Jonathan. You have been very helpful, and we appreciate it. Now, if you can just find those panties, we'll leave you alone."

After waiting for Jonathan to find the victim's panties, the two officers left the apartment.

"Maybe we should check out this Beacon Hill Pub, Lou. The victim apparently almost lived there."

Lou nodded. Once back in the cruiser, Gus lit his cigar, took a couple of puffs, and queried Lou: "What do you think of that guy?"

"I really don't know what to think, Gus. There are so many possibilities. We certainly don't have any solid evidence against anyone. There are a handful of people who could have done it, I suppose."

Gus put on the cruiser light and steamed through a red light on the way to Charles Street and the Beacon Hill Pub. He said, "According to the medical examiner's report, the victim died no later than 4:00 a.m. How do we reconcile that with Williams's statement that he is positive Sasha was at his home until at least 4:15?"

"And the panties being left at his place appears strange," added Lou.

"Yeah, how many broads forget to put on their panties while getting dressed?" responded Gus with a smirk as he continued to puff on his Garcia y Vega.

"But Gus, she was a strange broad from what we've learned from her friends."

"Still. Lou, even a kooky gal usually takes her panties with her."

"Hold it, Gus, there it is."

"Where?"

"Over there. See, in the big gold letters. Beacon Hill Pub."

The pub was a couple buildings up on Charles Street from Phillips drugstore. It occupied the bottom floor of a four-story brick building. On each floor above the bar were three windows evenly positioned across the front. The upper floors appeared to be occupied by apartments. The roof was slate. The gutter was washed with slashes of green that appeared to be the result of weathering. Directly in front of the pub was a restored nineteenth-century lamppost with a glass-enclosed false gas fixture. With the exception of the big, gold-lettered "Beacon Hill Pub" across the upper part of the face of the building, the front was all black.

Gus and Lou entered the pub. It was so dark, they had difficulty making out figures at first. On their right, the bar stretched thirty feet down the wall and curved in at the ends. There were about twenty barstools with red covers. A mirror stretched down the length of the bar on the wall behind it above the bottles. On the left were booths and a cigarette machine.

Far in the back, the officers made out several arcade video games and pinball machines with titles such as *Torch*, *Flight 2000*, *Mars*, *Star Castle*, *Pac-Man*, *Defender*, *Asteroids*, and *Space Invaders*. The only lighting came from isolated light bulbs with red shades that masked most of the light.

The two detectives sat at the bar. Even though they were not in uniform, they stood out like sore thumbs, as the crowd was a relatively young one.

"What can I get you?" asked the bartender.

"Two Becks," responded Gus. While the bartender filled the order, the detectives sized him up. He was approximately six feet and weighed about two hundred pounds. He wore glasses and was dressed in blue jeans and a tan polo shirt. His black hair was receding at both sides of his head, leaving only a thin line in the middle.

"Here are your Becks, fellows."

"Excuse me. My name is Gus Grazzi, and this is Lou Levitt. We're Boston Police detectives." Gus handed his card to the bartender. "We'd like to ask you a few questions about Sasha Lewis."

"Sure, officers. My name is Joe Kent. She was a regular here. She usually came in alone and met friends here. I knew her as Sash. She was quiet."

"Do you remember seeing her the night of the murder?"

"Yeah. I first noticed her about nine o'clock, and she stayed until closing, at about 2:00 a.m., as was her usual practice."

"What was she drinking?" asked Gus, as he rubbed out the stub of his cigar.

"She was drinking a mixed drink called TKO: tequila, Ouzo, and Kahlúa."

"Did you see her with anyone?"

"No one in particular."

"What did she do all that time she was here?" asked Lou.

"She loved to play those video game machines, and she was damn good at it. *Space Invaders* was her favorite."

The banging of the machines could be heard from the dim back of the pub. Cigarette smoke made the visibility even worse. But the officers could detect players intensely moving their hands and bodies as they addressed the machines.

"What else can you tell us about her?"

"Excuse me, officer. I have a customer." The bartender moved down the bar and pressed out two draft beers for two young men who had entered. He returned and sat on a stool across from the officers.

"She was the type of girl who you thought you knew well, but who you really didn't know. She got along good with people, if she liked you. If she didn't like someone, she didn't hesitate to tell them."

"Maybe that was her problem," Gus broke in.

The bartender continued. "You wonder about a woman who hangs out in bars and travels alone at night."

The officers turned their attention to the people in the bar. There were four young guys to their right, who appeared to be construction workers, in for a couple of pops after a hard day's work. They ordered turkey sandwiches. A bartender pulled them out of a large brown paper bag, as the bar apparently had no kitchen facilities. They ordered a round of Knickerbocker Natural Beer.

On the officers' left was a young girl about twenty years old. She was strikingly good-looking, with brown, curly hair falling to her neck. She was about five feet, eight inches, with blue eyes and large, extremely white teeth. Her lipstick was heavy red. She wore white painter's pants, a blue V-neck sweater, and moccasins.

Gus's eyes focused on her right nipple that could be clearly detected as the sweater clung tightly to her ample breasts. Lou nudged him and whispered in his ear, "Down, boy, down. I know you're nothing but a dirty old man, but we've got work to do!"

Gus took his business card out of his jacket pocket and placed it in front of the girl at the bar. She looked up at him with a broad smile and laughed.

Gus said, "We're investigating the murder of Sasha Lewis."

The girl immediately became subdued and responded, "I knew her. She was here all the time. I hope they castrate the guy who did it." She paused before adding, "By the way, my name is Sheila."

She got up and went to the jukebox, and soon the sound of "Back in Black" by AC/DC blasted forth. She didn't return to the barstool, but rather stood in front of the jukebox and kept time to the music with her body and hands. The next number was "Why Should I Care?" by The Who. Suddenly Sheila started singing.

When the second song ended, she returned to her place next to the two officers. Gus had ordered her another scotch on the rocks.

"Oh, thank you, officers. What can I do for you?"

Gus took the cigar out of his mouth and responded, "Any information you can give us would be appreciated."

Sheila sipped her drink and then put it down. "I'm actually a part-time waitress here. I usually work Sundays. I was here the night Sasha was murdered. I was with her for a short period of time."

"Did you see anyone else with her?" asked Lou.

"She was with an old boyfriend, I believe, named Richard."

"Do you know his last name?"

"No."

There was a brief silence. Sheila took another sip of scotch and continued. "I bought her a couple of drinks."

"When did she leave here?"

"About 2:00 a.m."

"Did she leave with anyone?"

"No. I don't believe so."

Gus lit up another cigar. "Sheila, do construction workers regularly come in here?"

"Yeah, from time to time."

"Do you know any that may have worked on or near 283 Beacon, where she was murdered?"

Sheila didn't respond immediately. She finished her scotch, and Gus ordered her another, as well as two Heinekens for Lou and himself. She sipped her new drink before speaking. "There are a few fellows that I think are working there or near there. But they usually hang at Father's Five Bar on Massachusetts Avenue at Marlborough Street. Sasha could be found there, too, on occasion."

"What are their names?"

"Ron Reed, Joe Grady, and a guy named Rick."

"Do you know where we can reach them now?"

"If they aren't at Father's Five, no, I don't."

The officers took their leave and returned to headquarters to get their cars and head home.

4

The Police Interrogate
the Defendant

SEVERAL DAYS WENT BY, BUT LITTLE PROGRESS WAS MADE IN determining the murderer of Sasha Lewis.

Gus and Lou sat in their office discussing the case. Gus had his feet up on the desk and was puffing away on his Garcia y Vega. Lou said, "I traced down that construction worker named Joe Grady, mentioned by Sheila at the Beacon Hill Pub. He lives on Beacon Street about five blocks up from the murder site. He's helping renovate a building there as well as the one at 281 Beacon, next to the murder scene. The contractor is letting him stay there in exchange for his acting as a custodian and watchman in the building." He is actually very close to the apartment of Jonathan Williams. Both apartments are a stone's throw from Massachusetts Avenue."

"Did you get in touch with him?"

"I phoned him to set up a time to talk, but he said he was too busy to see me and hung up."

"Well, fuck him," said Gus. "Let's go down to his worksite and try our luck there. With the murder occurring in the renovated building, and this construction worker hanging out at the Beacon Hill Pub, we have a relationship that should be checked out."

The two officers arrived at 281 Beacon Street at about noon. Gus asked one of the workers for the boss. He was directed to a stocky, redheaded man of about forty.

"Are you running this job?" inquired Gus politely.

"Yes, I'm the boss," replied the man, not without displaying annoyance.

At this point, Gus handed his card to him. The man's disposition improved immediately.

"What can I do for you, gentlemen?"

"Do you have a Joe Grady working for you?"

"Sure do."

"Do you mind if we ask you a few questions about him?"

"No, go right ahead. Why don't you come into my office?"

He led them into a partially renovated room that contained only a desk.

Gus took out his tape recorder. "And I don't suppose you mind if we tape-record it?

"That's fine with me. I suppose you are investigating that murder."

STATEMENT OF BOB WRIGHT

Q. What is your name?

A. Bob Wright.

Q. What is your position with the company doing this job?

A. I own it, and I was working at 486 Beacon Street and now here at 281.

Q. Do you have in your employment a Joe Grady?

A. Yes.

Q. Does Joe have anything at all to do with this building?

A. Yes, he's working on the renovation here. He is also actually living in the 486 building that we've nearly completed the renovation on.

Q. I am going to show you a picture of a white female. Have you ever seen this girl?

A. Yes.

Q. Where did you see her?

A. I've seen her on several occasions, in the alley, riding a bicycle.

Q. There is no question in your mind that this is the girl?

A. I recognize her by her glasses.

Q. So, that morning of October 30, did you have an occasion at that time to talk to Joe Grady?

A. Yes.

Q. What conversation did you have with Joe?

A. I asked him if he had heard about the murder, and he said he had.

Q. How did he look to you that morning?

A. Oh, he looked kind of washed out, like he had been out a couple of days on dope.

Q. Do you know if Joe smokes?

A. Yes, he does.

Q. Do you know what kind of cigarettes he smokes?

A. He smokes Marlboros.

Q. Does he smoke anything else?

A. Yes, marijuana.

Q. Are you sure of that?

A. I am positive of that.

Q. Why are you positive of that?

A. I have caught him smoking and have told him several times that if I caught him smoking on the job again, he would be dismissed.

Q. Did you have any other conversations with Joe relative to this homicide that took place at 283 Beacon Street?

A. No.

Q. How long has Joe lived at 486 Beacon Street?

A. Well, since around October 1.

Q. And how long has Joe worked for you?

A. Off and on for about a year.

Q. Has he been any problem to you?

A. Only a few times that I had to speak to him about smoking and being tardy.

Q. Does he have a temper, to your knowledge?

A. Yes, he does.

Q. How would you know that?

A. On several occasions, he has gotten into fights with coworkers. He has a reputation of getting into fights in barrooms.

Q. One more question. Did you happen to look at Joe's hands on the morning of the 30th?

A. Yes, he was removing rubbish off the roof, and he had gloves on.

Q. Do you know if he had a shirt on, a sweater, or anything else?

A. Yes. It was kind of chilly that morning. He had on a long-sleeved shirt.

"Okay. I want to thank you again, Bob, for talking to us." Gus turned off the tape recorder.

"Perhaps you guys want to talk to my foreman, Dick Brown. There he is." Bob pointed out the window to a clean-shaven man in his late twenties who was limping toward them.

"That would be great," Gus replied.

"Hey, Dick, come here a moment," Bob called out through the window. "I'd like to introduce you to these two Boston police officers. They're investigating the murder of that young girl on Beacon Street several days ago. They would like to ask you a few questions about Joe Grady."

Brown walked inside and extended his hand to Gus. "How do you do, officers? I'm Dick Brown. I don't mind talking to you guys if it will help get the maniac who butchered that girl."

Brown recalled seeing Joe Grady in the early morning of October 30. He was fifteen or twenty minutes late and was making excuses.

He also related running into Grady two or three days later. He met him in the hallway shortly after he had come out of his apartment. Grady had a tan shirt in his hands, which appeared to have bloodstains on it. Without any comment from Brown, Grady showed him the shirt, claiming he had been in a fight with three guys downtown the night before. When Brown observed no marks on his knuckles, Grady volunteered that he had been wearing gloves.

Word had gotten around the construction site that the cops were there, asking questions about Grady, so when Brown passed him on the way to meet the detectives, Grady looked at him and said, "No, I didn't do it." Brown was asked to ask Grady to come down from where he was working upstairs in one of the rooms under renovation to talk to the officers.

A few minutes later, Joe Grady strode into the office. "Dick told me you guys want to talk to me." He was dressed in blue jeans and a tan shirt with a pocket. He had a tattoo on his right arm depicting a skull and knife. There was a space between his big white upper teeth. He had big lips and straight black hair that fell down to his ears. He wore sneakers without shoelaces and dirty white socks. Joe's most distinctive characteristic was the stare of his one glass eye and his contagious smile. He smiled unconsciously, even when it wasn't appropriate to do so.

"We'd like to talk to you about Sasha Lewis's murder, Joe," began Gus.

"We just want to know where you were that evening," added Lou.

"None of your fucking business," retorted Joe.

"We're not interviewing you as a suspect, but rather as a witness," said Gus.

"My ass." He turned to leave.

At this point, Bob broke in. "Joe, why don't you talk to them? You have nothing to hide."

Joe hesitated before turning around and responding, "Okay, but only a few questions."

Gus began, "Do you know Sasha Lewis?"

"I'm not sure, unless I see her picture," responded Joe with a yawn.

Gus showed him the picture, and Joe acknowledged knowing who she was.

"Where were you on Monday, October 29, of this year?" Gus lit a cigar.

Joe sat on the desk and began: "I went to the Honey Lounge about 6:00 p.m., because it was right after I had cashed my check."

"And where did you go after that?" asked Gus as he drew on his cigar.

Joe smiled and continued. "I came home around 11:30 p.m. and visited two friends next door, Bill Jones and Henry Riggs."

"Did you go out again?" broke in Lou.

"Sometime after midnight I went to Frank 'N Stein's and watched the last flick. I met a broad there and took her home."

"What was her name?"

"I don't know. I only met her that night for the first time."

"Can you describe her?"

Joe got up off the desk and paced back and forth. "Why all these questions? You must think I did it."

"We're talking to everybody," replied Gus. He flicked his cigar ashes on the floor. "How about that description?"

"She was about eighteen years old with long hair to her shoulders. The most remarkable thing about her was her screwed-up makeup."

"When did you leave Frank 'N Stein's with her?"

"About 2:00 a.m. We walked along Massachusetts Avenue

toward Beacon Street. I hollered over to the group that was standing in front of Father's Five and invited anyone who wanted to come to a party at my house."

"Did anyone take you up?"

"Yeah, Ken and Lynn."

"Who are they?"

"Ken's a friend. Lynn is his girlfriend."

"What's Ken's last name?"

"I don't know."

Gus persisted. "He's a good friend, yet you don't know his last name?"

"Many of us who hang at Father's Five only go by first names."

"How long have you known him?"

"Three or four years."

"What does he look like?"

"Italian-looking. Black hair, slim build, mustache."

"So, who went to your place from Father's Five?"

"Me, Ken, Lynn, and the broad I picked up."

"How did you get there?"

"We walked. It's not far."

"And what did you do at your place?"

"Just partied."

"Did you leave there at any time?"

"Ken and I left after an hour or so, about 3:00 a.m., to go to his place."

"What about the girls?"

"They stayed at my place."

"When did you return to your place?"

"About half an hour later."

"And what did you do then?"

"Lynn had left. Only my girl was there. So Ken and I left again and took a cab back to Ken's place. Ken's old lady made him stay, so I came back alone with a six-pack."

"Did you take a cab back?"

"Yeah."

"Where did it leave you off?"

"At the corner of Massachusetts Avenue and Beacon Street."

"About what time was this?"

"After four. Maybe between 4:15 and 4:30."

"What did you do when you got back to your apartment?"

"The girl I had picked up was still there, and I spent the night with her."

Gus took out his cigar and sat on the corner of the desk. "You're sure you can't remember her name?"

"What are you guys trying to do to me?" protested Joe. The smile was still there. It seldom left Joe's face. He continued, "You're trying to frame me. I'll take a lie detector test. I'm incapable of doing anything like that."

Gus looked at Lou and shrugged. "We're talking to everybody who might in any way help us."

Gus continued the questions. Joe resumed pacing the floor.

"Did you go to work the next day?"

"Yeah. I went to work about eight o'clock. I stopped to get a cup of coffee at either the White Hen Pantry or the Hawk Shop."

"You can't remember which?"

"No."

Gus had been waiting to spring the next question. "What were you doing with the bloody shirt shortly after the murder?"

To Gus's surprise, there was no denial. "I got in a fight with some guys."

"When was that?"

"A few days before."

"Before the murder?"

"I believe so."

"Who were these guys?"

"I don't know," responded Joe calmly.

His smile irked Gus. "Can you tell me a little more about this fight?"

"Two guys and a girl went by me, and I said hello to the girl. One of the guys said to me, 'Fuck you, punk.' We started fighting, and then they both took off."

"Can you describe these people?"

"Not really. It was dark, and I was bombed."

Gus gave Lou an opportunity to pose a few questions. He pulled out the picture of Sasha again and showed it to Joe. "How well did you know Sasha?"

"I may have met her once, but I didn't know her. I may have seen her at Father's Five or the Honey Lounge. She's certainly not one I'd likely get tangled up with or murder."

Gus couldn't resist: "What's the type you would tangle with or—"

Before Gus could finish, Joe screamed, "You fucking bastards. You better finish up quickly because I've had about enough."

Gus retreated. "Okay, Joe, just a couple more questions. Did you ever go to the Beacon Hill Pub?"

"Yes, on occasion."

"Did you ever play the *Space Invaders* video game machine with Sasha?"

"I don't recall. I may have, but I can't remember. I've played the machines with a lot of people."

"Did you have a fight with Sasha about a week before she was murdered?"

"Not that I remember. For Christ's sake—how would I have had a fight with her if I can't even remember knowing her?"

"Do you remember how many drinks you had at Frank 'N Stein's that night?"

"I had about three or four beers."

"When did you first hear about the murder of Sasha Lewis?"

"Later that day."

"What did you think when you first heard about it?"

"I was surprised and a little scared of the people killing girls in the area because this is the second time this has happened. That's enough, you guys. If I'd let you, you would question me forever. I think I need a lawyer." Joe turned and left without another word.

Gus dropped his cigar butt on the floor and rubbed it out with his shoe.

On the way back to the station, he finally broke the silence. "I believe Grady is our man. But Goddamn it, we need more evidence to charge him." He followed his comment by spitting out the window.

"Maybe we should try that psychic. We haven't got anything else to go on now," suggested Lou.

"I guess we have nothing to lose. She's probably full of shit. But give her Grady's name. You can call her when we get back."

When the officers arrived at headquarters, they went directly to the homicide unit and their office. Gus threw himself into his battered wooden swivel chair and put his feet on the cluttered desk. The chair cushion was well worn and not very comfortable. He lit another cigar.

5

The Defendant Meets
His Lawyer

AFTER AN INITIAL INTEREST IN THE BROOMSTICK MURDER, RED CZEK had pushed it to the back of his mind and had fallen back into the routine of normal office business, when he received a call from a woman who had been referred to him by Sam Johnson, a neighbor, whose small family business had been incorporated by Red. She informed Red that her son Joe had been interrogated by the police relative to the broomstick murder. She implored Red to talk to him. She said that she had been told by Mr. Johnson that he was an excellent lawyer.

Red protested that he was not a criminal lawyer, but that he could refer her to one. But Mrs. Grady insisted that she wanted Red to talk to the boy.

Red let her babble on. She broke into tears. Rather than resist further, Red agreed that he would talk to Joe, but said he didn't want his involvement to go any further. The boy had not been charged. It wasn't even clear that he was a suspect. Red supposed it would do no harm to merely give him a consultation. He knew from watching *Perry Mason* that any criminal lawyer worth his salt always told his client to tell the police, "My lawyer has advised me to exercise my right to remain silent." So, at the very least, thought Red, he could advise Joe Grady to keep his mouth shut. However, from the way the mother was talking, and her excited state, he figured such advice might be coming too late. Red told Mrs. Grady to make an appointment with his secretary for her and her son.

A few days later Joe and his mother took the elevator to the fourth floor. Red's firm occupied the entire space. As they stepped off the elevator, they were greeted by the receptionist, who stiffly inquired if they were there to see Red Czek and then curtly told them to take a seat in the reception area.

While they waited, Joe and his mother had time to be impressed with the surroundings. The walls were brick, and natural beams were exposed throughout the ceiling. The carpets were plush, as was the sofa they sat in. Old prints of the Boston waterfront, framed in gold, hung on the walls. After waiting almost an hour, the receptionist ushered Joe and his mother into a spacious office at the end of a long corridor. Red Czek rose from behind his mahogany desk as they entered. "Please have a seat."

Before Mrs. Grady sat down, she exclaimed, "We appreciate so much your willingness to represent Joe!"

Red corrected her. "I do not represent your son, ma'am. I do not believe he has been charged yet, has he?"

"No, but—"

Red interrupted Mrs. Grady as he leaned back in his leather judge's swivel chair. "So, this is simply a consultation. Now let me ask Joe what this is all about."

"I don't know nothing. The cops are out to hang me for some reason," volunteered Joe without further prompting. He sat on the edge of his chair, anxiously awaiting a response from Red.

"But the police did talk to you, Joe?"

"Yes, but—"

Red cut in. "And you talked to them?"

"But I didn't want to. My boss talked me into it," replied Joe defensively.

"Well, what did you tell them?"

"Nothing, just where I'd been the night of the murder. But I guess they didn't believe me because they kept trying to talk some more, but I said I wanted to talk to a lawyer first."

"Good for you, Joe. Let's hope it's not too late." Red swiveled toward the window overlooking the central marketplace and looked at the milling crowds, and then back again.

Mrs. Grady asked, "What do you mean by that, Mr. Czek?"

"Only that the better practice is to not talk to the police at all. At least I know that much about criminal law. Whether you are innocent or guilty, that's the best course. If you're innocent, they will twist your words out of context and come up with some kind of incriminating statement. If you're guilty, you may give them the evidence necessary to convict you where they can't do so without it."

"But I didn't do it, Mr. Czek," pleaded Joe.

"I wasn't suggesting that," responded Red. "I'm speaking in generalities."

"Do you mind if I smoke?" asked Joe.

Red did mind, but he said no. There was a period of silence before Red addressed Mrs. Grady. "Perhaps it would be best, Mrs. Grady, if you leave Joe and me together alone for a few minutes. You know about attorney-client privilege?"

Mrs. Grady started to say something but thought better of it and bustled out.

Red addressed Joe. "I asked your mother to leave so that perhaps you would feel more comfortable with me. If I am to properly advise you, I must know the truth. I don't care what you say, as I'm bound to hold what you say in confidence."

"So, you don't believe me, either," complained Joe, as he squirmed in his chair.

"I didn't say that. However, the client must tell his lawyer the truth, or he digs his own grave. Of course, you're not my client, but we have an attorney-client relationship for the purposes of this consultation." The light flashed on the phone on Red's desk, and shortly after, Red was buzzed by the secretary. He talked briefly with someone about a real estate deal, apparently another lawyer.

"Excuse me, where was I?" continued Red as he put down the receiver. "Tell me what you were doing the night of the murder."

"I met this girl in a bar and took her and another couple to my place."

"Did you see the victim that night?"

"No, I don't even think I know who she is. I might have played some video games with her at Father's Five, but I really didn't know her."

Red didn't want to get any more involved, so he terminated the consultation. "The only advice I can give you, Joe, is to refrain from any further discussion with the police. You should be all right, as they haven't arrested you." Without thinking, he added, "If you have any problem in the future, give me a ring."

"Thank you very much, Mr. Czek," responded Joe as he rose and left the office. Red remained at his desk, hoping Mrs. Grady wouldn't demand to see him again, since he realized she was upset and did not want to increase her concern about Joe. After staring off into nowhere for a few minutes, Red relaxed, opened the file of one of his regular clients, and set to work on it.

6

The Astrologer, the Cabbie, and the Bar

LOU TELEPHONED THE ASTROLOGER, GERTRUDE GILLIS. GUS DIDN'T PAY any attention to the conversation. He was too depressed and too tired to do anything but sit there.

"Gus, she says she'll be right down," announced Lou as he hung up the phone.

About a half hour later, a tall, severe-looking woman in her forties with short black hair and dangling earrings was ushered into the detectives' office. Gus was struck by her bushy eyebrows and big white teeth. She wore a thin gold necklace, and her white blouse was buttoned to the top.

"So, you're the soothsayer, are you?" remarked Gus.

Gertrude did not crack a smile. She was all business from the beginning. "All I need is the names, dates, times, and places of birth of your suspects. I'll get your man."

"Can you give us any information now?" demanded Gus.

"The murder weapon is a hammer or a tire iron, something with a claw on it."

"Do you know where the murderer lived?" asked Lou.

"Probably four to four and a half miles south-southeast of the murder site. The weapon should also be found there."

Gus was skeptical, but he let her talk. "Do you have anything else that can help us?"

"The victim was killed at 4:15 a.m. My chart says a cab and a number—571—was involved. The number might be for a cab or possibly a telephone pole."

"How could you do a chart on Sasha Lewis?" queried Gus.

"I have my connections. I got the necessary information. If I had seen her chart earlier, I'd have told her there was a good possibility she would die that night."

Gus could not hide his skepticism. "You want us to believe that?" He flicked his cigar. He was still seated in his chair. Gertrude was still standing. She had not been offered a seat.

"You wouldn't go on a trip by car without a map," she replied flippantly. "The astrological chart shows there's possibility of something good or bad happening. It's a guide. It's up to you to pay attention to what it says or ignore it. Transitory planets will trigger homicides if the tendencies are in the natal chart."

"So you're, in effect, a psychic," alleged Lou.

Gertrude scowled at Lou as she retorted with a raised, hoarse voice. "Astrology is all mathematics. It's a science not accepted yet, but a science. I would like to see astrologers get the credit they deserve. I don't mean the lunatics, but the genuine astrologers."

There was silence when she finished. Then Gus inquired if she would mind leading them to the probable site of the murder weapon. She readily agreed, and they set out in a police cruiser.

They were led to a section of Queensberry Street in the Back Bay, where she pointed out a blunt instrument in a back alley. The officers seized the instrument and dropped Gertrude off at her home. They promised to telephone her soon with the information necessary to chart the suspect.

As soon as Gertrude had been dropped off, Gus remarked, "She doesn't know her ass from her elbow. But what she said about the cab being involved got me thinking. We should check out the cab company records. See if any fares were picked up at Grady's place on Beacon Street in the early morning hours of October 30."

"Sounds good to me. Should we also try to find the records of the cab that picked up the victim from Williams's place on Marlborough Street about 4:00 a.m.?"

"Good, Lou. Can you get on that right away? Get some of the police cadets and take them over to the big cab outfits so we can examine their waybills for the night in question."

Gus pulled up in front of police headquarters, and the two detectives headed up the steps and back to the homicide unit. They continued to discuss their latest approach to the case. "Another thing that might help us, Gus—federal regulations. I believe the ICC requires that records be made of all incoming calls requesting cabs. So we may be able to pick something up from that approach too."

"Very good, Lou. Good luck," said Gus as he continued to his office while Lou went to round up the cadets.

When Lou entered the office the next day, late in the afternoon, Gus knew he had struck pay dirt. Lou seldom smiled, but when he did, Gus knew he had good news. Gus put down the *Herald American* he was reading but left the cigar in his mouth. "Okay, big Lou, what is it? I know you have something good."

"I believe we have the cab driver who picked up Grady." He threw a waybill on Gus's desk. Gus took his glasses out of his top shirt pocket and put them on. Lou reached over his shoulder and pointed to the sixth entry. In the column labeled "FROM" were the words "486 Beacon Street"; under the column labeled "TO" was 31 Peterborough Street. Under the column labeled "FARE" was $3.42. The column labeled "T" for time was blank.

"So how do we know what time the fare was picked up?" asked Gus.

"We're in luck."

"You mean that federal regulation on the incoming calls?"

"Yeah, we found it. Take a look."

Lou handed Gus another piece of paper. On it was the number 486, with a big *B* underlined. Underneath those figures was the name Grady. A time of October 30, 4:02 a.m., was printed on the paper. It had clearly been machine stamped. The number 237 was written in the upper left-hand corner.

"What's the 237 mean?"

"Turn the waybill over!"

Gus did so, and studied it. "That's the number of the taxi!" He continued to study the two documents. "Have you noticed the three different types of writing on the slip of paper with Grady's name? A good lawyer could do a job on that bit of evidence. He'll claim we fabricated it to tie Grady into this."

"And look at the waybill again, Gus," remarked Lou. "See those checks next to some of the addresses?"

"Yeah, what do they mean?"

"I asked the guy at the taxi company. He said the check means a call-in. The only problem is, there is no check next to 486 Beacon."

"One more thing for the lawyer to play with," complained an exasperated Gus. "Let's get that taxicab driver in."

"Okay, Gus."

Sidney Goldberg, the taxi driver, arrived a half hour later and was directed to Gus's office. He knocked at the door.

"Come in," bellowed Gus.

Sidney Goldberg was short and fat. He was smoking a cigar. "What do you guys want?" he inquired.

Gus made his usual pitch for a statement. He offered Goldberg Lou's seat and one of his Garcia y Vegas. The taxi driver agreed to give a statement and said he had no objection to being taped.

Gus pulled a fresh tape out of the middle top desk drawer and flipped it into the tape recorder.

STATEMENT OF SIDNEY GOLDBERG

Q. At some time in the early morning hours of October 30, did you have occasion to pick up a fare on Beacon Street?

A. I believe so.

Q. Is there any way that you could consult records to determine where your pickups were that night?

A. Yes, sir.

Q. Do you recognize these two items?

A. This item I do recognize. It is my waybill for the night of the thirtieth. The other one I don't recognize because it documents when the call comes into the office.

Q. Do you know what the document is, though?

A. I know what it is. It states that the call was received in the office and then it's dispatched to me.

Q. In your best estimate, what time did you arrive at 486 Beacon Street?

A. Probably within a couple of minutes or so.

Q. A couple of minutes of what?

A. Of the time that the call was dispatched to me around five past four in the morning.

Q. Who did you pick up?

A. Now I remember. I picked up two gentlemen at 486 Beacon Street.

Q. Can you describe them?

A. No way.

Q. Can you give us any information as to their age or color?

A. Other than the fact that they were white, I couldn't give you any description.

Q. Where did you take them?

A. They got in and told me to take them to Peterborough Street. One of the gentlemen said he was coming back and the other one would stay. He told me to wait.

Q. What number Peterborough Street was it?

A. I think it was 31.

Q. How long did it take you to get from 486 Beacon Street to 31 Peterborough Street?

A. A few minutes.

Q. What happened when you got to Peterborough Street?

A. Both gentlemen left the cab.

Q. What did you do?

A. I waited for one of them, who said he would be right down.

Q. How long did you wait?

A. Roughly a minute or a minute and a half.

Q. And did one of the two fellows come back to the cab?

A. Yes.

Q. Where did you take him?

A. He told me to take him back to where I picked him up.

Q. Which was where?

A. I picked him up on Beacon Street.

Q. Where did you drop him off?

A. I dropped him off on the corner of Massachusetts Avenue and Beacon Street.

Q. Why did you drop him off there?

A. Well, in order to get to the address that he was going, I would've had to go down Marlborough Street, down Hereford Street, and up Beacon because it's one-way. It was a fairly nice night, as I recall, and when I got to the corner of Marlborough and Mass, coming up Marlborough Street from Charlesgate, he told me to take a left and leave him at the corner of Massachusetts

and Beacon instead of going all the way around. And that's
what I did.

Q. Did you see which way he walked as he left the cab?

A. No idea.

Q. When this man came out of the apartment, did he have anything
in his hand?

A. Nothing that I noticed.

Q. How would you describe the condition of each man?

A. Okay.

Q. Were they drunk or were they sober?

A. They looked sober to me.

Q. Was the partition in your cab open?

A. Half of it was.

Q. So the conversation was just between themselves and there
weren't any boisterous voices in the back seat?

A. Yeah, that's right.

"This is the end of the interview. Thank you, Sidney."

It was 7:30 p.m. when the taxi driver left. Gus and Lou decided
to call it a day. On the way out of headquarters, they discussed
where the case stood: "The girl left Williams's apartment around
4:15 a.m. She could have walked up to Massachusetts Avenue
to get a cab, for all we know. It's only fifty yards or so away. And
we probably have Joe Grady being dropped off on Massachusetts
Avenue only a block from the corner of Massachusetts Avenue and
Marlborough Street. Joe was probably flying high on cocaine. He
could have followed her down the alleyway from Massachusetts
Avenue toward her apartment and talked her into taking a look at
the half-renovated building."

Lou cut in on Gus. "That's all speculation. We still don't have
hard evidence. We certainly don't have enough to arrest the fucker,
let alone convict him."

"That's true. Not by a long shot," conceded Gus.

The two detectives paused on the sidewalk outside police headquarters. Gus lit a cigar, and both men buttoned up their worn-out overcoats, as the wind was brisk and frigid.

"I'd like to find that guy who went back to Joe's apartment with him and the two girls," mused Lou.

"All we have is his first name."

"He was in Father's Five the night of the murder. I'm going to check that place out tonight."

"Do you mind if I don't join you, Lou? I have to get home tonight. It's probably better if only one of us goes, anyway, so we don't stand out. Good luck."

The men parted, and Lou took a cab to Father's Five. It was in what had apparently been the basement apartment of the building at the corner of Massachusetts Avenue and Marlborough Street. The first thing to catch Lou's attention was a three-by-four-foot sign identifying the bar with huge black letters against a red background.

It was necessary to walk down several steps to gain access to the establishment. As one entered, there was a long, narrow bar to the left against the wall that stretched some twenty-five feet. On the right were three different arcade games—*Mars*, *Flight 2000*, and *Counterforce*. The game machine *Defender* was tucked in at the left before the bar. Several young men were gathered around each machine, watching as one man maneuvered his arms and body up and down and sideways, as if he were going through a strange ritual.

In the back of the bar were a series of tables and chairs, and against the back wall was a narrow counter with several stools.

The establishment was poorly lit, filled with smoke, and crowded with young people. Yet Lou found a seat at the bar.

There was only one bartender, and he was extremely busy. Lou ordered a Michelob. When he got the opportunity, he asked the bartender if he knew a guy named Ken who was regularly there. The bartender pointed to a tall, thin guy in his late twenties at the end of the bar. Lou focused in on the man, about six feet, two inches, with thick glasses and long, stringy black hair to his shoulders. He wore a black V-neck sweater with the sleeves rolled up, revealing his hairy chest. He wore jeans held up by what appeared to be an old U.S. Army belt. He had considerable facial hair, too, including a mustache that curved down at the sides of his mouth.

Lou made his way to the man through the crowd. He appeared to be drinking by himself. Lou tapped him on the shoulder and handed him his card. The man looked at it for a few seconds, then looked up at Lou as if to say, "So what?"

Lou said, "Your name is Ken?"

The man hesitated before answering "Yes" with a scowl that revealed small, yellow teeth.

"Do you know Joe Grady?"

Ken nodded. "Why, what's the problem?"

"Probably nothing, but I'd appreciate a few words with you. Can we get some privacy?"

"I'll get us a table at the end," Ken volunteered.

Lou watched him call the bartender over. He looked around the bar some more. The ceilings were low, with built-in lighting. The red and yellow bulbs made the lighting poor. There was another game machine called *Pac-Man* in the rear of the bar. The age of the clientele appeared to run between twenty and thirty.

Ken waved Lou to a table in the corner of the back of the bar. Lou ordered two more Michelobs.

Lou got right to the point. "We're investigating the murder of the girl on Beacon Street the day before Halloween. Joe tells us you were with him."

"What, is Joe a suspect?" asked Ken in surprise.

"We're talking to everybody," Lou said, noting Ken's glassy eyes. He appeared a bit stoned.

Ken didn't respond, so Lou went ahead.

"How long have you known Joe?"

"Three or four years."

"Could you describe the type of relationship you have?"

"We're friends."

"How often during the course of the week do you see Joe?"

"Not too much."

"More than once a week?"

"No."

Lou had to strain to hear the responses over the hard rock music pounding out from the speakers.

"Can you give an estimate as to how many times in a month?"

"No, I used to see him every night, but then he left town for a while and I see him only on occasion."

"Where would you see him?"

"Here."

"Do you mean this bar?"

"Yeah."

"Have you seen him tonight?"

"No, I haven't seen him in a while. Officer, do you have a smoke?" Lou pulled out a pack of Marlboros and offered it to Ken. He took one, Lou took another, and both lit up.

"On the night before Sasha Lewis was found, do you recall whether you were at Father's Five?"

"Yeah."

"Do you recall who you were with?"

"Yeah."

"Who?"

"I was with my girlfriend."

"Did you see Joe that night?"

"Yeah."

"What time did you meet Joe?"

"Between one and two, about."

"Where did you meet him?"

"Outside the bar."

"Had you left the bar for the evening?"

"Yeah."

"When you first saw Joe, where was he?"

"Outside the bar."

"On the sidewalk?"

"Yeah."

"Was he with anyone?"

"He was with a girl."

"At that time, were you with anyone?"

"I was with Lynn. She was being harassed by two guys, so I was protecting her."

"Did the four of you go somewhere?"

"To Joe's house."

"Where is that located?"

"Beacon Street."

"What's Lynn's last name?"

"I don't know."

"How long have you known her?"

"About two weeks. No one uses last names here."

"How far is Joe's place from Father's Five?"

"Block away."

"How did you get there?"

"Walked."

"What time did you arrive?"

"Well, if we left at one, we got there at, like, ten after. If we left at two, we got there at ten after."

"So, you're uncertain as to what time you left Father's Five?"

"Yeah."

"How long did you stay at Joe's apartment?"

"Half hour, forty-five minutes."

"What were you doing?"

"Lit a fire, listened to music."

"At some point, did you leave Joe's apartment?"

"Yes."

"Where did you go?"

"My house."

"Did you go with anyone?"

"Yes, Joe."

"Where did you live at that time?"

"Peterborough Street."

"What number?"

"31."

"How did you get there from Joe's apartment?"

"Took a cab."

It was like pulling teeth, as Ken did not volunteer much. Lou continued questioning.

"When you went to your house, did Joe go into the house with you?"

"Yeah."

"How long did you stay there?"

"Half hour, forty-five minutes."

"What were you doing there?"

"Sitting and talking."

"When you left Joe's apartment, were the two young ladies still there?"

"Yeah."

"At some point, did you return to Joe's apartment?"

"Yeah."

"Can you give us an estimate as to the time you returned to Joe's apartment?"

"Not accurately."

"In any event, it was approximately forty-five minutes after you went to your apartment?"

"Yeah."

"How did you get from your apartment back to Joe's?"

"Cab."

"When you arrived at Joe's apartment, who was there?"

"A girl."

"Was it one of the two girls that had been there previously?"

"Yeah."

"Do you know where the other girl had gone?"

"No."

"Was it Lynn, the girl you were with, that had gone?"

"Yeah."

"And the girl that remained was the one Joe brought along?"

"Yeah."

"Do you know her name?"

"No."

"When you became aware that Lynn had left, what did you do?"

"Nothing."

"Did you stay at Joe's house?"

"No."

"What did you do?"

"We went back to my house."

"When you say 'we,' to whom are you referring?"

"Joe."

"You and Joe went back to your house?"

"Right."

"Where did the cab pick you up?"

"I think outside Joe's house."

"And you went directly to Peterborough Street?"

"Yeah."

"What happened when you went to your house?"

"We went upstairs."

"Both of you?"

"Yeah. And Joe left."

"How long did Joe remain in your apartment this second time?"

"About a minute."

"Do you know whether or not the cab remained waiting for him?"

"Yeah."

"When was the next time you saw him?"

"I haven't seen him since."

"Do you recall what Joe was wearing that night?"

"No."

"What did the girl look like that Joe was with?"

"She had dark hair, weighed about 115 pounds, about eighteen years old."

"And for what reasons had Joe accompanied you for the second time back to your apartment?"

"He came to get something from my house."

"Like what?"

"I don't know why I'm telling you all of this, but it was a needle."

"And for what purpose was he getting the needle from you?"

"Well, he was going to use it, I guess. Why the fuck do you think he wanted it?" Ken was losing patience with the cop's methodical questioning.

"When you returned after the half-hour or forty-five-minute stay in your apartment, the first time back to Beacon Street, where you said Joe lived, were you both high?"

Again Ken was hesitant, and before he could answer, Lou broke in. "We're not interested in any drug charge against you or Joe or anyone else. The murder is the only thing we're concerned with."

"Okay, we were both high," conceded Ken.

"And you had both gotten high in your apartment?"

"Yeah."

"Why did you leave Joe's place shortly after you arrived?"

"We first went back to Joe's house because we thought the girl wanted to snort the coke, but she wanted to shoot the coke. So we went back to my house to get the set of works to bring back there. I stayed at my place, and Joe returned alone."

"So, the last time you saw Joe was that morning, when Joe left you to bring back the works to the apartment to the girl waiting to shoot up?"

"Right," responded Ken. He pushed himself up from the table. "Hey, look, mister, I shouldn't even be talking to you. All my friends are here. What are they going to say?"

"How do they know I'm a cop?"

Ken could hardly contain himself. "You stand out like a fucking sore thumb."

Lou realized he wasn't going to get much more out of this guy, but he did want to talk to Lynn. "I appreciate your talking to me. One more thing, Ken. Could you tell me where I might find this Lynn?"

Ken pointed back at the bar to a strikingly pretty girl with long black hair. As Ken left the table, Lou instructed him: "Send her over, please."

While Lou waited, he gazed around the bar again. The bartender was drying his hands with a dirty white dish towel. Lou's eye caught the two old-fashioned cash registers at each end of the bar. On the wall opposite him, a large professional door sign read "KING BUDWEISER BOTTLE—$.75."

"Can I get you another one?" asked the bartender, who had walked over to the table.

Lou's attention had been diverted. Before him stood the black-haired girl. Up close, she didn't appear as pretty. Her features were hard, and she wore a frown.

"What do you want?"

"Didn't Ken tell you?" responded Lou.

"Hey, I'm busy, mister. I don't know anything about any murder."

"But you were with Ken and Joe the night Sasha Lewis died."

"So what?"

"Look, miss, I'm not trying to give you a hard time. I'm talking to everybody. That's my job." His response calmed the girl. "Take a seat. It will only take a minute."

Her story corroborated Ken's. When Lou asked her why she left Joe's apartment before the men had returned, she replied that she was tired of waiting for them. She said the other girl wanted to shoot up real bad, so she stayed. Before Lou could press her for more details, the girl was called away by some friends. As she left, she said, "That's all I know, mister."

7

The Key Witness Is Found

THE DAYS WENT SLOWLY BY. DAYS BECAME WEEKS AND THEN MONTHS.
Gus and Lou vigorously checked out all new information and
attempted to develop all previous leads. But the proverbial smoking
gun was missing. They felt they knew who the murderer was, but
they still did not have the goods on him. Depression set in. They
needed a break in the case.

And then it came, when they had almost given up hope. The
call arrived at headquarters. Sergeant Francis from Station Four
called to report that one of his patrolmen had picked up a young
lady earlier that morning and that she claimed to have important
information related to the murder of Sasha Lewis. Gus requested
that Sergeant Francis send the officer to homicide immediately.

When Officer Cremans arrived, Gus and Lou were drinking

their morning coffee and munching on doughnuts. They asked him to take a seat.

He didn't want coffee. They wasted no time in requesting him to describe what he knew, having just come from an accident on the corner of Commonwealth and Exeter Streets. He said, "It was extremely cold, and we were heading toward Kenmore Square on Newbury Street to get ourselves a cup of coffee before we went to the station to make out a report. In the vicinity of Exeter and Fairfield Streets on Newbury Street, we observed a woman in the street waving at us. I stopped the wagon, and this young girl came over to me and she says, 'I'm freezing to death. I'm trying to get a cab. There is none around.' I asked where she lived. She stated she lived at 40 Berkeley Street, the YWCA. I says, 'Well, ma'am, we're heading toward Kenmore Square. We're going back to the station right now and that's right next to the station. Do you want a lift?' She says, 'That would be great, thank you.'"

Gus broke in with a question: "Did you learn her name at that point?"

"She told me her name, but I can't exactly remember now. I think her first name was Julie. On my way toward Kenmore Square, there was a brief conversation, and she asked me, 'Have they found that guy that killed Sasha?' And I says, 'Sasha who?' And she said, 'Sasha Lewis, I believe her name was.' And I says, 'Gee, I really don't know.' She says to me, 'Well, I know who killed her.' And I looked at her and says, 'Who?' She says, 'Joe Grady.' I says, 'Really?' She says, 'Yes.' I stopped her there, and I asked was she willing to talk to the detectives. She said she was going for a job interview at eleven o'clock, but if they came earlier, she'd be able to talk to them. She told me that she was at a bar, Father's Five, about a week and a half earlier when he had come into the bar."

"He being who?" asked Gus.

"This Joe. She looked kind of scared when she was telling me this. She said she was sitting at the bar with a guy, and Joe came over to her and said, 'You are my main alibi,' or something to that effect."

"Did she mention the name of the fellow she was sitting with when this Joe came over?"

"She might have, but I don't remember his name."

"After that conversation, what did you do?"

"I took her to Kenmore Square, and I got a cup of coffee for myself and my partner. I asked if she wanted one and she said no, and I took her back to the YWCA."

"As a result of the conversation with this person, what did you do?"

"I contacted Sergeant Francis, who is at the District Four station. I told him the circumstances, and he said, 'I think this should go right up to homicide.'"

After dismissing Officer Cremans, Gus called Sergeant Francis and discovered that the name of the girl officer Cremans had picked up was Julie Connors. Gus and Lou headed for the YWCA. They called for Julie at the front desk.

After only a short wait, a young girl appeared. She struck the detectives as being no more than eighteen or nineteen years old. She was slender, with long black hair. Her face was narrow. She wore dungarees and a T-shirt. Gus introduced himself and Lou. As there was no convenient and private place to talk, Gus requested the girl come down to headquarters later that day.

A few hours later, Gus and Lou anxiously awaited the girl's arrival.

"Gus, do you want me to set up the tape recorder?" asked Lou as he stirred the cup of coffee in front of him with his fingers.

"No, Lou. Let's dry-run her first. If we tape-record, we'll have to turn everything she says over to some fucking asshole of a defense counsel down the road." Gus shifted in his chair and threw his left leg up on his desk.

"Let's hope this is the break we've been looking for," said Lou.

The phone rang. It was the desk man. The girl had arrived. Gus left to fetch her and then ushered her in. She was wearing the same jeans but now had on a tight sweater. Her nipples appeared to Gus to be even more pronounced. She wanted sugar in her coffee. After she sat and crossed her legs, Gus began. "We appreciate your coming down. Julie, is it?"

"Yes."

"And what did you say your last name was?"

"Connors."

Gus scanned his desk for a pencil. None had decent points. He opened his desk and found a halfway sharpened one. He scribbled her name on a yellow pad.

He continued: "We're told you have some information on the Sasha Lewis murder."

Without hesitation, the girl responded, "Yes, I was with Joe Grady the night before the murder. He took me to his place for a party. I don't remember much. But he did leave me for a couple of hours in the early morning between 3:00 and 5:30 a.m. or so. I didn't think too much about it at the time, but a month later he approached me in Father's Five and threatened me." Gus wrote furiously in an attempt to keep up with her.

The girl paused at this point. Gus asked, "What did he say?"

"I was sitting with another guy at the bar, and Joe came up and taps me on the shoulder. I turned around, and he says, 'Remember me?' I told him I did, and he blurts out that he is the number one suspect in the Sasha Lewis murder. He then adds: 'I'm going to use you as my alibi witness.' At this point, the guy I was with told Joe to get the hell out of the bar. He and a few other guys dragged and pushed him out. Joe had been barred from Father's Five and wasn't supposed to be there. My friend Rick returned and said Joe was an asshole."

"Can you tell us, Julie, a little more about this party you went to at Joe's house?"

"I can't remember much," she said. "All I remember is his leaving and then coming back much later. He appeared very tired when he got back."

"Did you ask him where he had been?"

"No."

"Why can't you remember more, Julie?"

"I don't know. It was quite a while ago."

"Did you have anything to drink that night?"

"A few beers."

"What about drugs?"

Julie hesitated and crossed her legs again. She asked Gus for a cigarette. He lit it for her.

"You must tell us everything," Lou said softly.

"Joe brought back some coke and we shot up," responded Julie as she stared at the ceiling. She added, "He already appeared to be flying high when he returned. I figured he'd already done most of it."

"Can you remember anything Joe said?"

"No, it's all hazy now."

"Can you remember where you met him?"

"Yeah, at Frank 'N Stein's."

"And what happened before you went to his apartment for the party?"

"He said he could get any drugs he wanted and at any time he wanted. We left Frank 'N Stein's and walked down Commonwealth Avenue toward the Charles. We waited outside Father's Five until it closed. Joe invited everybody to a party. He told me he was going to see some guy about some coke, and I saw him going down to the bottom of the steps and talking to some guy. Some girl came up to me and introduced herself as Lynn, and she started to talk to me and tell me what a good guy Joe was." Julie drew deeply on her cigarette.

"And then what happened?"

"The four of us took a cab to Joe's place."

"And what happened at his house?"

"I can't remember any more than I told you except I woke up at his place at about 8:30 a.m., and after seeing him sleeping, I got dressed and left."

Gus stood up. "Lou and I will be right back. Just make yourself at home. We have another matter that we must attend to."

Gus and Lou went out into the corridor. "I think we should call Ben Ripley, over at the hypnosis unit. This girl knows more, I believe, than we're getting out of her."

"I'll call now, Lou. Go back and keep her company."

Gus called District Fourteen and was put through to Detective Ripley: "Hey, Ben, I've got some business for you. Can I come over?"

"What is it, Gus?"

"It's this broomstick murder case. We've got a girl who was with our chief suspect around the time of the murder. But she's very hazy on the details."

"Don't tell me anymore, Gus. Just bring the incident report. And be sure the subject is willing to be hypnotized."

"Okay, we'll probably see you soon," concluded Gus, and he hung up the phone.

On his return to his office, he found Lou and Julie in animated conversation. He caught something about a father-daughter relationship. As he slumped back in his chair, he addressed Julie: "Do you know what hypnosis is?"

"Well, like anyone else, I've heard a little about it."

"We police use it to help witnesses remember. We think it would be appropriate in this case. Are you willing to give it a try?"

"Sure."

"Okay, good. I've already made a call and set it up. We can go over right now."

8

The Key Witness Is
Hypnotized

THE TWO DETECTIVES AND THE GIRL LEFT POLICE HEADQUARTERS AND headed for Station Fourteen. On the way over, they stopped at Julie's room at the YWCA to allow her a few minutes to freshen up.

When Julie and the two detectives arrived at Station Fourteen, they went to the second-floor office of Detective Ben Ripley, who headed up what was called the Hypno-Investigative Unit.

The secretary ushered them into a small, neat office that was remarkably different from those found in most police stations. The walls were painted light blue, and the ceiling was low, with track lights overhead to darken the room, as well as wall-to-wall carpeting. On one of the walls was a series of framed certificates. Opposite a simple metal desk was a comfortable-looking vinyl "induction" chair with an adjustable back.

As the three were still in the process of fully surveying the room, Detective Ripley entered the office and introduced himself. He was young and handsome with an engaging smile. His hair was curly and black, and he wore a plaid sports jacket with gray flannel slacks. His teeth were even and gleaming white. Julie liked him immediately.

He invited her to take a seat. Gus handed him the incident report and briefly conversed with him at the far side of the room near the door. When Detective Ripley returned to the desk, he began explaining what hypnosis was and what he intended to do in order to induce the state of hypnosis.

In the meantime, a young woman, who was a police cadet, and an assistant district attorney entered the room as observers.

"Hypnosis is slowly being accepted around the nation. Eventually," Detective Ripley remarked, "I feel it will be a regular part of police investigation procedure, simply because it works. Hypnosis induces hypermnesia, the opposite of amnesia, and enhances the capacity to remember details. It also produces 'revivification,' or the reliving of an event."

He continued as he moved to lower the backrest of the leather easy chair to make the girl more comfortable. "The mind is constantly taking pictures. It has a great storage capacity, but a weak retrieval system. That is what hypnosis attempts to call up. So that any fears you may have are dispelled, let me assure you that a person under hypnosis will not reveal any deep, dark secrets. You will not be put to sleep but will hear everything going on around you.

"And, Julie, let me dispel another myth. It is not true that once under hypnosis, the subject will not come out of it. We have had no adverse reactions since we started." Detective Ripley had returned to his desk and was now sitting opposite the subject. "It merely gives you a heightened concentration and awareness. Under hypnosis, you are talking about a particular event, so you have focused your attention on it. You have an altered state of consciousness. You block out everything else but that one event. We all allow ourselves to be hypnotized every day. We can do it by reading a book or watching television. Hypnosis, Julie, is not magic. What we are doing is talking to the subconscious. Once I have regressed you to the time of the event, you will be able to see the event taking place and will be much more aware of the circumstances."

"How long will it take?" asked Julie, as she shifted in the chair.

"The induction can take anywhere from fifteen minutes to half an hour."

"And what is done to induce hypnosis?"

"One technique is referred to as levitation. I will tell you your arm is getting lighter, and it will raise itself without your conscious effort. As the hypnosis takes hold, breathing goes from the chest to the lower torso."

Gus and Lou, the assistant attorney, and the police cadet encircled the young subject as they stood at various places in the small room.

"I guess we're all set to go, Julie. Are you game to try it?" asked Detective Ripley.

"It sounds like fun," replied Julie.

"Good. Now I'm going to turn on the tape recorder on my desk, and we'll start." Into the tape recorder, he said, "Today is Tuesday, February 5, 1980, and the time is approximately quarter past four. We're at District Fourteen, in the Hypno-Investigative Unit. My name is Detective Ripley, and we have a young lady here, one Julie Connors. Is that correct, Julie?"

"Yes."

Detective Ripley explained what would happen. That they would use progressive relaxation, that she would feel good, and that it would help her concentrate on the time in the past they wanted to know more about.

"Okay, well, why don't we begin? Now, basically, what's going to happen is I'm going to have you stare at this ring, and you'll find that your eyelids will get very heavy and you'll begin to relax more and more. Then what will happen is . . . do you have a television at home?"

"Yes."

"You'll be able to watch the events of the twenty-ninth and thirtieth as if you were watching it on a television set. You'll be very comfortable, very relaxed, and you'll see this happening, and you'll relay to me exactly what you see transpiring. It will be like watching a documentary."

"Okay."

"Fine. All right, I want you to look at the center of the ring. As I bring it closer, you'll find that your eyes will begin to break, and that will be a good sign. Very nice. And you'll see that as I bring it closer, your eyelids are starting to get heavier. Heavier and heavier as you concentrate on the center of that, and they are getting heavier and heavier as your eyes start to follow the ring. You'll notice that your eyelids are going down and down, getting heavier and heavier.

"Your eyelids are getting heavier and heavier. Your eyes may start to smart or tear, but that's all right. And as your eyelids start to come down because they're getting so heavy, you can shut them at any time it's comfortable. As you breathe in and out, you feel this relaxation coming all about your body. Almost like a sensation of floating, and you may close your eyes now. Each breath that you take, you'll feel this wonderful relaxation coming over you, a kind of floating, dreamy feeling.

"I want you now to concentrate on the top of your head and imagine, if you will, tiny fingers, massaging the scalp. And as this massaging takes place, you can feel all the tiny muscles begin to relax, and the relaxing is moving down the sides of your head and the back of your head and down your forehead, almost like a warm, magic fluid. All the muscles in the forehead and the eyebrows are beginning to relax more and more, as well as the tiniest muscles in the body. The eyes are relaxing more and more. Relaxation now is going down the sides of your face and you feel it in the cheeks and in the lips and the chin. You are relaxed, and with each breath you find that you're able to drift deeper and deeper. Drifting deeper still and this relaxation now is going down the sides of your neck and throat. You feel it in the front and rear, starting down further and further, and all the tiny muscles in the back of your neck and the sides relax, and your head is begging to become very heavy. If it becomes too heavy, you might find that it's drifting forward, and if that happens, it's all right. Relaxation now is spreading through your shoulders and down your back. Feel it now coming from your neck and chest. Feels so good. Relaxation now is in the upper part of the stomach and coming down the back as well. Down and down, your whole body is becoming heavier and heavier and so relaxed. With each breath, you will find yourself drifting deeper and deeper still. The voices in the background will soon disappear, although you'll be aware of them. You'll concentrate more deeply on the sound of my voice. So relaxed, so comfortable, you feel so good. As you breathe in and out, this relaxation is coming down the bottom of your back now and your lower stomach, going down, spreading through your hips, buttocks, and thighs, starting to descend now down the tops of your legs. Going down to the knees, down the shins, as it's starting to go down from the knees, you feel the calves of your legs, down through the ankles and heels, tops of the feet, the arches, right down to the tips of your toes. Your toes may get a tingling sensation. If they do, that's all right. Relaxation is spreading down from your shoulders and down your arms as your whole body becomes more and more relaxed. So relaxed, so comfortable. With each breath, you're going deeper and deeper and deeper still. Relaxing is coming down your arms now to the area of the elbows. Down to the forearms, the wrist, the top of the hand, the palms of the hands, relaxing down through each finger, right to the very tips. It feels so good, so good.

With each breath now, you will find that you will start to drift so
beautifully and peacefully into this lovely state that we call hypnosis.

"With every breath, your head will become heavy and heavier,
so heavy, so relaxed, so heavy and so relaxed. And now, if you would,
I'd like you, Julie, to see yourself in a beautiful, luxurious hotel on the
twentieth floor. You're feeling so good, so comfortable. And you're
walking across a lush carpet, and we're getting into the elevator.
Inside this elevator, you will find yourself going deeper and deeper
than you are now. This, then, is your elevator of relaxation. The
doors are closing . . . twenty, nineteen . . . this elevator is descending
. . . eighteen, seventeen . . . deeper still . . . sixteen, fifteen, fourteen
. . . deeper and deeper . . . thirteen, twelve, eleven, ten, nine, eight,
seven, six, five . . . so deep, lower, lower . . . four, three, two, one.
You're doing so good, Julie, so good and you're so comfortable.

"Now the elevator door is opening, and you're walking down
this lovely carpeted corridor. You see a beautiful carved door, and it's
open. You walk into this room. The interior can be any way you like,
such a comfortable room, so secure. This is your security room, such
a comfortable room, so secure. This is your security room, and there's
a beautiful couch there, and you lie down, and it feels so good. And
you're so relaxed and you feel so good, so relaxed. Now with each
breath, you will still go deeper and deeper in this beautiful relaxed
state. I want you to concentrate on your right arm from the shoulder
down, and you'll find that it becomes heavier and heavier, as if there
were leaden weights on it. It becomes limp, almost like a warm, wet
towel. So heavy. And in a moment, I will lift your hand near the wrist.
It will be so heavy and so limp, and on the count of five, it will drop
to your side, and you will be five times more comfortable. As you
go deeper and deeper still, your arm is limp and just so heavy like a
warm, wet towel, so heavy, so beautiful. One, so heavy, two, heavy
and heavier, three, heavier still, four, and five.

"Now I'm going to press the muscles in your neck. Your head
is getting heavier and tending to go forward. So heavy and so

comfortable. You're doing so, so good, so good. And now, I want you to think of when you were a child and very happy and you're on a slide. Do you like slides?"

"Yes."

"Okay, now I want you to imagine yourself at the top of the slide and as I press on your shoulders. You can go even deeper when I press down. You'll find that you feel relaxed ever further as you drift deeper and deeper. At the count of three, I will press down— one, two, three—so good. Very good. I'd like you to go deeper still as I press down, and you'll picture yourself going down this beautiful slide as I press down, and one more time as I press down. So relaxed, so deep and relaxed. Are you relaxed?"

"Yes."

"I want you to think of yourself now on a lovely carpeted staircase without any shoes on. There's a banister there. It looks so nice and feels so good. And you're going to descend down these stairs. The rug feels so nice under your feet, and I will count from one to ten and you descend, and you will feel even more relaxed than you are now. Ten, nine, eight, seven, six, five, four, three, two, one. You're doing so good. I would like you now to picture your television set. And the television set is where it always is, the particular room. And I want you to sit in front of the television where you usually sit, rest, or recline, and tell me what this television looks like."

"It's brown, square, moderately small."

"All right, and you can see it?"

"Yes."

"I'd like you now to get up and walk over and see yourself walk over and turn it on. When the picture tube is illuminated, I want you to tell me."

"It is now, but I can't really tell you what's on it."

"That's all right. I don't want you to right now. Because what I'm going to do is, I'm going in a moment to turn the channel, and when I do, you're going to see two little kittens playing with a ball of string. That will be kind of fun to look at, won't it?"

"Yes."

"Okay, one, two, three. I want you to tell me when you see the little kittens frolicking over a ball of string."

"Yes."

"Could you describe these kittens to me?"

"One's black, and one's gray."

"What are they doing?"

"Playing with a white ball of yarn."

"Do they seem to be enjoying themselves?"

"Yes."

"Fine, fine, so good. And now, at the count of three again, I will turn the channel to another channel, and we will begin by watching a documentary of what took place early in the evening of October 29, and you will see this and tell me what is happening, adding nothing or detracting nothing, just as you watch it on the screen. One, two, three, and I'm going to change the channel now and the documentary begins. Now where are you?"

"I'm at the bar. I think it's the Back Bay Lounge."

"Are you with anyone?"

"No."

"What are you doing?"

"Trying to avoid the people. They're bothering me in there."

"How are they bothering you?"

"Lots of Black pimps in there."

"Are they talking to you?"

"Yeah."

"What is the conversation?"

"Can I buy you a drink and do you want to go home with me? Crap like that."

"And what's happening now?"

"Still sitting there by myself. Can I rest my head? I'm getting a stiff neck."

"Yes, certainly. Does that feel better?"

"Yeah."

"Be as comfortable as you like. And what's happening now, Julie?"

"I'm at Frank 'N Stein's."

"What are you doing in Frank 'N Stein's?"

"Just sitting down."

"And what's happening now?"

"Someone's talking to me."

"Do you know who this person is?"

"No."

"What is this person's name?"

"Joe."

"And what is happening now?"

"He asked me if there are any parties around."

"Did you answer this?"

"Yeah."

"What is he saying?"

"That he's gonna start one in his apartment probably, and he can get anything he wants for it. Booze and drugs and stuff."

"And what's happening?"

"Just watching a movie. Looks like something with Robert Redford. I'm not sure, 'cause I can't really see."

"Why can't you see?"

"I don't have my contact lenses in."

"All right, and what's happening now?"

"Buying another beer, and I'm getting mad 'cause the guy's not paying for my drinks."

"What's happening now?"

"I keep asking him who's going to the party and what he's gonna have there. He keeps saying we'll start one at Father's Five."

"And tell me what's happening?"

"Just watching the movie."

"And tell me what is happening now?"

"Standing outside of Father's Five."

"Who are you with?"

"Joe, it's like 2:10 or something. There's no one out there even yet."

"What is Joe wearing as you're looking?

"Blue sweater, dirty jeans, white and blue sneakers."

"What's happening now?"

"He said he'd be back in a second, and he walked down the stairs, talking to someone."

"Can you hear what they are saying?"

"No, he is sending some girl to talk to me."

"He's sending a girl up to you? Do you know this girl?"

"No."

"What is she saying?"

"'Hi, how are you doing? Are you a friend of Joe's?'"

"And what is happening now?"

"Joe's coming back out."

"And what's happening now?"

"Everybody's ignoring us."

"And now, what do you see now?"

"Joe's just saying, 'Let's go. Let's get out of this place. It's a dump anyway.'"

"You're doing so good."

"He's trying to hail a cab."

"Where is he standing when he's hailing a cab?"

"By the side of the road, across the street from the bar."

"And what's happening now?"

"We're in the cab."

"Then what's happening?"

"Getting out of a cab. Going up the stairs. Could you open the window a little more, Detective Ripley?"

"Sure. And what's happening now?"

"I'm standing in the middle of the room. I keep asking if he has any drugs or anything. Lynn does too."

"Who's in the room?"

"Me and Lynn and Joe."

"Do you know Lynn's last name?"

"No."

"And what's happening?"

"He went down the hallway for something. Lynn's asking me how long I've known him. He came back and said he was gonna get some coke."

"And what's happening now?"

"He's leaving again."

"And what's happening now, Julie?"

"Lynn's talking to me. She said her boyfriend got arrested."

"Why?"

"Dealing drugs, and she has to go to court tomorrow for something. She's in trouble for hooking and for dealing."

"What's happening now?"

"She says she's known Joe for a while and he's really nice. I'm lucky to be there."

"Who's lucky to be there?"

"That I am."

"Why?"

"That he's really nice, and I'm lucky to be there, to be with him."

"What's happening now?"

"Still talking to me, telling me I should be a hooker."

"Why?"

"She told me I was good-looking enough to do it, and they make a lot of money, and that it wasn't that bad. Boyfriends got her jobs."

"And what's happening now?"

"Just sitting there, wondering where the hell Joe is."

"Do you have any idea what time it is?"

"No, there's no clock around."

"I'm going to press the screen to fast-forward a little. All right, one, two, three, and the picture is on again. What's happening now?"

"Lynn's getting bored. She said she's tired of waiting around. He probably took all the drugs and did them all himself."

"And what's happening?"

"She's leaving. Said, 'See ya around.'"

"What's happening now?"

"Joe just got here."

"And what's he doing?"

"Sitting down next to me, telling me he got what he looked for."

"Does he have blood on him?"

"Yeah, and his jeans are ripped."

"The jeans are what?"

"Ripped."

"Where are they ripped?"

"The side of the right leg."

"And where is the blood?"

"On his hand, his lower arm, a little bit on his neck."

"Which side of the neck?"

"Left. He's pulling out the coke and there's a needle. I told him I never shot it before. He just said to try it, and I'd like it."

"And what's happening now?"

"Shooting up coke."

"How does it feel?"

"Like taking speed or something. Like I'm really shaky."

"And what's happening now?"

"He's moving over nearer to me on the mattress, moves his arms around me, pushing me backward on the mattress."

"What's happening now?"

"Kissing me and telling me to take off my pants and shoes, to relax, that he's tired."

"Continue, Julie."

"Taking off most of my clothes, throwing them halfway across the room, rolling over on top of me."

"Does he have his clothes on or off?"

"Off. His pants off, his shirt on."

"And what's the conversation?"

"There is none."

"Fine, and what's happening now?"

"He's fucking me."

"And what's happening?"

"He rolled off me pretty quickly and said he's going to sleep."

"What are you doing?"

"Going to sleep."

"Can you see his clothes?"

"I can see his shirt. He's wearing it, but he threw his jeans over by my clothes."

"Can you describe the jeans?"

"They're like twenty feet away."

"Okay, is there blood on them?"

"Yeah, I think so."

"Are his sneakers in the same direction?"

"Yeah, they are with the pants."

"Okay, fine. And what's happening?"

"Starting to get tired."

"What are you thinking about?"

"Just that he was gone a long time and that I didn't get high off the coke, and he had a dump for an apartment with crap all over the floors."

"What's happening?"

"Just lying on my side, starting to fall asleep."

"Are you both asleep now?"

"Yes."

"Now I'll continue to fast-forward this film until the time that you're awaking. Are you waking up now?"

"Still sleeping."

"And what are you doing?"

"Looking around for my clothes. Got shit all over them, throwing them around."

"What is on them?"

"Dirt, dust."

"What's happening now?"

"Getting dressed and putting my pants on, missing a sock."

"And now?"

"Gonna leave."

"And what's happening now?"

"Going downstairs."

"Did you have a conversation before you left?"

"No."

"And what's happening?"

"Trying to figure out what direction I have to go to get home."

"Where are you standing?"

"On the sidewalk, right outside the building."

"I'm going to back up this film now until the time he came in and you described him as having blood on his lower arm. Do you see this?"

"Yes."

"And what are your thoughts?"

"I don't know. I wonder where the hell he got it. It's his business."

"Are you asking him?"

"No."

"Does he go somewhere to wash or does he leave this substance on his clothes and arms?"

"He stays in the room with me."

"Why do you say it's blood?"

"I know what blood looks like."

"Is he commenting on the blood?"

"No."

"Are you questioning him about it?"

"No. Said it's been a rough night."

"What does he mean by a rough night?"

"I don't know."

"What else is he saying?"

"He's tired out."

"Why?"

"I don't know."

"And what's happening now?"

"He's taking out coke."

"Did he mention to you the name of Ken?"

"No, Lynn did."

"What did Lynn say? I'm gonna back this up from the time that you're having the conversation with Lynn to the time that you first heard this name, and I will do it on the count of three. One, two, three. Where are you now?"

"Standing by the window with Lynn."

"And what's happening?"

"Saying Joe's friend has some good coke."

"Good. How long do you think it will take him to get it?"

"She answered that she doesn't think it will take too long."

"As you're listening to this conversation, I want you to repeat it for me."

"What?"

"I'd like you to repeat the conversation the way it goes, the way you hear it."

"'Joe has a friend who has some excellent coke.' 'Good, will it take a long time to get it?' 'Not very long. He doesn't have to go far for it.' 'Good, I'm sick of waiting around all night.'"

"Where is he getting the coke?"

"From one of his friends."

"What is his friend's name?"

"She said a friend of his named Ken might have some."

"All right, do you know this Ken?"

"No."

"All right. Okay, you're doing so good, so good, so relaxed. Your body is so relaxed, so comfortable, peaceful, and secure. So comfortable, so peaceful. Did she mention Peterborough Street?"

"No."

"You're doing so good, Julie, so good. And you're so secure, so relaxed. Feels so nice as you're watching this and you feel so refreshed. When did you first hear the name Sasha Lewis? And at the moment that you first heard it is where I will be putting the film. On the count of three, you will begin telling me about the first time you heard the name Sasha Lewis. One, two, three."

"In the news. Lying in bed in my room."

"What news?"

"On the news or in the papers, I'm not sure which."

"And what's happening?"

"Thinking about how Joe was gone all that time and how he had blood on his hands."

"And what do you think about that?"

"That it's weird that he was gone all that time, and he got blood on his hands and stuff."

"Have you seen Joe since that morning?"

"In December."

"Fine. What I'd like to do now is I'd like to move the film forward to the time that you see Joe. On the count of three, you'll be able to observe this. One, two, three. What's happening?"

"Sitting up at the bar at Father's Five."

"Where are you sitting?"

"Six seats down from the door."

"Who is sitting to your immediate right?"

"A guy name Rich."

"And Rich's last name?"

"I don't know it."

"All right, and what's happening now?"

"There's a big crowd of people there, and someone just tapped me on the back."

"And what's happening?"

"Joe's standing there. I turned around when I felt someone tap me. Not really sure if it's him at first."

"Why?"

"Just dark, and something looks different."

"What do you mean, something looks different?"

"I don't know what, something's different."

"All right, what's happening now?"

"He's talking to me and saying, 'I don't know if you remember me.' I just said, 'Yeah, yeah, I do.' Rich grabbed me and whispered in my ear, 'Where the hell do you know that asshole from?'"

"All right, and what are you saying to Rich?"

"I told you already. How stupid are you?"

Detective Ripley gulped but continued the interview.

"Joe said he's looked all over for me and that I'm a hard person to track down. He wants to know if I remember about the girl that was murdered. He said he's a suspect."

"Can you tell me exactly what he is saying to you now?"

"'Do you remember when Sasha Lewis was murdered?' 'Yes.' 'Well, the cops think I did it, and they said I'm the number one suspect.' I said, 'So what? I don't give a shit. It's not my problem.' He said, 'You better give them an alibi for me, or else. Say you were with me.' And Rich jumps up and pushes him."

"Pushes who?"

"Joe."

"Are you upset?"

"No. Had about fourteen gin and tonics."

"Has Joe done this to other girls before?"

"Done what?"

"Has he assaulted anyone?"

"He smacked one of the waitresses."

"Really?"

"That's what Rich told me."

"And what's happening now?"

"Rich is coming back in, and he says that chickenshit just ran, scared even to fight. 'Someday, I'm gonna blow his fucking head off.'"

"And what's happening now?"

"He's ordering me another drink."

"What kind?"

"Gin and tonic."

"Fine, and now what's happening?"

"Sitting there drinking. He said Joe's a real asshole."

"As he's saying that, I want you to look down at your drink, and you can see it. Can you describe the glass?"

"Just a plain, tall glass, one of those, like . . . pretty much clear. Looks like it could be frosted. There's a lot of ice in it."

"Is the ice crushed or is it cubed?"

"It's cracked, but I think it was originally cubes."

"Does the drink taste good?"

"Yes."

"Is the drink weak or strong?"

"Strong."

"Is there more than a shot in there, if you know?"

"I don't think so. The bartender's pretty cheap, so I doubt it."

At this point, Detective Ripley slid his foot to the outlet to the left of the desk and squeezed out the tape recorder plug. He wanted to dig deeper with the witness on the crucial question of the blood on Joe. If she pulled back, he certainly didn't want it on tape.

"Now what I'd like to do, Julie, is return to when Joe came back to the apartment on the night of the murder. I'm just going to press this down and return there for a moment, and I'm going to slow this down frame by frame. Now tell me more about the blood on Joe that night."

"I have a hard time seeing it."

"Try harder, Julie. It's very important. What's happening when Joe returns?"

"He has the shit, and he sticks me."

"He what?"

"We're on the mattress, and he has the needle. I want it so bad. He sticks it in. It feels so good."

"Was it good stuff?"

"Oh, yes, I got a good high."

"And the blood. Describe the blood on Joe."

"I can't see it well."

"Well, what happened next?"

"He fucked me, and that was so good too. It was big and hard and strong."

Detective Ripley suppressed a smile. He could see he was getting no further with the witness, so he brought her out of the hypnotic state. He raised his voice to a normal tone and said, "That's it, Julie. It's all over. You're no longer under hypnosis."

Julie sat up straight, smiled, and remarked, "It wasn't so bad after all."

9

The Defendant Is Arrested

GUS AND LOU ARRIVED AT HEADQUARTERS LATE THE FOLLOWING DAY. For the first time in months, they felt they could relax, as progress was being made. It was Gus's turn to make the coffee. He poured Lou his cup and topped it off with a dash of milk from the half-size refrigerator shared by the whole floor.

"How do you think things stand now, Lou?" began Gus.

"You mean can we arrest Joe?"

"Well—yes, I guess that's what I'm asking." Gus lit his usual morning cigar and threw his legs up on his desk.

"We've made some real progress, but you know as well as I do it isn't enough. The blood itself can be explained away. We desperately need something else, like an admission of sorts."

"What about the taxicab driver's testimony?"

"But he can't identify Joe as his rider, and it's doubtful we could even get that guy to testify. Even if it was Joe, it only puts him in the same area at the same time as Sasha."

"We know the fucker did it, but we have to deal with that damn reasonable doubt."

"You're right."

"And that hypnosis could create problems."

"We'll have to make the best of it."

"Wait, Lou. I say fuck the hypnosis. It will kill us if some smart-ass lawyer gets wind of Julie only 'remembering' the blood while under hypnosis."

"Well, what do you propose?" inquired Lou.

"Don't be stupid, Lou. I'll write up her statement without mentioning any hypnosis. I believe the girl will cooperate with us."

"You're right, Gus. The hypnosis thing compromises the credibility of our best witness's testimony."

"Okay. That's that. Now to get back to work. I think we should try and locate Joe again. If we can get some type of admission out of him, we're all set."

"You asked me some time ago to contact him, but I haven't had much luck."

"What do you mean, Lou?"

"I've talked to him three or four times. I call him up and ask him to come in and talk to me. He always agrees but never shows. I also bumped into him in person down in the vicinity of the Charles Street area. Once again, he said he would be in the following day. I waited around the office, but he never showed up. I called him about a week later, and I asked him if he had intended to come in and talk to me for any reason whatsoever, and he said that he didn't want to talk to me until he talked to his lawyer."

"Who's his lawyer?" Gus inhaled and slowly blew the smoke out.

"He didn't say. I don't even know if he has one yet."

"The key is to work on one of his friends if we are to get any admission. Have you had any luck with any of them?"

"There's one guy who has promised us he'll keep his ears open. He's that no-good B and E man who's always getting busted. He's worried they'll send him away the next time, so he should be real cooperative."

"What's his name?"

"Ed Lovett."

"Does he hang at Father's Five?"

"Yeah, he's usually there with the rest of Joe's buddies."

"Well, there's not too much we can do now but wait for a break."

Lou shrugged and nodded in agreement.

A FEW MONTHS LATER, A call came from officers at District Ten. They had picked up an Ed Lovett on an extortion charge. He had requested to talk to the homicide detectives on the Sasha Lewis murder case. Gus and Lou wasted little time in getting to the District Ten police station.

Ed Lovett looked like something the cat dragged in as the officer came upon him in his cell. He wore a tattered and dirty T-shirt and dungarees with holes in the knees. He was heavyset, and his face was pockmarked. His big red nose and reddened face gave the impression he was an alcoholic, and he had cauliflower ears. He greeted Lou with a smile. "I think I have something that will interest you guys."

"What you got, Ed?" questioned Lou.

"It's about Joe Grady. He made some interesting statements to me."

"Well, what did he say?" asked an impatient Gus.

"Wait a minute, you guys. What's in this for me?" demanded Ed.

"Don't worry, kid. If you've got something good, we'll take care of you the next time you're busted," promised Gus.

"You got a cigarette?"

"Yeah, here."

"Thanks. Okay. This is what went down. Me and Joe were heading back from that big steak house on the North Shore. We had eaten a nice lunch there."

"When was this, Ed?"

"I believe it was last Wednesday."

"You mean February 25?"

"That sounds right."

Gus lit his cigar. "So, continue."

"I was driving."

"Whose car?"

"I don't know the guy's name, but we were going to burn it for him so he could get his insurance money."

"And what happened, Ed?" inquired Gus in his most pleasant voice. He didn't want to lose this one.

"Joe says to me all of a sudden, 'Quick, there's District Four,' and I turned to him and says, 'Joe, they're watching you. They think you did the Sasha Lewis murder case, and they's keeping an eye on you.' Joe then grabbed the stick shift and put it in neutral and says, 'Ed, pull over. I want to drive.' I kept on saying, 'Just a few more minutes.' Then he says, 'Ed, pull over or I'm going to pull a Sasha Lewis on you.' I said, 'Joe, you probably killed the girl,' and he said, 'Yeah, I did it. So what, I'm leaving anyway. They're going to hang me on the seventeenth.' I pulled the car over, and he drove the rest of the way to Boston."

Gus took a few seconds finishing his note-taking before he spoke. "What does that 'District Four' expression mean?"

"It's what we say when we're doing something wrong," responded Ed as he paced back and forth in the cell.

"What did he mean in his reference to getting hung on the seventeenth?"

"Oh, he's got some assault and battery with a dangerous weapon charge for that date in the municipal court. He got into a fight with some guy and beat the shit out of him."

"What was the dangerous weapon?"

"Only a shod foot."

"Have you ever seen Joe with Sasha Lewis, Ed?"

"She occasionally came to Father's Five to play the video machines. I once saw her playing with Joe."

"When was that?"

"I don't know, some time ago."

"Did he ever mention Sasha?"

"One time he did."

"When was that?"

"About ten days before her death."

"What did he say?"

"We were sitting at the bar, and we spotted her playing the *Space Invaders* machine. He leaned over and told me that she was 'a fucking whore.' I think he also said, 'She thinks she's too good for me,' or something like that."

"What did you say?"

"I just chuckled."

"Where's Joe now?"

"He was staying at some motel in Somerville, but I believe he was busted last night for a B and E in the suburbs. He's in the House of Correction."

"Okay, thanks, Ed. We appreciate your help." Gus dropped his cigar butt to the floor and squashed it out with the toe of his shoe. He turned to leave.

"Hey, wait a minute, you guys," screamed Ed. "I got defaults all over the place. You promised you'd take care of me."

"Don't worry, kid. I'll send someone to take you around and clear them up. You'll be on the street in a couple of days."

Gus shook Lou's hand as they left the station. "Congratulations, old man, I believe we have enough now to move."

"I believe you're right, Gus. Hopefully, we'll get more as a result of the arrest so that we can tie this case up once and for all."

"Okay, you go over to the municipal court and get a warrant for his arrest. Then both of us will go serve it to him at the House of Correction."

When Gus and Lou arrived at the House of Correction, they sent word to Joe through one of the correction officers that they wished to speak with him. The officer reported back that Joe would only talk to Gus.

Gus was ushered into one of the interview rooms. He took a seat and placed his tape recorder on the makeshift table and waited for Joe.

When Joe entered the room, Gus told him to take a seat. Joe replied, "What the fuck do you want?"

Gus retorted with a slight smile. "I have a little present for you, Grady. It's a warrant for your arrest for the murder of Sasha Lewis."

Joe's face stiffened. He caught sight of the tape recorder. "Turn that fucking thing off."

"Okay, but would you like to give me a statement, Grady?"

"What fucking statement are you talking about? I already told you where I was."

"I must read you your rights. You have a right to remain silent—"

Joe cut in. "I know my Goddamn rights, and I won't give you the time of day now. You're trying to frame me. I know your little games."

"Look, Grady, I just presented the facts to the court, and it was satisfied, so it issued the warrant."

"What fucking facts?"

"We found that girl you were with, Grady. She says you had blood all over you when you returned to your place the day Sasha Lewis was murdered."

"Well, she's full of shit."

"And your buddy, Ed Lovett, tells us you confessed to the murder."

Joe's face reddened. "That stupid asshole can't be trusted further than he can be kicked. He's ripped off more people than anyone else in the city."

"I'm just telling you what we got," protested Gus.

Joe got up and moved toward the door. "You make me sick. You're trying to frame me." He left the interview room and called the guard.

JOE GRADY'S MOTHER HEARD THE news of her son's arrest for the murder of Sasha Lewis over the radio while she was driving home from work. Although the news was not a complete surprise, she broke into sobs and drove directly to the House of Correction. She filled out a visitor request form and waited in the visiting room. When Joe arrived, she went to him, threw her arms around him, and hugged him as tears rained down.

Joe was the first to speak. "Don't worry, Mom. I didn't do it. They're trying to frame me."

Mrs. Grady sobbed. "Ever since your dad died, I've tried to do the best I could. . . ."

Joe consoled her. "It's not your fault, Mom."

"You needed the strong, guiding hand of a man in the house—"

Joe cut in. "But I didn't do it."

"If only I didn't have to work and could have stayed home with you and your brothers and sisters," lamented Mrs. Grady as the sobbing became more sporadic.

"Okay, Mom, what I need now is a lawyer. I need a good lawyer who is going to fight like hell for me. They're trying to frame me, Mom. Get me someone who's not afraid to take on the powers that be," pleaded Joe.

"Okay, son. I'll do the best I can, but where am I going to find you a lawyer? I can't afford one."

"Don't worry about the money, Mom. I'll get the court to

appoint him. But if you don't get a good one, the judge will appoint some seat-of-the-pants lawyer who hangs around the courthouse and who couldn't try his way out of a paper bag."

Mrs. Grady sighed.

"Have you got some cigarettes, Mom?"

"I brought some, but they made me leave them out at the desk for you."

"I bet the screws have already ripped them off."

"What about that Mr. Czek we consulted with?" suggested Mrs. Grady.

"Oh, I had almost forgotten about him," mused Joe. "But didn't he say he wouldn't defend me because he didn't do this type of law?"

"Don't worry about that, son," responded his mother. "I'll get in touch with him right away."

Red Czek visited Joe at the House of Correction the next day, at the insistence of Mrs. Grady and against the advice of his partners. They had cautioned Red that the publicity would reflect badly on the firm and that the case would be a losing proposition financially. His billable hours, at $600 per hour, would be lost. As it was a murder trial, hundreds of hours of work would be necessary.

"You realize, Joe, that it's going to be a long haul, as the cops and the district attorney want a conviction badly. It was a brutal murder, and the DA hopes to ride a conviction in this case to reelection."

"I realize that," responded Joe. "That's why my mother contacted you. I told her I wanted a real tiger."

"We can expect the prosecutor to play games with us. It will be my job to keep them as honest as possible." Red had no sooner spoken than he realized he had agreed to represent Joe Grady.

Joe relaxed. He felt at ease with Red and confident he was in good hands. "What about getting me out of here?"

"But you don't have any money, do you?"

"Oh, I can get some."

"From where?"

"I have friends."

"Look, Joe," observed Red, "you're going to need a lot of money even if they don't hold you without bail, as is the usual procedure in murder cases. I doubt your friends will be able to come up with the necessary funds."

"What about my mom?"

"You know damn well, Joe, she doesn't have any money, and what she has she needs for the other kids."

"I guess you're right."

"I hate to say this to you, but it looks like you will have to be patient and wait it out." Joe groaned, but Red continued: "It's important that we are fully prepared before the trial commences, since the stakes are high. If you lose, you spend the rest of your life in prison."

"I understand, but it's so hard waiting in this fucking hole."

"I've read that the district attorney is pushing for an early trial, so you may not have too long to wait."

"Who's going to prosecute?"

"I believe they will send their number one heavy hitter, Tim Tuesday. He wouldn't think twice about prosecuting his own mother if it meant sending another body to prison. We will have to be on our toes to keep him in line."

Red visited the district attorney, Tim Tuesday, at his office a few days later. He was of average height and in his late forties. His receding black hair was tinged with white, and he brushed it straight back. He was meticulously dressed in a button-down white shirt with cuff links, gray tie, gray pants, and blue blazer. A gold watch dangled always from his waist. Tuesday promised that the district attorney's complete file would be made available to the defense.

As the months glided by, the trial date rapidly approached, but Red could not locate the key government witnesses. Gus and Lou had, in fact, kept their word to Ed Lovett and had taken him from court to court in order to clear up his defaults. He was back on the street, and even the detectives could not locate him. They had their fingers crossed that he would show up for trial.

The other key witness, Julie Connors, now lived out of state, as she had returned home to her family, but the prosecution would surely have her available for trial. Red would use the monies in court allowed for investigators to interview her. Tuesday would have to give the defense her address. However, the prosecutor would encourage her not to talk to the defense, as was her right.

Red did manage to track down some acquaintances of Ed Lovett, who reluctantly agreed to testify at the trial as to the latter's reputation in the community for not telling the truth.

10

The Semen Defense

ONE DOCUMENT IN PARTICULAR IN THE DISCOVERY PACKAGE FORWARDED by district attorney Tuesday caught Red Czek's attention. It was the report of the chemist, Brandon Block, relative to the debris collected from the anus of the victim. Under the heading "Results of Examination," the state chemist working out of state police headquarters stated his rather cryptic findings:

> Chemical and microscopic examination of an extraction of the anal debris demonstrated the presence of semen. Immunohematological tests demonstrated the presence of group-specific substances. At such time as whole blood and saliva samples are submitted from any suspects, the

blood group of the person depositing the semen found in
the anal debris may be determined.

The state chemist was claiming that he needed the blood
and saliva samples of the suspect before making any specific
determination. Certainly his examination of the semen in the anal
debris could determine a blood type. Only at the completion of that
stage of the examination would it be necessary to have the suspect's
blood sample for comparison. Red knew he would feel a lot more
comfortable with the accuracy and reliability of the test results if
he had a written report of the specific finding before Joe's blood
sample was taken and compared.

Red called Tim Tuesday and complained. Tuesday was not
sympathetic, until Red threatened to bring a motion to force a
written report of the specific results. At that point, Tuesday agreed
to obtain a more detailed report.

When it arrived a couple of weeks later, Red read it with interest.
Immunohematological tests were conducted on the extraction of the
anal debris. Both A and O group-specific substances were detected.

Due to the complexity of the interpretation of results
from secretion typing of mixed specimens, no significance
can or should be placed upon the foregoing data until a
proper interpretation can be made.

Normally, such an interpretation would be made
only after receipt and testing of blood and saliva samples
from both the victim and from any suspects.

In this case, however, a saliva sample was not received
from the victim (deceased) so as to determine if she were
a secretor.

It is, therefore, all the more necessary to receive the
blood and saliva from any suspects in order to attempt
exclusions.

CONCLUSION

Given only the data presently at hand—there is the blood group of the victim (group A), the finding of semen in the anal debris of the victim, and the finding of A and O group-specific substance in the anal debris from the victim—the following are the only conclusions concerning the origin of the semen at this time (the order of presentation is *not* significant):

1. A person of blood group A, secretor, is not excluded.

2. A person of blood group O, secretor, is not excluded.

3. A person of any blood group, nonsecretor, is not excluded.

4. A person of blood group AB, secretor, may not have deposited the semen.

5. A person of blood group B, secretor, is unlikely to have deposited the semen.

More definitive statements concerning a particular individual can only be made after determining his blood group and secretor status on submitted blood *and* saliva samples.

This report hedged a bit too much in its conclusion by using the words "may" and "unlikely," when a person with AB or B blood types should be absolutely excluded. The language wasn't strong enough. It didn't make the findings sound as certain as they were. Nevertheless, the state was bound to certain blood groups as being found in the semen.

Before agreeing to submit Joe's blood and saliva samples for analysis, Red hoped to learn Joe's blood type. He knew that eventually, the prosecution could obtain samples by court order, since they are not encompassed within the Fifth Amendment of the U.S. Constitution's protection against self-incrimination. Joe didn't know his blood type but had given blood to earn a few bucks to a private blood bank. After obtaining the necessary authorization from Joe, it was with trepidation that Red opened the envelope with the crucial information relative to the blood type. Great was his elation when the capital letters "AB" shot out at him. But he realized that it was too early to be certain that the defense had a good issue. For if Joe was not a secretor, then he could have been the depositor of the semen and yet not left any trace, since a nonsecretor does not give a blood type. However, since only 20 percent of the population are nonsecretors, the odds looked good. Red didn't trust the state chemist, but he knew that he was well aware that Red would have his own expert determine the secretor status of Joe if the chemist's determination came out "nonsecretor." Furthermore, neither the chemist nor District Attorney Tuesday were aware that Red already knew Joe's blood type. Thus there was an added check on the accuracy of the chemist's work.

Now Red allowed the taking of Joe's blood and saliva samples. The prosecution did not toy with the results, as Joe's blood type came back as AB. But of course the result Red was most concerned about was the secretor information. To Red's great relief, Joe's saliva sample revealed he was a secretor—thus, if he had deposited the semen, type AB would have shown up.

Red called Tim Tuesday. "Say, Tim, how about dismissing the rape charge? You're in trouble now. Joe is excluded as the rapist."

"But the chemist says only that a person of blood AB secretor status 'may not have deposited the semen,'" retorted Tuesday.

"He was trying to protect himself from not having to exclude an AB secretor as the rapist, but my expert tells us that an AB secretor could not possibly be the depositor of the semen detected in the anal debris, if no type B shows up to make out an AB blood type."

"Not so fast," responded Tuesday with a sneer, "because the medical examiner will testify that the so-called 'anal debris' did not come directly from inside the anus but rather from the perineum, the area between the vagina and the anus. Thus, the fact that there was no type B means nothing, because Williams, the guy who said he had intercourse with Sasha before her death, could have been responsible for the semen in that area outside the anus."

"But you don't know his type," responded Red.

"Oh, yes, we do. Williams is an O secretor. Furthermore, since the victim is group A, the semen substance is consistent with Williams and the victim. The chemist says the A type in the semen may be the contribution of the victim from her secretion."

"You bastards aren't going to get away with this," screamed Red. "The Goddamn medical examiner labeled the semen sample as 'material from anus.' Now he's trying to fudge it and draw back. I won't let him. Wait until I get him on the stand. That fuck would say anything to help you guys get a conviction."

"Calm down, Red. Let me explain our position again. Your guy cannot be eliminated as the depositor, as the types A and O found can be attributed to Williams and the victim."

"If we take your argument, then your chemist is highly incompetent not to take a sample from the anus. Furthermore, he was also negligent in not taking a saliva sample from the victim. We know she was blood type AB. She could have been a nonsecretor, thus the A blood type in the debris could have come from the rapist, as the O blood type found would be Williams's."

Tuesday gave no response.

"How are you going to deal with reasonable doubt?" asked Red.

"I'm not worried about any jury taking reasonable doubt seriously in this case. Once they see the gruesome picture of Sasha, they will convict in short order."

"You mean you're going to use those pictures?"

"You bet your sweet ass I am. And you know damn well the judge will let them in, no matter how strenuously you argue against it. He'll give you the customary cautionary instructions."

"Okay, let's change the subject. Have you given me all the discovery I have a right to?"

"You have everything," promised the district attorney.

"How about you and me and Gus sitting down and discussing the case? Every time I ask you a question, you say you don't know and will have to ask Gus."

"If you really want it, I'll set something up."

"For when?"

"How about next Tuesday in my office at 10:00 a.m.?"

"Okay, see you then."

The following Tuesday, Tuesday, the prosecutor, and Red Czek met Gus Grazzi, the cop. Red had a few specific questions relative to matters raised through the statements of the witnesses. Gus answered the questions Red posed, but in a vague way, so that no more information than necessary was turned over to the defense. "Yes, an address book was found," he said, and, "Yes, you can have access to it with Tuesday's okay."

Both Gus and Tuesday were anxious to quickly terminate the conference. Red only had time for one last question. It was a shot in the dark, but he had recently read an article in *The Boston Globe* about a new hypnosis unit in the Boston Police Department that hypnotized witnesses in important cases. He asked Gus, "Have any witnesses been hypnotized in this case?"

Gus hesitated, but without glancing at Tuesday, he mumbled a hardly audible "Yes," to minimize its importance.

"Well, who was it?" probed Red.

Gus looked at Tuesday, but the latter remained poker-faced.

Red pressed on: "What's the big secret?"

Having observed no reaction from Tuesday, Gus softly stated, "Julie Connors."

Red eyed Tuesday. The latter threw up his hands and responded: "I thought you knew."

"You thought I knew," complained Red. "How the fuck was I to know? No one told me."

"I thought I told you," Tuesday responded meekly.

Addressing Gus, Red asked: "And do you have a tape of the hypnosis session?"

"Yes, I believe it was taped."

"I want a copy."

Tuesday said, "That's the first I've heard of any tape. I'll have to call the hypnotist at District Fourteen who did it."

Red was furious when he left. He didn't believe the district attorney further than he could kick him in his claim that he thought the defense was aware of the hypnosis already. Red was anxious to listen to the tape. He figured the prosecution was attempting to hide some damaging aspect of its case by not revealing the fact of the hypnosis. He knew the law clearly required that the defense be informed of any hypnosis of witnesses, yet the bastards tried to get away with not disclosing it. Only due to a lucky fluke did the secret come out. "Well," Red thought, "we'll make full use of the hypnosis issue. They may well have blown the case by trying to be too sneaky for their own britches."

11

Other Suspects

AS THE TRIAL DATE QUICKLY APPROACHED, THE DEFENSE RECEIVED another surprise. District Attorney Tuesday called one morning. "I don't feel I am required by the law to inform you," he said, "but we have received information that a woman in New York named Ann Goode claims a man other than your client has admitted to the murder of Sasha Lewis."

Red cut in. "Wow, are you kidding?"

"Before you reach a climax, let me tell you that the woman's present address is a mental hospital. We intend to check her story out."

As he hung up, Red thought to himself, "Who does he think he's kidding, when he says he is just being a good guy in telling me? That's exculpatory evidence if there ever was any, and he's required to tell me."

Red called District Attorney Tuesday to obtain the address of the new witness. Tuesday reported that the matter was presently under investigation and that he would convey her address to the defense at a later date. He added that he and Gus were taking the new development seriously enough that they intended to fly to New York to interview the woman.

Two weeks later, Red received Tuesday's report of what the woman had told Gus and him, with the name of the new suspect excised:

> She states she had an occasion to meet, about a week before Thanksgiving of 1979, one XXXX, whom she describes as a white male, approximately five foot six, with blond hair and a heavy build. He deals in art from his town house, which is located on Beacon Hill. She states at that time she was in the antiques business and that a dealer was taking her to small claims court, which necessitated being introduced to him by a friend of hers. The purpose of the meeting was to have him evaluate some paintings that she had in her possession. She states that she met him twice after that, but just on a friendly basis. She states that somewhere in the vicinity of about 3:15 a.m., she had trouble sleeping one night, and she went down to Phillips Drugstore at Charles Street Circle, where they ran into each other. He invited her to have a cup of coffee, and they went somewhere in the North Station area in his large vehicle, which she believed to be maroon in color. She states that they were there approximately two and a half hours and had several cups of coffee and a bowl of oatmeal. During their conversation, he stated how he had known her whole family, relating the fact that he grew up in Dorchester with her uncle and also that he went to his wedding. In

her last conversation with her uncle, he told her at that time to stay away from him, meaning XXXX, because "he's weird." She also said he gave up smoking because he had heart trouble and he wanted to lose some weight and because he had insomnia.

Throughout the conversation, it appeared to her that he was very nervous. He told her all he did was go into the Beacon Hill Pub and play the machines at night because he could not sleep and he had terrible nightmares and did not know what to do with himself. He told her he got married at forty years old, and he talked about his wife and why they had no children, and that he had no relations with his wife because they lived on separate floors.

He gave her the impression that he was fascinated by physical illnesses in females. He told her how when he had lived in a Back Bay apartment, how the police kept bothering him about his roommate, whom they believed to be a pyromaniac. But she got the impression that he was talking about himself. He kept repeating to her not to tell Dede, his wife, about the conversation.

He kept worrying about her safety, but she told him she didn't make a habit of going out late at night. He asked her about her sex life, and she told him she didn't have one at the present time. He gave her no details as to what type of sex he liked. When he dropped her off, he asked her if she wanted to go down to the parking garage where he parked his car, and she told him no.

She said the next time she saw him was in the daytime, when she was with a friend, and while talking to her he looked at her and gave her the impression that he had terror in his eyes. She also informed us of the fact that another friend, who lives right over the Beacon

Hill Pub, had told her she had seen him on different occasions in the Beacon Hill Pub. She had known about the Sasha Lewis murder before she had met XXXX at the cafeteria, so when he asked her if she had read about it, she told him yes. The first time she knew about the broomstick was when he mentioned it. He started talking like he knew her (meaning Sasha Lewis) and the fact that she was wealthy, independent, and when a bar closed, she would be outside and would be fresh to whatever police officers were telling them to move on. He seemed to know a lot about Sasha and the fact that she preferred boys instead of men, and he seemed to resent that very much. He told her how he got Sasha, because when she left the bar that night, she left with a white male with blond hair, and that he followed them up Beacon Hill to possibly Revere or Myrtle Streets, and her being independent, he knew that when she went anywhere she would not stay the night. He said, "You know what the murderer did, he broomsticked her." When she asked him how he knew that, he said he did it. She said, "All you have to do now is kill yourself," and he said he tried but did not elaborate on how. He told her not to tell anybody about their conversation.

Red telephoned Tuesday to get his reaction to the interview he had with the woman in New York. "Well, how did it go, Tim?" asked Red, hiding his anxiety.

"She was fairly convincing, and we began to have our doubts about your man as the murderer until we were about to leave. The last thing she said that I didn't put in the statement was that she was going to marry her doctor. We talked to her doctor afterward, and he stated he was happily married with three children and had absolutely no social relationship with Ann."

"But aren't you intending to check out her story here?"

"Of course, we'll try to talk to this guy. But I believe we have a crazy on our hands. I have my doubts about whether your guy is the murderer, but Gus is absolutely convinced he did it."

Red's initial optimism was gradually diminishing. "Why won't Gus keep an open mind?"

"You know cops. Once they make an arrest, they hate to even think they may have the wrong man. It's human nature. I never told you, but Gus got a tip that your man was seen near a dumpster shortly after the murder. Gus traced the contents of the dumpster to a waste removal company in South Boston. It was a Friday, and he ordered them to hold that collected material until Monday; but somehow signals got crossed, and that material was trucked away and dumped. Gus has always believed that he would have found the smoking gun, so to speak, in that dumpster, and that it would have tied up the case against your man."

"Hey, look, Tuesday, when are you intending to give me the name and address of this guy?"

"Pretty soon, pretty soon. We want to check him out ourselves first."

"Well, if I don't get it soon, I'm going to get a court order."

"You'll have it soon. Don't worry, Red."

A summary of the statement of one David Dickens arrived a week later. Red was pissed once again that it was not verbatim and that the prosecution could selectively present what it wanted him to hear:

> Mr. Dickens stated that he knew Sasha Lewis from the Beacon Hill Pub and had played the pinball machine with her on two or three occasions. He stated he would go to the pub to relax, even though he does not drink liquor, because of some of the pressures at work. He would never stay very late, because young people would frequent it at night,

and because he is a married man and felt no necessity to remain. He read and heard about her death and how she was killed (a lot of talk in the bar and on Beacon Hill). He respected her because she was not the type of girl who expected men to buy her drinks. He saw her arrive at the pub on one occasion but never saw her leave.

He was asked if he knew an Ann Goode and states that he did know her. He indicated he tried to help her out in the antiques business as a favor to a friend. He informed us that Ann is mentally ill, and on one occasion she went crazy.

He states he did take her for some breakfast at Dom's cafeteria and does not remember the specific date but thinks it was during the winter. He talked to her about current events and his relationship with his wife, because of his insomnia, and discussed a former roommate. The conversation lasted about one hour.

He denied killing Sasha Lewis when informed of what Ann Goode had stated to Detective Grazzi. He states that Miss Goode is seriously ill and imagines people being killed and murdered. He advised us to check with some people who know her to corroborate that fact.

Mr. Dickens was asked if he would take a polygraph test, and he replied in the affirmative. However, on the following Monday morning, he called and stated that he spoke to his brother, who advised him not to get involved and not to take the polygraph test.

After reading the statement, Red called Tuesday.

"Do you think he'll talk to me?" Red asked.

"I doubt it. He's not talking to us anymore. Once he talked to his brother, he backed down on his offer to take a lie detector test and clammed up."

Red was surprised that Tim Tuesday had opened up so much but surmised that it was Tuesday's way of appeasing his guilty feelings over possibly prosecuting an innocent man. Red had decided to take full advantage and obtain as much information as possible. "What else bothers you about this guy?"

"He initially denied ever knowing Ann. It was only after we alleged that Ann had brought him a painting to appraise that he 'recalled' knowing her."

"Why isn't that in the statement I was given?"

"Gus wrote it up. Ask him," replied Tuesday matter-of-factly.

"But Goddamn it, you're the district attorney and an officer of the court. And you're responsible for turning over exculpatory matters to me," protested Red as his voice rose.

"That's why I'm doing so much yapping to you now. You can't complain later and ask for a new trial. I sympathize with you, but the guy certainly isn't going to help you, since he'll deny the murder. I doubt you'll ever get Ann here from New York. Her psychiatrists will never let her come, and no New York court will order her to if the shrinks say it will jeopardize her mental condition."

"So what else can you tell me about him, since apparently you're not worried it will affect your case against Joe?"

Tuesday continued, "He also lied about sleeping with his wife. He later conceded he no longer did. By the way, is that guy ugly! During the interview he paced up and down and chain-smoked."

"Did he say anything else about Sasha, apart from what's in the statement?"

Tuesday paused for a few seconds before responding, so it wasn't clear if he was drawing on his memory or deciding whether to tell Red all he knew. "You'll love this, Red. He said Sasha smelled like a pig, even though she wore ninety-dollar blouses."

12

The Jury Is Chosen

"HEAR YE! HEAR YE! HEAR YE! ALL PERSONS HAVING ANYTHING TO DO before the Honorable Kermit Regan, the Justice of the Superior Court, now sitting at Boston, within and from the County of Suffolk, for the transaction of Criminal Business in the Sixth Session thereof, draw near, give your attention, and you shall be heard. God save the Commonwealth of Massachusetts."

The court officer boomed out this opening proclamation in a strong, firm voice as everyone in the courtroom rose at the judge's entrance. The court officer was smartly dressed in a dark-blue double-breasted suit with four gold buttons and two large pockets on the jacket front. He wore a black tie, white shirt, and shiny black shoes with thick soles.

The courtroom was huge, some sixty feet wide and one hundred feet long with a twenty-five-foot-high ceiling. There were four large arched windows on each side of the courtroom, stretching from three feet off the floor to some five feet from the ceiling. The walls were ornate, with columns highlighted by ivory arches in relief. The lighting was provided by twelve metal chains dropping from the ceiling with large globes.

The judge's bench was of solid, carved oak, completely surrounding him and elevated. Directly behind the high-backed judge's chair was a large, built-in oak bookcase with a complete set of Massachusetts Reports.

A delicate, ivory-faced clock with roman numerals, approximately two feet by two feet, hung on the wall behind the judge. To the left of the clock was the American flag, and to the right was the flag of the Commonwealth of Massachusetts.

Tim Tuesday slumped in his chair with his arms folded in front of him. To his left was his assistant, a woman in her forties with short brownish hair, blue eyes, and delicate features. She wore short earrings and a trace of lipstick. She was dressed in a red- and purple-striped suit with a red velvet collar. Her purple blouse matched the suit, and she wore high-heeled shoes. She rested her head on her left hand as she awaited the commencement of the proceedings.

With Red and Joe at the defense table was a female law student who had been carefully selected by Red. Since the murder was so brutal and ugly, with the suggestion that the victim had been raped, Red, for tactical reasons, wanted an assistant who would win a favorable reaction from both male and female members of the jury. As they observed her interact comfortably with the defendant, it would, so the theory went, be more difficult for them, unconsciously or not, to see the defendant as the type of monster who could commit the crime charged. Thus, Susie was selected for her feminine charm and physical attractiveness. She was from the South, with a Southern drawl. Red was thinking for a way to allow the jury to hear it. Her hair was long and blond and her features smooth. It would be difficult to say she was beautiful, but she exuded femininity. Although her breasts were small, she was dressed so smartly in a blouse and sweater that they could not be ignored. But it was her ass that gave her that special sexy air. It was ample but tightly controlled by the clothes she wore. Her skirt was slit up the side, revealing sensuous legs that complemented her ass. Red's only concern was that the jury would be distracted by her from hearing the evidence. But by the time it came for the defense case to be presented, he figured they would have adjusted to her.

The Chinese stenographer was also a very attractive female with her traditionally long black hair and trim figure. She sat to the right of the clerks' desk in front of the witness stand.

The judge, Kermit Regan, swiftly exited his office to the left rear of the podium and took his seat. At approximately sixty years of age, he had a full head of white hair combed straight back, and his face was literally as red as a beet. He had a hook nose and blue eyes with bushy eyebrows. His white dress shirt and dark tie were visible above his black judicial robe. He had been appointed to the bench after a career as a prosecutor, and his sympathies had not altered with his change of position. He sat straight as a board in his high-backed brown judge's chair. His head came within six inches of the top. As he addressed those in the courtroom with a "good morning," a finger from his right hand rested on his nose.

THE CLERK: May I proceed, Your Honor?
THE JUDGE: Yes.
THE CLERK: Your Honor, before the court this day is the matter of Indictment No. 678321, Commonwealth v. Joe Grady. The defendant is present in court this morning, Your Honor, represented by Mr. Czek. The Commonwealth is represented by Mr. Tuesday. Your Honor, may the record indicate that the prospective jurors are present in the courtroom and also that the defendant is at the bar.

MR. TUESDAY: May I proceed at this time, if Your Honor pleases?

THE JUDGE: We will select sixteen jurors; twelve will sit and four will be alternates in case one of the sitting jurors needs to be replaced.

MR. TUESDAY: Ladies and gentlemen of the jury, the Commonwealth moves for trial on Indictment No. 678321, charging the defendant, Joe Grady, with murder in the first degree.

THE CLERK: Joe Grady, please stand. You are now set at the bar to be tried, and these good men and women whom I shall call are to pass between the Commonwealth and you upon your trial. You have a right to challenge sixteen of their number without assigning a reason therefore. If you do so, or if you object to others for cause, you must do so as they are called and before they are sworn.

Would the jurors please stand and raise your right hands?

The jury venire is sworn.

THE CLERK: Please be seated.

THE JUDGE: By way of introduction, my name is Kermit Regan, and I am an associate justice of the Superior Court who will preside at this trial in the sixth criminal session of the Suffolk Superior Court.

This is the trial of Joe Grady, who has been charged in Indictment No. 678321 with the murder of Sasha Lewis on October 30, 1979, in Boston. Timothy Tuesday is the assistant district attorney who will represent the Commonwealth. The defendant will be represented by Mr. Red Czek of Boston.

If any one of you are related to the defendant, Mr. Grady, or to the victim, Sasha Lewis, or if you are acquainted with either the defendant or were acquainted with the victim, or are either related to or acquainted with Mr. Tuesday, the assistant district attorney, or with Mr. Czek, please make it known to the court at this time.

No responses.

THE JUDGE: I want to make a statement now while everybody is here. And this is very important. This is a first-degree murder case. Let me, at the outset, make one thing perfectly clear. If you are excused either by the court or by counsel in exercising a challenge, you must not, and I emphasize must not, discuss with any other jurors in the jury pool what occurred in this room. If we don't obtain sixteen jurors from this group of seventy-five, we will draw from an additional pool. And therefore, you must not discuss with any juror upstairs what happened in this room: not the nature of the crime, the name of counsel, or anything at all. And if you do and I learn it, I will take the proper action and deal with it accordingly. Do you understand? As long as we understand.

Red thought the judge was being a little too rough with the jury. He looked back at the potential jurors but could detect no reaction.

THE JUDGE: It is alleged that the murder occurred in Boston on October 30, 1979, at 283 Beacon Street, and that that victim was a twenty-four-year-old woman living in Boston.

Now, if any of you have read or heard anything about this case, or have any interest in this case, or have expressed or formed an opinion as to the guilt or innocence of the defendant or are sensible or conscious of any bias or prejudice you may have, please make it known to the court at this time.

No response.

I have some more questions that we have to ask the entire panel. Listen carefully, if you will. Are you or any member of your family or close personal friends engaged in any profession or occupation which may be included in the term "law enforcement"? If so, please stand, and we will further interview you individually.

No response.

Now, to this question, please listen carefully. Have you or a close friend or relative ever been the victim of, or a witness to, a violent crime? I'm concerned about your prior involvement in the judicial system, in the sense that it may very well be that your car has been stolen, that your house has been broken into, or that your purse has been stolen. Regardless of the nature of the matter, you should apprise the court of your involvement at the appropriate time.

No response.

THE CLERK: May I proceed, Your Honor?

THE JUDGE: You may. How many names are you going to draw?

THE CLERK: Three, Your Honor. At this time, the jurors' names will be placed in this barrel and mixed, and the three names that I now call will remain in the courtroom. Number 74, Linda Bates; number 114, Joanne Dugan; and number 46, Patricia Bono.

THE JUDGE: Now you will be inquired of individually, and other questions will be asked of you by the court. The rest of you will be escorted upstairs here. You are not to discuss this case among yourselves. At lunchtime, you're not to discuss this case with anybody. And I will give further instructions this evening to those who are chosen. It's doubtful we will have sixteen jurors by four o'clock this afternoon, but we will attempt to do it. So all those whose names have not been called, please go upstairs with the court officer. And talk about the Red Sox, the Celtics, the Israeli attack, anything you want, but do not talk about this case at all.

THE CLERK: This is number 74, Linda Bates.

THE JUDGE: All right. You're still under oath, and I will ask you some questions.

Q. And you're Linda Bates, is that it?

A. Yes.

Q. Is it Miss or Mrs.?

A. Miss.

Q. I note that the list indicates that you're at home. In what capacity?

A. No, I'm working now, Your Honor.

Q. For whom are you working?

MR. CZEK: Excuse me. Could the witness speak up?

A. I'm working at the Malden Public School System as a METCO teacher aide.

Q. May I be so bold to ask your age?

A. Thirty-nine.

Q. Do you have any direct or personal interest in this case?

A. No.

Q. Have you expressed or formed any opinion about this case or this defendant?

A. No.

Q. Are you conscious of any bias or prejudice either for or against the defendant or the prosecution?

A. No.

Q. Have you or any of your relatives or close friends been the victim of a crime?

A. No.

Q. There will be evidence that a broomstick was found inserted in the victim's vagina at the time her body was discovered. Do you feel you could still remain impartial in spite of that fact?

A. *(Without hesitation)* Yes.

The defense was content with Linda Bates, as she was Black and not too young. Red saw Blacks as neutral jurors with a white victim and defendant. They were, as a general rule, streetwise and could understand the rough environment Sasha lived in.

THE CLERK: This is number 114, Joanne Dugan.

Q. Do you have any relatives or close friends who were victims of a crime?

A. My twenty-four-year-old cousin was found murdered in Franklin Park.

Q. Do you feel that fact would prevent you from being impartial?

A. No.

Q. There will be evidence that a broomstick was found in the victim's vagina at the time her body was discovered. Do you feel you could remain impartial in light of that fact?

A. *(Long hesitation)* My God! I just don't know.

Q. Would you try to be impartial?

A. Well, of course, but that's quite shocking!

Q. But your job will be to determine if this defendant committed the murder. Can you give him a fair trial?

A. I'll try to do so. I believe I can.

Red leaned over to talk to his student-assistant, Susie. "I don't think we should take a chance with this one. Did you see her expression when the judge mentioned the broomstick? And this murder—what do you think?"

"I agree," replied Susie.

"Okay. I'm going to challenge."

THE JUDGE: I find this juror indifferent.

MR. TUESDAY: The Commonwealth is content with this juror.

MR. CZEK: Your Honor, could the young lady be asked whether anyone was convicted of the murder of her cousin?

THE JUDGE: I would ask that.

Q. Did you testify in the case?

A. No.

Q. Was the person who was charged with the crime convicted?

A. Yes.

MR. CZEK: The defendant respectfully challenges.

THE JUDGE: All right. You've been challenged. Now, remember, you are not to discuss anything with anyone upstairs at all. Thank you very much.

The third juror called stated she was "scared" and that the testimony relative to the sexual aspects of the case would "embarrass" her. She was excused by the judge, and additional jurors were escorted downstairs.

Red challenged the fourth juror called, as he did not appear relaxed and open to hearing all the evidence before he made a decision. The defense wanted jurors who would not assume the defendant was probably guilty simply because he was charged. Even though the following juror called had a hearing problem, Red did not challenge him, as he smiled often and did not answer the questions in a clipped, cold fashion. His house had been broken into, but Red felt that fact might help the defense as one of the key government witnesses, Ed Lovett, had a prior criminal record of several breaking-and-entering convictions. Thus, he might be hostile to this witness.

The judge excused for cause one juror who said she was "nervous" and in therapy. Red challenged a woman who had a son in the district attorney's office in Los Angeles. He didn't want her consulting him as to how to vote. Even though jurors are sworn not to discuss the case with others, everyone knows they do. Red also challenged the following juror, who had a court officer as a good friend and whose brother was beaten with a bat. Red wanted to stay away from jurors who had personal experience with violence. Furthermore, court officers as a rule are sympathetic to the prosecution. The next juror was an investment banker whom Red feared might have particular influence with the jury. He didn't want to risk an apparently conservative, blue-blood Yankee dominating the jury. He preferred to have no one strong personality on it.

As the defense only had sixteen peremptory challenges, Red was concerned, as he gradually used them up with but two jurors seated. He challenged for cause a Black juror who stated he was "paranoid about violence." The judge inquired further of the man, and he eventually agreed in response to a leading question that he would be impartial. The challenge for cause was denied, and Red was forced to use another peremptory challenge. Finally, a third juror was chosen. He was an easygoing Italian with three sons who smiled regularly and appeared relaxed.

A one-eyed retired postal worker was excused for cause. Red reluctantly challenged a fifty-year-old Black construction worker with daughters aged twenty-three and nineteen. As the victim was twenty-four, Red was wary of individuals on the jury with daughters about the same age, who might feel they didn't want to take any chances that the defendant might possibly be the murderer, out of fear their daughter might be next. The reasonable doubt instruction would be meaningless under those circumstances.

The district attorney at last made his first peremptory challenge of a young, unemployed Black man, who stated that a friend of his had been charged with murder too. The next juror was an elderly, single woman who, when asked if the nature of the crime might affect her impartiality, stated, "I don't think so." Red read between the lines and challenged, as he didn't want to take any chances.

A pregnant juror was excused by the judge. An older woman with daughters in their early twenties was excused for cause when she volunteered that she favored the death penalty.

When a young male juror stated that he would tend not to believe a policeman, he was challenged by the district attorney. A juror who stated he would tend to give more credibility to a police officer's testimony than to that of a layman was challenged by Red. A young, single white male with longish hair was challenged by Tim Tuesday. The judge excused an older woman with several daughters in their twenties when she stated: "I would prefer not to sit." Red challenged another cold, Irish postal worker with several daughters in their twenties.

Red had commenced to be seriously concerned that he would not obtain a jury with which he could feel comfortable, as only three jurors had been seated and he had used eleven of his sixteen challenges. He knew he would have to become less choosy and only challenge peremptorily those jurors whom he felt very strongly about not having. Although he was reluctant to have young women on the jury, he felt the right sort of intelligent, open-minded person, regardless of age, was better than someone coming to the case with a closed mind. Thus, he accepted as juror number four a twenty-four-year-old single Italian clerk, as she did not bat an eye when informed of the horrendous nature of the crime.

Tuesday challenged a male supervisor of children. Red was sorry to see him go, as he felt he would be one to look closely at the individual facts of the case. A second Black juror was chosen. He was tall, immaculately dressed, and carried an umbrella. Red was not entirely happy with him, as he appeared too ordered to be flexible enough to keep an open mind and listen to others. But Red knew he must now exercise his peremptory challenges carefully.

The sixth juror chosen to sit was a young Irish college student who, although he stated he was "not overly comfortable sitting on a crime of this type," remarked, "I believe I could be fair." Neither Tuesday nor Red thought he would be a risky juror, either way. Juror seven was a young Black female switchboard operator who once had someone break into her house. Red wanted her again for her expected attitude toward Ed Lovett, the key prosecution witness. Red didn't believe that Tuesday grasped why he (Red) was not challenging these jurors, since, on the surface, they appeared to be victims of crime who would be prosecution-oriented.

Juror number eight was a young Black mechanic who appeared to have street sense. Red felt he would compare the prosecution witnesses to people he knew in the street whom he wouldn't trust farther than he could kick them.

Juror thirteen was a short-haired, straight-looking supervisor with the telephone company, who had police acquaintances but who came across as open and forthright. With only one peremptory challenge left, Red reluctantly accepted him. An elderly juror candidly admitted to having served prison time some forty years before. Red would not have minded having him on the jury, but the district attorney challenged. A grandmother remarked, "It makes me sick to think of this case. I'd gladly sit if I could keep my food down long enough." Needless to say, she was excused by the judge.

Jurors fourteen and fifteen were selected with dispatch, as Red had exhausted his peremptory challenges. Juror fourteen was an elderly Black female, a part-time bookkeeper with two daughters in their twenties whose husband was a security guard. Juror fifteen was a young, childless engineer of Italian background who appeared open to hearing all the facts before forming an opinion as to the guilt or innocence of Joe.

Red was basically content with the final jury selection, even though he had exhausted his peremptory challenges. It was representative of the community, with a mix of Blacks, young single men, young single women, middle-aged men, and middle-aged women. There appeared to be no one person who would dominate the jury. Thus, if there was to be a conviction, there would have to be a solid general consensus from a varied group of individuals who would most likely listen carefully to the evidence and decide for themselves.

The jury was sworn, and the judge dismissed them until Monday morning at 10:00 a.m., as it was already late Friday afternoon. The judge informed them that they would hear opening arguments at that time.

After the jury had filed out of the courtroom, the court officers handcuffed Joe and led him out.

13

A Weekend on Nantucket

RED WANTED TO SPEND THE WEEKEND BEFORE THE COMMENCEMENT OF the trial putting the finishing touches on his trial preparation. He felt he had to get away from home if he was to have time away from everyday distractions. This was necessary for adequate preparation.

As he needed someone to critique his opening statement and discuss trial strategy, he invited his law student, Susie, to join him. They took the 9:00 p.m. ferry from Hyannis to the island of Nantucket. Red had vacationed there on several occasions and loved its quiet beauty, its quaintness. The two-and-a-quarter-hour ferry ride allowed Red time to draft an outline of his opening statement.

The ferry ride was pleasant, as the night was clear, with a full moon and calm seas. Red and Susie arrived shortly after 11:00. After disembarking the boat, they wandered down Steamboat Wharf and veered to the left toward the cobblestone Main Street. They stopped at the first inn on the corner of tree-lined Chestnut Street. The old, swinging sign informed them it was the Four Seasons Guest House.

All was dark. Red rang the bell. There was no response. He rang it again.

Finally, they heard movement. The owner arrived in her robe with a yawn. She mumbled, "You're damn lucky I have space left. Probably all there is on the island."

Red requested two rooms. She gave them each a key and retreated to the interior of the first floor, where she apparently lived. Red and Susie had rooms 19 and 20, which they found four stairways up at the top of the nineteenth-century structure. Both were exhausted; soon they were asleep in their separate rooms.

The next morning, over espresso and croissants at a popular breakfast place, Downyflake, Red and Susie planned a trial strategy. They discussed the pros and cons of Joe testifying in his own defense. Red was inclined not to put him on if he could do enough damage to Julie Connors and Ed Lovett, the key prosecution witnesses, on cross-examination. He believed they were both vulnerable: Julie because of her "refreshed memory" after hypnosis and Ed Lovett because of his long criminal record and motive to lie to please the government.

Susie listened to Red's analysis but played devil's advocate by putting herself in the place of a juror's reaction to a defendant's failure to testify. The first thing that came to his mind was, "Why is the defendant not testifying if he is innocent?"

The balance of the day was spent in Red's bedroom as Susie listened patiently and critiqued Red's opening statement.

In the late afternoon, they called it quits and Red suggested they take a walk on the beach. "We can't work all evening, can we, Susie?" Red said with a mischievous smile.

Susie agreed they needed a break.

They rented bicycles and pedaled across the island to Ladies

Beach, with its impeccable sand and crashing waves. Most bathers had left, as it was late in the day. They walked away from the entrance. Finally, they came upon isolated nude bathers among the sand dunes, enjoying the last rays of the late-afternoon summer sun.

Susie remarked, "You never told me there was a nudist beach here."

Red only smiled.

After walking a little farther, Red and Susie settled down near the dunes in a spot that was protected on one side by the flowing green beach grass and on the other side by a dip in the beach contour. They lay on the blanket Susie had brought.

Red thought of the weekend as a strictly professional outing. He was a happily married man, and Susie was married as well. Besides, there was work to be done, and heavy responsibilities awaited that Monday. But in the utter beauty and stillness of the moment, he focused his attention on Susie as more than his legal assistant.

Red smiled at Susie, and she smiled back. Soon their smiles faded.

Susie pulled her polo shirt over her head, unhitched her bra, and slipped it off. They both took off their shorts.

Red grabbed Susie by the hand and they ran toward the water, plunging into the breaking waves of the rough surf. They rode the waves and dove in, frolicking and laughing, oblivious to their nakedness. Finally, they returned to the blanket and toweled down.

They watched the sun start to disappear, taking with it the warmth they had basked in. Red reached out to Susie and brought her to him. She came easily, and he held her close.

"That feels good. I was getting cold," she said.

Red turned her head and leaned in to kiss her. She weakly protested, "We really shouldn't, Red."

"I know, Susie, but the moment has seized us. Let's not lose it. Tomorrow we have to return to reality. To the trial, our families."

She answered by rolling over into Red's arms. Their lips met and their tongues searched each other out.

Red slid down to suck each pleading breast. Her nipples hardened. His hand moved down and her legs spread. She was wet.

With her right hand, Susie searched out his cock and played with its tip. "I want to fuck you, Red," she said. "I want as much as you can give me."

"I want you, too, Susie." He slid down, swung his feet, and made a sixty-nine position. His finger felt her wetness, moved back and forth. He licked and sucked her with relish. She responded in turn, sucking his hard prick.

Finally, she whispered, "Oh, please fuck me now, Red. I'm ready."

Red rolled her over and helped raise her up onto her hands and knees. He moved in from behind.

Back and forth he rocked as he cupped her breasts with his hands. Susie moaned. As Red drew near climax, he withdrew and lay on his back. He eased her into a saddle position and reinserted his cock. He pulled her head down and they French-kissed as she rode him. He stopped kissing from time to time to suck on her hanging breasts.

"Red, it's so good! I've never done it outside before, in nature like this. I feel no guilt. The beauty of this place—it makes it so natural."

Red responded by turning her on her back and mounting her. He grabbed her ass, drove back into her. He moved back and forth in a quick rhythm. She moaned louder.

"You fuck so good," he said. They increased the tempo and he felt it coming. She sensed his climax and reached hers too.

When it was over, they lay on their backs and enjoyed the last moments of the spectacular Madaket sunset.

14

Opening Statements

THE JUDGE: ALL RIGHT, MR. TUESDAY, YOU MAY PROCEED.
MR. TUESDAY: Thank you very much, Your Honor.

OPENING STATEMENT ON BEHALF OF
THE COMMONWEALTH BY MR. TUESDAY

MR. TUESDAY: Justice Regan, Mr. Foreman, and ladies and gentle-men of the jury. By now, you know that my name is Timothy Tuesday, and that I am the assistant district attorney in Suffolk County who has been assigned to prosecute the single indictment against Mr. Joe Grady, charging him with murder in the first degree of a young lady, approximately twenty-four years of age, by the name of Sasha Lewis.

What I say concerning the facts of this case should not be considered as the evidence, for the evidence in this case is only what comes out of the mouths of the various witnesses that will be called.

For the benefit of those jurors who have not had the opportunity to sit on a jury trial in a criminal case, what I am presenting to you is an opening statement. An opening statement has a specific function, and that function is to provide you people, the members of the jury, with a brief synopsis, or outline, or a blueprint, if you will, of what the intended evidence will be, at least on behalf of the Commonwealth of Massachusetts.

Yesterday, the clerk read to you a single indictment, and I'd like to discuss that indictment with you now in a very informal manner.

May I have the indictment, Mr. Clerk, please?

It's one paragraph and it states: "The jurors for the Commonwealth of Massachusetts on their oath present that Joe Grady, on the thirtieth day of October, in the year of our Lord one thousand nine hundred and seventy-nine, did assault and beat one Sasha Lewis with intent to murder her, and by such assault and beating did kill and murder the said Sasha Lewis."

The Commonwealth will prove to you beyond a reasonable doubt that Joe Grady, by murder with extreme atrocity and cruelty, killed Sasha Lewis on October 30, 1979. And let me tell you at the outset that during the course of my trial, I will not present any witnesses for your consideration who will testify that they were present with Joe Grady and saw Joe Grady take a blunt instrument and strike Sasha Lewis seven or eight times to the head. Nor will we present any witnesses who were present and saw Joe Grady drag Sasha Lewis up a series of stairs, causing her head to hit those stairs. Furthermore, we will not present any witnesses who will testify that they were present and observed Joe Grady insert a broomstick into her vagina.

Red Czek pondered whether he should interrupt Tuesday's opening at this point, since it was a blunt appeal to the emotion and verged on argument, rather

than a statement of evidence to be presented, but he thought that to do so might
do more harm than help to his case by emphasizing in the jurors' minds the
damaging statement by Tuesday.

Now, what we will do is to present a series of witnesses that will
supply the pieces of the puzzle. And after all those witnesses have
been called by the Commonwealth, you will see a picture of the
murderer. You will, in fact, see Joe Grady as the murderer of Sasha
Lewis. We will prove to each and every one of you that Joe Grady
did, by murder with extreme atrocity and cruelty, take the life of
Sasha Lewis on October 30, 1979.

We will call as a witness Dr. Philip Richmond, who will tell
you that he's the medical examiner in Suffolk County and that
he received a telephone call concerning the finding of a body. He
will testify that Sasha Lewis met her death by being struck on her
head at least seven or eight times, resulting in a cracking of her
skull and a fracturing of her jaw. He will further testify that she had
lacerations about her face and that part of her brains did ooze out,
having separated from her skull. He will also render his professional
opinion as to when Sasha Lewis met her death.

Additionally, we will present evidence that at approximately
quarter to seven on the morning of October 30, 1979, at 283
Beacon Street, a construction worker, upon entering the building,
observed something different than what he had left when termi-
nating his work the prior evening. He saw blood. He followed the
blood to a point where he observed a body lying on the floor. He will
testify that he observed the body of a female that was nude except
for a sweater pulled up over her left breast, and that there was a
broomstick protruding from her vagina. Upon seeing this horrific
scene, he telephoned the police.

There will be evidence that, based upon that telephone call,
police officers responded to the scene of the crime and conducted
an investigation. They will also tell you what they observed. They
searched for the murder weapon, and none was found. They

attempted to lift some fingerprints, but there were no prints of any value that would indicate who had been in the area. You'll hear some testimony concerning a box of Marlboro cigarettes that was found on one of the stairs near the body of Sasha Lewis. Some prints were lifted off the Marlboro box, and there were some comparisons made with certain people, but there was no so-called matchup; that is, the prints on the Marlboro box did not match any person whose fingerprints were on file.

There'll be evidence that the police attempted to discover what Sasha Lewis did that day and who she was last seen with. You will hear from one or two of Sasha Lewis's friends, who will testify as to when they last saw her. One witness will testify that she saw Sasha Lewis sometime around one o'clock in the morning of October 30.

A Jonathan Williams will testify that sometime around 2:30 in the morning, Sasha Lewis came over to his house. She had come to obtain a cape to wear to a costume party. Mr. Williams will tell you that they talked for about twenty minutes before they then got into bed and had sexual intercourse. He ejaculated. He will indicate that Sasha Lewis left his apartment sometime between 4:15 and 4:30 a.m.

As you'll learn through the witnesses, the body of Sasha Lewis was found sometime around 6:45 a.m. Thus, sometime between 4:30 and 6:45 a.m., Sasha Lewis was murdered. And again, we say by our indictment, and we will prove to you beyond a reasonable doubt, that it was Joe Grady who was the last one to see Sasha Lewis alive and who killed Sasha Lewis.

Now, there'll be further evidence that sometime around midnight on October 29, 1979, Mr. Grady met a young lady by the name of Julie Connors at a place called Tom Foolery's. It was formerly called Frank 'N Stein's. They engaged in some conversation and consumed some alcoholic beverages. Mr. Grady and this Julie Connors left Frank 'N Stein's and proceeded down to Father's Five. Outside Father's Five, they met Lynn Clemente and a fellow named

Ken. Mr. Grady invited Julie Connors, Lynn, and this fellow Ken back to his apartment at 486 Beacon Street. They arrived there sometime around 2:15 in the morning of October 30. There was some conversation concerning obtaining some cocaine.

Julie will testify as to approximately what time Mr. Grady left the apartment with Ken, and that she expected Mr. Grady to come right back but that he did not return until sometime around 5:30 in the morning, or thereabouts. She will tell you that Lynn Clemente, who I mentioned before as one of the people that came back to Joe Grady's apartment, couldn't wait any longer, and left sometime between 3:30 and four o'clock in the morning.

Julie Connors will further testify that when Mr. Grady returned to his apartment, where she had remained, he had blood on him. She'll describe to you what she observed about Joe Grady's demeanor, that his eyes were bloodshot, and that he appeared to be nervous and tired. She will describe that his pants appeared to be ripped, and she will tell you that he took out a hypodermic needle and syringe, and that she and he were injected with cocaine to get high before they engaged in sexual intercourse.

You will hear also from a cab driver by the name of Sidney Goldberg, who will testify that sometime around four o'clock he received a dispatch to go to 486 Beacon Street, where he picked up two males, and he was told to drive to an address on Peterborough Street. He took the two males from 486 Beacon Street to Peterborough Street, where both went into the building. He was told to wait, and one male came down, and he brought back the single male to Joe Grady's apartment at approximately 4:15 a.m.

Furthermore, there will be testimony that Julie Connors was hypnotized and made certain statements concerning this case while under hypnosis. And you will hear from Detective Ben Ripley, the hypnotist, and he will tell you what procedures he used to place her under hypnosis and give you a general description as to what hypnosis is all about.

You will also have testimony that at some time, approximately seven to ten days prior to the finding of Sasha Lewis, the defendant Joe Grady was with a friend of his by the name of Ed Lovett. He will tell you that Joe Grady referred to Sasha Lewis as a "fucking cunt," complained that she wouldn't go out with him, and that she was an asshole. This same individual will testify that on Wednesday, February 25, 1980, Mr. Grady and he were riding in an automobile, a red Mustang. Mr. Grady demanded that he drive. Mr. Lovett refused to let Joe Grady drive. Mr. Grady then stated: "If you don't let me drive that automobile, I will pull a Sasha Lewis on you." And Mr. Lovett said to Mr. Grady, his friend: "You killed Sasha Lewis, didn't you?" Mr. Grady responded, "Yes. So what? I'm leaving because they're going to hang me on the seventeenth of March anyway."

You'll also hear from a fellow construction worker of Mr. Grady by the name Dick Brown. He'll tell you how he knows Mr. Grady and how long he's worked with him. He'll describe an incident that occurred two to three days subsequent to the finding of the body of Sasha Lewis. He observed Mr. Grady exiting his apartment with a short-sleeved shirt in his possession with blood on it. And without Mr. Brown asking any questions of Mr. Grady, the latter stated that he had been involved in an argument and a fight with three people. Mr. Brown will also testify that he observed Mr. Grady's hands and that they were absent of any bruises or scrapes. Mr. Grady's response was that he was wearing his gloves at the time that he had gotten into that argument with those supposed three people.

That, ladies and gentlemen of the jury, is a brief summary as to the evidence with which the Commonwealth intends to prove beyond a reasonable doubt that Joe Grady is in fact the person who took a blunt instrument and, on seven or eight occasions, struck the head of Sasha Lewis, causing her to meet her death. Thank you.

As District Attorney Tuesday finished, his voice reached a crescendo with his arms outstretched toward the jurors.

THE JUDGE: Thank you, Mr. Tuesday. Mr. Czek?

Mr. Czek: Yes, Your Honor, I would appreciate the opportunity to make my opening statement at this time.

The Judge: You may proceed, Mr. Czek.

Mr. Czek: Thank you, Your Honor.

Red Czek left his seat and approached to within a few feet of the jury box. He made eye contact with the jurors.

OPENING STATEMENT ON BEHALF OF THE DEFENDANT BY MR. CZEK

Mr. Czek: Mr. Justice Regan, Mr. Foreman, ladies and gentlemen of the jury. As Mr. Tuesday has already told you, opening statement is that time when the attorneys have the opportunity to attempt to put the case in some focus; that is, give you some idea as to what evidence will be presented. And, of course, what I say is not evidence, and what Mr. Tuesday said is not evidence, and is not to be considered by you in any way in terms of deciding on the guilt or innocence of the defendant.

I hope you'll keep an open mind. It is vitally important that you not come to any conclusions at this point. You've heard an emotional address by the district attorney as to what he intends to produce by way of evidence. But I think you'll agree that it's very important that you hear from the defense attorney and to hear what the defense intends to produce by way of evidence, for there are many things that Mr. Tuesday neglected to tell you. And most of these things he neglected to tell you are pieces of evidence that will suggest that this defendant was not the murderer. And that's what I want to discuss with you now.

Mr. Tuesday: Objection.

Mr. Czek: I didn't interrupt him. I gave him some flexibility.

The Judge: Please approach. I know why he's rising. It's not for you to make a critique of the district attorney's opening. Your job is to tell the jury what you intend to prove.

MR. CZEK: I understand that.

THE JUDGE: That's what I'm just trying to keep you to. Is that all right, Mr. Tuesday?

MR. TUESDAY: Yes, Your Honor. The court is aware of the proper function of an opening statement. One doesn't describe all the evidence that will be presented. Your Honor, if I may?

THE JUDGE: Well, I understand that. Go ahead.

The attorneys returned to their places.

MR. CZEK: Certainly one doesn't discuss every bit of evidence in the opening statement. The point is that I would like at this time to bring to your attention certain important pieces of evidence that will come into this trial that Mr. Tuesday did not discuss with you. There will be evidence that there was seminal fluid in the rectum of the victim. That evidence will come from Mr. Philip Richmond, the medical examiner who conducted the autopsy and who was mentioned by Mr. Tuesday.

There will be testimony from Mr. Block, a state police chemist, and from an expert witness called by the defense, Mr. William Wise, that there is now a technique whereby a chemist in a lab can determine in some cases the blood type of the person depositing the seminal fluid. And these experts will discuss with you the procedures that are used in making such a determination. They will state to you their findings. They will inform you as to the blood types they found in the seminal fluid in the rectum of the victim.

There will also be evidence that the defendant gave blood for the purposes of analysis. You will be informed as to the blood type of this defendant. The experts will discuss with you the fact that 80 percent of the population are secretors, and twenty percent are nonsecretors. If you are a secretor, and that can be determined by looking at saliva as well as blood, you leave traces of your blood type. If one is a nonsecretor, he does not leave any trace of the blood type.

Based on the analysis of all these factors, Mr. Block, the state police chemist, as well as the expert called by the defense, will testify that they can absolutely exclude the defendant as the depositor of the seminal fluid in the rectum of the victim because the semen was type O and the defendant is a secretor with blood type B. If he were type O, then he could not be eliminated as the depositor.

Mr. Tuesday also neglected to tell you that Mr. Williams, the gentleman who had intercourse with the victim right before her death and was the last one, according to the evidence, to see her alive, absolutely denies rectal intercourse with the victim. Thus, even though his blood type is O, he cannot be the depositor, as he says he did not have rectal intercourse. So the type O in the semen in the rectum came from the rapist and not Mr. Williams, nor the defendant, who is type B.

The expert witness whom we are calling is Mr. William Wise, head of a nonprofit blood institute in San Francisco, California. He will inform you that all the relevant evidence relating to blood and body fluids was sent to him in California for analysis. He will discuss with you the procedures that he went through in analyzing the material. And he will testify that by using a certain technique, he determined that there was a large amount of seminal fluid in the rectum of the victim.

The defense will also call a Dr. Otto Ox as an expert witness in this case. Dr. Ox is director of the Unit for Experimental Psychiatry at Massachusetts General Hospital. He will be called as an expert on forensic hypnosis. He will testify that, in his opinion, a witness is so contaminated by the suggestive nature of the hypnotic process that the testimony of that witness is unreliable. He will discuss with you exactly what is the nature of the phenomenon of hypnosis. He will state that even if the person conducting hypnosis does not intend to give suggestions, he unwittingly will necessarily do so, and that the process of hypnosis is a very suggestive one.

He will testify that once a person has been put under hypnosis who is a prospective witness in a criminal trial, he cannot distinguish his original memory of what happened from the created, or enhanced, memory that remains after the hypnotic process. Suffice to say, this expert will assist you in analyzing the hypnotic process and the weight, if any, you should give to the testimony from the witness who was hypnotized.

Mr. Tuesday also neglected to tell you many important things about the witness Julie Connors.

MR. TUESDAY: Objection.

THE JUDGE: Sustained.

Red wanted to be certain the jury understood what a one-sided version of the case they had received from Tuesday, even if the DA again objected.

MR. CZEK: She will testify that on the night of this murder, she was very depressed, and at about nine o'clock she went to a bar called the Back Bay Lounge. She started drinking at that time. After she was there for a period of time, she then went to Frank 'N Stein's, another bar. She continued drinking at Frank 'N Stein's. There she met the defendant, Joe Grady.

There will be conflicting testimony as to whether or not the witness, Julie Connors, was wearing her contact lenses that evening. She will testify that without those lenses, she sees very, very poorly.

She will testify that she met up with other people, and that they went to Joe Grady's apartment. She will admit that under hypnosis she said they took a taxi from Father's Five to the apartment. Her testimony in court, we anticipate, will be that she is now rejecting that testimony and will state that they walked over.

MR. TUESDAY: Objection.

THE JUDGE: Sustained. Just state what you intend to prove from your witnesses. Go ahead.

MR. CZEK: She will also testify that, under hypnosis, she said only three people went to that apartment, but now her present memory is that four people went.

There will be testimony from a Lynn Clemente, who also went to the apartment with Joe and Julie Connors and a man named Ken, that Julie that evening was "messed up," staggering about and slurring her speech. She will testify that Julie Connors smoked some pot while Joe Grady was gone. The reason Julie stayed around the apartment after Lynn had left was that she wanted some cocaine, and she was going to wait to get that cocaine.

There will also be testimony that Julie Connors did not report what she had allegedly seen that night to the police, and that it was only several months later when she was in the middle of the street at two in the morning, on a very cold night, that this information came to the attention of the authorities. She flagged down a police cruiser because she was cold and requested the police take her to her residence, which at that time was the YWCA.

The defense will call as a witness one Molly Rondo. She was the roommate of Julie Connors at the time of this crime. She was with her at about six o'clock p.m. on October 30, 1979, when news of the murder of Sasha Lewis came over the radio. She will testify that at that point Julie remarked: "I was with Sasha Lewis last night." Julie appeared very shocked at the news. Julie then added, "At a certain point, Sasha Lewis left myself and four men to go get some cocaine, and one of the men left after her." She will testify that at no time did Julie ever mention to her seeing blood on one of the men that night.

Mr. Tuesday told you that there will be testimony from a witness by the name of Ed Lovett. You will learn that this Lovett informed the police of this alleged admission by the defendant at a time when he was under arrest at District Fourteen for a crime. You will hear that he has a criminal record and that at the time he made this statement, he had several charges pending against him in various courts. Today, these charges are still pending. Mr. Lovett's understanding is that the police will inform these various courts as to his cooperation in this case at the time that the cases are disposed of. In fact, the police took this Mr. Lovett to these various courts about the time he made his statement, in order to clear up defaults that were pending at that time.

A Mary Katz will testify that very, very recently, she ran into Ed Lovett, that she had a conversation with him, and that he told her that he had lied about Joe Grady being involved in this murder. She will state that he said he understood he had committed perjury, and that he realized he would have to go to jail for committing such perjury. You will hear from several different witnesses concerning the reputation of Ed Lovett for telling the truth. These witnesses knew Mr. Ed Lovett around the time of the murder and frequented the places he did. They will testify that his reputation for telling the truth is poor.

Ladies and gentlemen, as you've already been informed by the district attorney, this is not the time to indicate to you every bit of evidence that will be offered. It's only designed to give you some idea as to what you're going to hear from the witness stand. I hope that, after hearing some of what the defense intends to present, you can now put the case in better perspective. And once again, I cannot urge more strongly that you try as hard as you can to keep an open mind until you've heard all of the evidence. Do not rush to any early conclusions. Listen to every witness carefully. And only then, when you've heard all the evidence, make the critical decision that is so important to all of us.

Thank you very much.

THE JUDGE: Thank you, Mr. Czek. The court will take its morning recess now.

15

The Evidence Begins

DISTRICT ATTORNEY TIM TUESDAY CALLED AS HIS FIRST WITNESS THE
construction worker who found the body. He described what he
observed upon entering the building at 283 Beacon Street. There
was no cross-examination by defense counsel Czek.

He was followed by the first police officer who arrived at the
scene, as well as officers from the identification section and the
crime lab. They testified that the murder weapon was not found, in
spite of a thorough search by the officers. Nor were they any more
successful in obtaining usable fingerprints.

They were able to lift a smudged print in blood from the thigh
of the victim. Prints lifted from a Marlboro cigarette box found at
the scene did not match those of the defendant. Photographs of the
crime scene, including shots of the prostrate Sasha Lewis and the

broomstick, were introduced despite objection by the defense. The judge allowed them to be passed to the jurors.

The first important witness called by District Attorney Tuesday was Jonathan Williams, the last known person to see Sasha Lewis alive. He related that the victim arrived at his apartment about 2:00 a.m. and that he had intercourse with her. He recalled her making a telephone call for a taxi prior to her leaving the apartment, sometime shortly after 4:00 a.m. He claimed he could pinpoint the time from looking at the clock at his bedside.

On cross-examination, Williams adamantly denied having rectal intercourse with the victim. He could not explain why Sasha Lewis had left her panties at his apartment after getting dressed and leaving. Red Czek left it for the jury to evaluate Williams's story, in light of that odd piece of the puzzle. The defense hoped it would raise a question as to the credibility of Williams's claim of noninvolvement.

Without a further laying of foundation, District Attorney Tuesday called his key witness, Julie Connors, to the stand. All eyes were on the side door entrance when he called out her name.

DIRECT EXAMINATION OF JULIE CONNORS

Q. Miss Connors, kindly speak up loud enough so the court and everyone in the rear of the courtroom can hear you and understand you. Would you kindly state your name, please?

A. Julie Connors.

Q. And could you tell us what state you currently reside in, please, without giving your specific address?

A. New York.

Q. All right. And how old are you, Miss Connors?

A. Eighteen.

Q. And with whom do you live?

A. I live at home with my parents.

Q. Where were you residing in October of 1979?

A. I was living at the YWCA on Berkeley Street in Boston.

Q. Did you have occasion to be at a bar by the name of Frank 'N Stein's on the evening of October 29, 1979?

A. Yes.

Q. What time did you arrive at Frank 'N Stein's on October 29?

A. About midnight.

Q. How long did you remain at Frank 'N Stein's?

A. About two hours.

Q. Did you have anything to drink there?

A. Two beers.

Q. At some point in time, did you have occasion to meet a young man known as Joe Grady?

A. Yes.

Q. Do you see Mr. Grady in this courtroom?

A. I need my glasses.

Q. All right. Put them on. Now can you point out Mr. Grady for us, please?

A. Yes, right there.

Q. Would you describe the person that you are pointing to?

A. I am pointing to the second man from the left.

Q. This person who my hand is over?

A. With the sweater and blue shirt.

Q. Do you wear any other seeing aids besides glasses?

A. Yes, contact lenses.

Q. What were you wearing on the evening of October 29 and early morning hours of October 30, 1979?

A. Contact lenses.

Q. Any doubt in your mind whether you were wearing contact lenses at that time?

A. No.

Q. At what time did you meet Joe Grady?

A. At about one o'clock.

Q. How did that come about?

A. I was sitting next to him at the bar, and he started talking to me.

Q. Did he introduce himself to you?

A. Yes.

Q. What did you say?

A. "Hi, I'm Julie."

Q. What did you discuss with him?

A. We were talking about there being nothing to do, and then we started discussing drugs.

Q. What did he say concerning drugs?

A. He said he could get whatever kind he wanted, and he said that he might have a party later on with some drugs.

Q. Did he mention any specific drugs?

A. Cocaine.

Q. And he indicated he could get some cocaine?

A. Yes.

Q. What did you say?

A. I said it would be fun to go to his party.

Q. And at some point in time did you leave this establishment?

A. Yes, around 2:00 a.m. We both left and went to Father's Five.

Q. Where is Father's Five located in relationship to Frank 'N Stein's?

A. It is several blocks away up Massachusetts Avenue.

Q. Approximately how long a walk would it take if you are walking at a normal pace?

A. Five to ten minutes.

Q. While en route from Frank 'N Stein's to Father's Five, was there any conversation between you and Mr. Grady?

A. Yes.

Q. Do you recall the gist of the conversation?

A. He said he knew some people at Father's Five that he could start a party with and that we would go down there and see if he could find any of them.

Q. What happened when you arrived at Father's Five?

A. Everybody was coming out of the bar at once because it had just closed. Joe started asking people if they wanted to come to his place and have a party.

Q. Prior to leaving the area of Father's Five, did you have occasion to meet anyone?

A. Yes, I met two of his acquaintances, Lynn and Ken.

Q. Could you describe Lynn for us?

A. She is about five-five, with long black hair and fair skin.

THE JUDGE: And a girl, I assume?

MISS CONNORS: Yes.

THE JUDGE: All right.

Red looked at Joe with raised eyebrows. Judge Regan had asked another foolish question.

Q. And at some point in time did you have occasion to leave the area of Father's Five?

A. The four of us went to Beacon Street, to Joe's apartment.

Q. Give your best estimate as to what time it was when you, Lynn, Joe, and Ken left to go to Joe's apartment.

A. About 2:15.

Q. When you say that "we discussed getting drugs," could you tell us who you were referring to when you used the term "we"?

A. All four of us said we wanted to get some drugs, and Joe and Ken were talking about going out and getting some cocaine.

Q. Do you recollect what Mr. Grady was wearing that evening?

A. Jeans, a short-sleeved shirt, and sneakers.

Q. Do you recollect what color sneakers he was wearing?

A. I am not positive, but I think blue and white.

Q. What was the first thing that happened, Miss Connors, upon arrival at Mr. Grady's apartment?

A. We all talked for several minutes.

Q. Could you describe, as best you can, what Mr. Grady's apartment looked like?

A. Sparsely furnished, with a mattress on the floor.

Q. Were there any sheets on the mattress?

A. No.

Q. Just a bare mattress?

A. Yes.

Q. And do you recall the gist of what your conversation was about?

A. Ken and Joe discussed going out to buy some drugs.

Q. Did something happen after you had talked about drugs?

A. Yes. Joe and Ken left.

Q. Can you tell us how much time passed from when you arrived at Joe's apartment with the three others until the time that Joe and Ken left the apartment?

A. Ten or fifteen minutes.

Q. And now what time would it be, approximately, keeping in mind that you have indicated that you left Father's Five sometime around 2:15 a.m.?

A. About twenty of three.

Q. Did anyone remain with you after Joe and Ken had left?

A. Lynn stayed there with me.

Q. Did you converse with this young lady by the name of Lynn when Mr. Grady left?

A. Yes.

Q. And how long did you talk with Lynn?

A. An hour to an hour and a half.

Q. Could you tell us what you talked about with Lynn?

A. Lynn was telling me that she knew both Ken and Joe, and they were nice and that they could get any kind of drugs they wanted to. We talked also about local bars and prostitution.

Q. Could you elaborate on the conversation concerning Joe and Ken getting drugs?

A. Lynn said, "I have known them for quite a while. They should be able to get good stuff if they want to." I said, "Do you think they will be able to get coke?" and she said, "Yes."

Q. Was there any further conversation concerning the area of drugs, other than what you have just told us?

A. Lynn and I discussed what drugs we preferred.

Q. Tell us what the conversation was about as to what drugs you and Lynn preferred, if you recall.

A. Lynn asked me what kinds of drugs I have done. I told her I've tried just about everything. I said that I didn't like downers but that I like speed and cocaine, and she said the same.

Q. Could you elaborate on the conversation that you had concerning prostitution with Lynn?

A. She said she had been involved in it, that she made good money, and that she knew people who could set me up if I was interested.

Q. Was there any further conversation?

A. She said that she was sick of hanging around there, they probably did all the drugs themselves, and they would come back with nothing. She said she was going to get out of there.

Q. Can you tell us the next thing you recall occurring after Lynn left Joe's apartment?

A. I waited for a long period of time.

Q. What do you mean by that?

A. For at least another hour by myself.

Q. Did you notice anything unusual concerning Joe's hands or arms or clothing when he left with Ken?

A. No.

Q. Did you have any conversation with Mr. Grady prior to him leaving with Ken?

A. He said he would be back in a while, and I said I'd wait.

Q. Did Mr. Grady take anything from you prior to his leaving, if you recall?

A. I gave him a pack with a few cigarettes left in it.

Q. What kind of cigarettes do you smoke?

A. Marlboro.

Q. Was it a soft pack or hard pack of Marlboros?

A. Hard pack.

Q. A flip top on it?

A. Yes.

Q. Now, keeping in mind what Mr. Grady looked like upon his departure, did you notice any difference in Mr. Grady upon his arrival back sometime around 4:00 a.m.?

A. His eyes were bloodshot, and he had some spots of blood on his clothing.

Q. And where did he have spots of blood?

A. On his forearm, his upper arm, his neck, and I am not sure about the hands.

Q. What did Mr. Grady do then?

A. He took out a syringe and some cocaine.

Q. And was there any conversation concerning the use or nonuse of the hypodermic syringe and cocaine?

A. I believe I told him that I had never used drugs intravenously before.

Q. And what did Joe say?

A. He said that was okay and that I'd get a good high off of it.

Q. Who injected that cocaine into your blood system at that time?

A. Joe did.

Q. Where did he inject you?

A. In my right arm.

Q. And did he do anything to your arm prior to injecting you with cocaine?

A. He put something around my upper arm to get the blood vessel up.

Q. Get your veins tight?

A. Yes.

Q. As a result of being injected with the cocaine, did you feel high?

A. Yes, I did.

Q. Somewhat euphoric?

A. Yes.

Q. Did Joe take cocaine himself?

A. Yes, he injected cocaine into his system.

Q. Do you know where on his body he used the hypodermic syringe?

A. In one of his arms.

Q. Did he use the same syringe?

A. Yes.

Q. And after that took place, what was the next thing that you recall occurring between you and Mr. Grady?

A. We had intercourse.

Q. Did Joe take his clothes off?

A. His pants.

Q. What about his sneakers?

A. Yes.

MR. CZEK: Objection, leading question.

MR. TUESDAY: All right.

THE JUDGE: Rephrase the question.

MR. TUESDAY: I will rephrase it, Judge.

Q. Other than his pants, what other items of clothing do you recollect that he took off?

A. His shoes and socks.

Q. What kind of shoes?

A. Sneakers.

Q. What about his underpants?

A. Yes.

Q. Did you remove any of your clothing?

A. My shoes, socks, pants, and underpants.

Q. Did you have sexual intercourse?

A. Yes.

Q. After you had sexual intercourse, what was the next thing you recall occurring between you and Mr. Grady?

A. We put our clothes back on, and he started to fall asleep on the mattress, and I lay there for several minutes.

Q. Did you fall asleep?

A. No.

Q. What was the next thing that happened?

A. I went home.

Q. At some point in time, did you tell anybody about what you had observed concerning Mr. Grady with blood on him and the length of time that he had been absent from his apartment while you stayed there?

A. Yes.

Q. Who did you tell?

A. My roommate.

Q. Do you recall what you told her?

A. I told her that I had taken drugs intravenously, which upset her very much. I think she brought up the subject of there being a murder in the area that night. I told her about the blood, and she said I was getting myself into trouble, and I was going to get hurt one of these days, and I better watch out.

Q. Did you tell any law enforcement officials what you knew?

A. Not until several months later.

Q. How did you come into contact with the police?

A. I was walking home alone, and it was late at night, and the police officers stopped me and asked me if I was all right. It was about February 1.

Q. And did you, pursuant to the conversation, get a ride from the police officers?

A. Yes, I told them I wasn't sure in which direction my roommate was. I was living at the YWCA on Berkeley Street at that time, and I told them I didn't have any money for a cab, and they drove me home.

Q. And did you have a conversation with the police officers while en route to the YWCA?

A. Yes, I did.

Q. Could you relate to the court, please, what the conversation was that transpired between you and the two police officers?

A. I asked if they had found out who killed Sasha Lewis, and I said

I knew something about it. They told me they would send police officers down the next day to my room at the Y to speak to me.

Q. Now, other than what you have already told us you discussed, can you elaborate on what precisely you told the two police officers concerning what you knew about the Sasha Lewis murder?

A. I told them I knew somebody who claimed he was a prime suspect in the Sasha Lewis murder, and that he wanted me to go to the police and give an alibi for him.

Q. Do you recall the circumstances of how and where you saw Mr. Grady the second time?

A. I was sitting in Father's Five on Marlborough Street with a friend at the bar, and somebody tapped me on the shoulder, and I turned around and it was Joe.

Q. Will you tell the court, as best as your memory allows, as to the conversation, if any, that transpired between you and Mr. Grady upon his arrival and tapping you on the shoulder?

A. He said, "Hi, I don't know if you remember me. I am Joe Grady." And I said, "Yeah, I remember you." And he said, "Well, you won't believe this, but I am a prime suspect in the murder of Sasha Lewis." And he said I better give the police an alibi for him for that night or else, and then somebody removed him from the bar.

THE JUDGE: He said: "I am a prime suspect in the murder of Sasha Lewis." Is that right?

MISS CONNORS: Yes.

THE JUDGE: Then what did he say?

"There goes the judge trying to be prosecutor too," remarked Red to his assistant and Joe.

A. He said that I had better give the police an alibi for that night I was with him or else.

Q. He said, "Or else?"

A. Yes.

Q. And did you respond to his statement?

A. I didn't get a chance to say anything. I was sitting there looking at him. I was nervous and also very surprised to see him.

Q. What happened then?

A. Several people escorted him out of the bar.

Q. What do you mean by "escorted?"

A. They didn't pick him up and physically throw him out the door, but they took his arms and pulled him out.

Q. Would you describe the manner of Mr. Grady's voice when he addressed you?

A. When he said that I had better give the police an alibi or else, he sounded rather threatening.

THE JUDGE: Do you need some water, Miss Connors?

MISS CONNORS: Yes.

Q. At some time did you go to police headquarters after you were picked up that cold morning?

A. Yes.

Q. Did you know the purpose of your going down to the homicide unit at Boston Police headquarters?

A. To make a statement.

Q. A statement about what?

A. About what I knew in connection with Sasha Lewis's death.

Q. Will you try to keep your voice up just a little bit higher so everybody can hear you? Now, did you in fact make a statement to the police officers?

A. Yes.

Q. Was it Detective Gus Grazzi and another police officer who took you down to the homicide unit?

A. Yes.

Q. What did you tell them? Give us your best memory.

A. It is basically a discussion of how I knew Mr. Grady, of what night I was with him, how I met him, the length of time that he was gone from his apartment, the reasons why I had not said anything to the police sooner, and what was the conversation that went on at

Father's Five a month after the murder.

Q. Did any of the officers take any notes?

A. I think there was somebody there who was taking down my statement and they were listening. They told me it was being taken down word for word.

Q. Do you remember telling Detective Grazzi that you heard about what happened to Sasha Lewis on the radio that day and kept thinking about how long Joe was gone and how he looked when he came back? So you tried to contact him by phone, and his line was disconnected?

MR. CZEK: Objection. What's going on here? He's leading the witness.

THE JUDGE: I am going to sustain the objection. Show her the statement. I note your objection on the record. See if it refreshes her recollection.

Q. I show you this document, Miss Connors. Read it to yourself. Have you finished reading it?

A. Yes.

Q. Does that paragraph you have read refresh your recollection as to what you told Detective Grazzi concerning Sasha Lewis's murder?

A. Yes. I recall saying that I had tried to get in contact with Joe several weeks after the Sasha Lewis murder, and I couldn't reach him by phone. It was either disconnected or out of order.

Q. Did you have some difficulty remembering the events of the evening you were with Joe?

A. Yes.

Q. Did you go anywhere with Detective Grazzi after the conversation?

A. Yes.

Q. Where did you go?

A. I believe it was to Station Fourteen.

Q. Was there some purpose for your going there?

A. Yes, the police asked me if I would be willing to undergo hypnosis.

THE JUDGE: Raise your voice.

MISS CONNORS: The police asked me if I would be willing to undergo hypnotism as a means of refreshing my memory. The detective named Gus said there was a man down there who specialized in that, and I could go down there with them and see him.

Q. And who took you down to see him?

A. Sergeant Grazzi—and I believe Detective Levitt may have been with us.

Q. Why don't you tell us, Miss Connors, as best you can, what took place from the time that you arrived at the hypnotic unit?

16

The Hypnosis Begins

A. THERE WAS A DESK WITH THE HYPNOTIST, DETECTIVE RIPLEY, behind it. I was opposite him and to his left in a chair. The other people, including a police cadet, were sitting and standing to my left.

Q. Do you know who else was in the room?

A. Sergeant Grazzi and the other police officer.

Q. Anyone else?

A. And one other person whose name I don't know. I think he was a district attorney.

Q. Can you describe the tests that were conducted to see whether or not you were conducive or suggestible to hypnosis?

A. He had me look at his ring to see if I would start relaxing. He used television images to induce a hypnotic state.

Q. Do you know how long you were under hypnosis?

A. I'd say about fifteen minutes.

Q. And were you conscious or unconscious during the hypnotic sitting with Detective Ripley?

A. I was conscious.

Q. Were your eyes open or closed?

A. I am not sure on that.

Q. Do you recall being asked some questions and responding?

A. Yes.

Q. Were you asleep at any time?

A. No.

Q. Will you tell us in your own words what Detective Ripley said to you while you were under hypnosis?

A. Yes. He got me totally relaxed first, from head to toe. He then told me that I was looking into a large television screen, and that I could see myself riding in an elevator in a hotel and then getting out and walking on shag carpeting and feeling very relaxed. I was supposed to be able to see myself on the screen, and I had to describe what I was doing and where I was.

Q. And do you recall any other questions that were asked of you by Detective Ripley, after you say that you were relaxed and that you were imagining looking into a television screen, as you have described?

A. Yes. He asked me to describe where I was, whom I was with, what time of day it was, and what I was wearing. He then seemed to be able to move the time back and forth. He said, "Okay, move the time ahead now to later in the day or later in the evening and tell me where you are." And I responded that I was sitting in Frank 'N Stein's, and he moved the time back and forth, and he just said, "Well, where are you, and what happened?" and I responded and told him what was going on, and I was able to see everything in much clearer detail.

Q. Do you remember any specifics, as far as what was asked of you and what you responded?

A. Yes, I was able to remember much more vividly what was on the movie screen in Frank 'N Stein's. I saw Robert Redford on the screen, which I hadn't been able to recall before.

Q. Would you continue, as best you can, recalling what you believed was asked of you and what you responded?

A. Okay. I was asked all the same questions as I was asked when I made my original statement, only with some of them, I responded with more detail. For example, I remembered the blood on Mr. Grady.

MR. TUESDAY: No further questions.

CROSS-EXAMINATION OF JULIE CONNORS

Q. Did you come to Massachusetts for the purpose of testifying in this case?

A. Yes.

Q. When did you arrive in Massachusetts?

A. Sunday afternoon.

Q. Did you fly here?

A. Yes.

Q. Did anyone meet you at the airport?

A. Mr. Tuesday and Mr. Ripley.

Q. Did you have a conversation with the district attorney and Mr. Ripley on the way from the airport into Boston?

A. Yes.

Q. What did you talk about?

A. Where I would be staying and what time I needed to be in court the next day.

Q. Did you discuss the information you had relative to this murder?

A. Not on the way from the airport, no.

Q. Did you discuss that with them at any time before you testified Monday?

A. Yes.

Q. Where did you discuss what information you had on this murder with them?

A. At my hotel room.

Q. When?

A. Sunday afternoon.

Q. Were you willing to talk to me outside of court?

A. No.

Q. Why not?

THE JUDGE: You can answer.

Q. Why are you looking at the district attorney?

A. He was starting to stand, and I was waiting to see if he was making an objection or not.

THE JUDGE: Is there any reason why you do not want to speak to Mr. Czek, counsel for Mr. Grady?

MISS CONNORS: Yes, I don't want to help the defendant.

Q. You think it would help Mr. Grady's defense if his lawyer had a chance to talk to you as to what information you had about the crime with which he is charged?

A. Yes.

MR. TUESDAY: Objection.

THE JUDGE: She has the right of talking or not talking to anyone, whether he is a lawyer or not a lawyer, and if that's her personal reason as to why she doesn't want to talk, whether it is good or bad, that's her privilege. Maybe she doesn't like Mr. Czek or his tie, but for whatever reason, she declined to talk to him.

Q. Is it because you don't like my tie?

Laughter in the courtroom.

A. No.

Q. Is the basic reason you won't talk to me that you feel it would help Mr. Grady to have me talk to you?

A. Yes.

Q. And you feel it would hurt the district attorney to have you talk to me?

A. Yes.

Q. But nevertheless, you talked to him, didn't you?

A. Are you referring to Mr. Tuesday?

Q. Yes.

A. I had to talk to him.

Q. You felt you had to talk to Mr. Tuesday?

A. Yes.

Q. And why was that?

A. Because I am testifying.

Q. Why couldn't you have simply said to Mr. Tuesday, "I will give my testimony in court, but I am not talking to you or to Mr. Czek?"

MR. TUESDAY: Objection.

THE JUDGE: Sustained.

MR. CZEK: Note my exception.

Q. Did I ask to talk to you on Monday out in the corridor?

A. Yes.

Q. And did you refuse to talk to me on Monday?

A. Yes.

Q. Why?

THE JUDGE (addressing witness): Tell him why you don't want to talk to him.

MISS CONNORS: Because I have already talked to about eight people. I don't think if I spoke to you it could help me any. I think you would try to confuse me and get me on the stand and try to make it look like I don't know what I am talking about.

THE JUDGE: All right. Move on. Next question.

Q. So you think if you talk to me it would confuse you?

MR. TUESDAY: Objection.

THE JUDGE: Sustained. She didn't say that.

Q. Do you remember my asking you why you were willing to talk to the district attorney if you weren't willing to talk to me?

MR. TUESDAY: Objection.

MISS CONNORS: Yes.

THE JUDGE: I will allow that question.

A. Yes.

Q. Miss Connors, do you remember responding that you were talking to the district attorney because he told you he would subpoena you if you didn't?

A. I said I was talking to him because if I refused to testify, I would be subpoenaed.

Q. That isn't what you told me, is it?

MR. TUESDAY: Objection. Mr. Czek has now made himself a witness in this case, and he cannot go into that area now since he is now the defense attorney.

THE JUDGE: I will sustain your objection in that regard.

MR. CZEK: There is no way I made myself a witness. It is perfectly proper for an attorney who's talked to a witness to say, "Didn't I tell you something?" It doesn't make the attorney a witness. It is in the finest traditions of proper cross-examination.

THE JUDGE: I am allowing you to interrogate this witness in the manner you feel best under the circumstances.

Q. So at some time, the district attorney told you you'd be subpoenaed if you refused to cooperate, didn't he?

A. No, I asked him.

Q. You asked him what would happen if you refused to cooperate?

A. Yes.

Q. What did he say?

A. I think I was told I would be subpoenaed.

Q. So, you were thinking of refusing to cooperate?

A. No, I was just curious what happened if a witness doesn't cooperate.

Q. Just curious?

A. That's right.

Q. You say that you had a discussion with the district attorney at the Parker House Hotel on Sunday night concerning what you knew about this murder.

A. Yes.

Q. So everyone went up to your room after you arrived at the hotel?

A. Yes, they came up with me when I arrived.

Q. Did Detective Ripley come up with Mr. Tuesday?

A. I believe so.

Q. Was Detective Grazzi there?

A. Yes.

Q. So there was Detective Grazzi, Detective Ripley, and Mr. Tuesday?

A. Yes.

Q. Was there anyone else present?

A. No.

Q, And everyone sat down in your room and discussed your knowledge of the case?

A. Yes.

Q. Could you please describe how that discussion took place?

A. I sat down and Mr. Tuesday reviewed what my testimony would be.

Q. How did he go about doing that?

A. We just went over my statement.

Q. He gave you a copy of the transcript of the testimony under hypnosis, didn't he?

A. Yes.

Q. And he told you to read it?

A. Yes.

Q. And you read it?

A. Yes.

Q. And he left that copy with you to read over the night, didn't he?

A. Yes.

Q. And you studied that transcript Sunday night before your testimony Monday?

A. Yes.

Q. And you spent how much time with it?

A. About one half-hour.

Q. So, in effect, when you don't know the answer to a question, you often answer it anyway based upon what you assume you probably did?

A. No, I make it clear I am not sure.

Q. Well, you didn't tell me you are not sure, did you?

A. I assumed I did.

Q. You said, "I believe so," didn't you?

A. Yes.

Q. Now you're saying you don't know for sure, aren't you?

A. Yes, that's right.

Q. Do you see a distinction between saying, "I believe I went," and, "I am not sure I went?"

A. Yes.

Q. What did you do on October 30 immediately after you got up?

A. I brushed my teeth.

Q. Do you remember distinctly brushing your teeth?

A. No.

Q. But you assumed you brushed your teeth because you always brush your teeth?

A. That's correct.

Q. So the answer is based on assumption, not on whether you knew for a fact you did it, isn't that correct?

A. Yes.

Q. Can you remember what you did in the morning?

A. No.

Q. Would it be fair to say you went to work?

A. No, it wouldn't be fair to say that.

Q. Would it be fair to say maybe you went to work and maybe you didn't, but you just can't say?

A. That's right.

Q. Did you start at Berklee College of Music in the fall of 1978?

A. Yes.

Q. Why did you leave Berklee?

A. Because I was failing my classes and got kicked out of the dorm.

Q. Why were you kicked out?

A. For doing drugs.

Q. What kind of drugs?

A. Heroin and cocaine.

Q. And were you a heroin addict?

A. Yes, I was.

Q. When did you start taking heroin?

A. In the fall of 1979.

Q. When in the fall of 1979?

A. October.

Q. When in October?

A. I don't know the date.

Q. What drugs were you involved with at that time?

A. Dexedrine, pot, cocaine.

Q. You were into cocaine before October?

A. Yes.

Q. But you say you weren't an addict?

A. That's right.

Q. How heavily were you into cocaine before October?

A. I was doing it frequently.

Q. What do you mean by frequently?

A. Several times a week.

Q. How were you doing it?

A. I was snorting it.

Q. How were you getting the money to buy cocaine?

A. I was getting it at parties, and I was getting it from friends.

Q. What were you giving the friends in exchange for the cocaine?

MR. TUESDAY: Objection.

THE JUDGE: Sustained.

Q. What else were you taking besides cocaine?

A. I was smoking pot, and I was taking Dexedrine occasionally.

Q. What is Dexedrine?

A. It is a form of amphetamine.

Q. How often were you taking that?

A. Once or twice a week.

Q. So it would be fair to say that before November, your chief interest in the area of drugs was cocaine.

A. Not really, no.

Q. But you took more cocaine than any other drug?

A. No, I smoked more pot.

Q. But you took cocaine several times a week?

A. Yes.

Q. But you smoked pot even more than that?

A. Yes.

Q. When did you smoke it?

A. You mean what hour of the day?

Q. Yes.

A. Afternoons and evenings, mainly.

Q. So on the afternoon of October 29, you smoked pot.

A. No, I didn't.

Q. On the evening of October 29, you smoked pot?

A. No, I didn't.

Q. So that was the one day you didn't smoke pot when basically you smoke pot every other day?

A. I smoked it nearly every day. Some days I didn't, but most of the time I smoked it.

Q. But you have a distinct memory you didn't smoke pot on October 29?

A. Yes.

Q. Still you can't remember what you did on the morning of October 30?

A. That's correct.

Q. You were certainly an alcoholic in December, weren't you?

A. No.

Q. Isn't it correct that that day in December when Joe Grady came in to Father's Five and asked you about the alibi, you had had fourteen gin and tonics by the time he arrived?

A. I don't know if it was fourteen, but I had quite a few drinks, yes.

Q. You were drunk, weren't you?

A. I wasn't sober. So I was close to drunk, yes.

THE JUDGE: Give me that again.

Q. You say you weren't sober?

A. That's right.

Q. You refuse to say you were drunk?

A. It depends on what your definition of drunk is.

Q. Well, is it fair to say you had fourteen strong gin and tonics?

A. I am not sure if it was exactly fourteen, but I had quite a few.

Q. When did you start drinking that day?

A. When I arrived there.

Q. And how many drinks did you have before Joe came in?

A. Quite a few. I don't know how many.

Q. Do you remember what you told Detective Ripley when you were hypnotized as to how many?

A. Yes.

Q. How many?

A. Fourteen.

Q. Well, is that the truth?

A. I assume it was somewhere around that number, but I don't know the exact number for sure.

Q. So you wouldn't stand on fourteen necessarily?

A. No, I would not.

Q. But you did give that number when you were hypnotized?

A. Yes.

Q. And you kept drinking after Joe was thrown out, didn't you?

A. Yes.

Q. So how many drinks did you have that night in all?

A. I don't know.

Q. So, in light of the fact that you had all that to drink, would it be fair to say you were drunk when Joe Grady came in?

A. Pretty much so, yes.

Q. Would it be fair to say you were drunk?

A. Yes.

Q. Of course, you had smoked pot that day, too, hadn't you?

A. Yes.

Q. When did you smoke pot?

A. I don't know.

Q. You had some in the bar, didn't you?

A. Excuse me?

Q. In Father's Five, you smoked a joint?

A. I don't recall if I did in Father's Five.

Q. Do some people smoke pot in Father's Five?

A. Occasionally, yes.

Q. Can you get away with it?

A. Sometimes.

Q. But you do admit you had pot sometime that day?

A. Yes.

Q. Where did you smoke it?

A. I don't remember for sure.

Q. How can you remember you had it if you don't remember where you had it?

A. Because I remember smoking in the dormitories that day, but I don't remember the room number.

Q. Why do you remember that particular day?

A. Because I remember smoking with a number of my friends that day.

Q. But how can you remember that it was the same day that you saw Joe Grady come into the bar?

A. Because that night I was feeling very inebriated and that was partially the cause of it.

Q. And you smoked quite a bit of pot?

A. Yes.

Q. And on top of the pot you had fourteen gin and tonics?

A. I don't know if that's the exact number, but I had quite a few.

Q. And they were strong, weren't they?

A. Yes.

Q. What did you do after dinner on October 29?

A. I went down to the Back Bay Lounge.

Q. Where is the Back Bay Lounge located?

A. On Massachusetts Avenue, across the street from Berklee.

Q. Why did you go there that night?

A. Because I was upset, and I had nothing else to do.

Q. Why were you so upset?

A. Because I had an argument with the guy I was dating.

Q. What was the argument about?

A. He said I spent too much time partying, drinking beer, and smoking pot, and that I didn't do enough studying and that I should shape up and get myself together and get to work more.

Q. Everything he said was absolutely true?

A. Yes.

THE JUDGE: Did you feel it was true at the time?

MISS CONNORS: At that time I was just angry, and I said it was none of his business.

Q. So what time did you arrive at the Back Bay Lounge?

A. I am not sure of the time.

Q. Would it be fair to say that you arrived in a state of depression?

A. Yes.

Q. So you didn't stay long there, did you?

A. I don't drink that quickly. I may have been there as long as two hours.

Q. You took those insults for two hours?

A. I didn't say I was constantly insulted.

MR. TUESDAY: Objection.

THE JUDGE: Sustained.

Mr. Czek: This is a murder case and cross-examination. You won't let me try this case!

The Judge: One more comment like that, and I'll hold you in contempt. Don't you think I know it's a murder case? Do you take me for some type of nincompoop?

Red perfunctorily apologized to the judge and prepared to continue his cross-examination. But the judge interrupted and ordered Red to the bench. He dismissed the jury.

The Judge: And I think that I should declare a mistrial. Then you can try it all over again.

Mr. Czek: Well, I'm doing this in good faith, Your Honor.

The Judge: I think you're doing it in bad faith.

Mr. Czek: I am not, I'm telling you.

The Judge: You made a totally improper comment.

Mr. Tuesday: He knew the comment was improper. He caused the damage in front of the jury, as he has done, if I may suggest, on other questions. Do I want a mistrial? There is a course of conduct here that is egregious. I would like to think about it, because again my witness has gone through hell. She has been trembling, fidgeting with the wire of the microphone. This is an ordeal. She has been struggling. I don't know what my position is. It's too bad for the Commonwealth for defense counsel to engage in this conduct to prejudice this jury so much against my witness. But I'm in a bind. What am I going to do, try this case a second time? Mr. Czek knows the consequences of that.

Mr. Czek: Do you think I want a mistrial? I don't want a mistrial. He's more concerned with convicting me than the defendant.

The Judge: I just want to say this, Mr. Czek. I believe that the comment you made in front of the jury is the basis of a contempt hearing. I believe that it was totally inappropriate and improper, and you know better. I think that after the trial, I'm going to apply sanctions. You, sir, I advise you now, are walking a very thin line. So when we go back out there in this case, we will just try it in a straight, low-key manner. I'll consider appropriate sanctions in respect to this particular issue at the conclusion of the trial.

MR. CZEK: Are you suggesting I should retain counsel?

THE JUDGE: That wouldn't be necessary, but the next time you make a comment that I deem is totally inappropriate and solely for tactical reasons to inflame the jury, I am going to discipline you. This comment, I think, was totally, absolutely inappropriate, and you knew better. You're not a vestal virgin. Some of these stunts you've pulled, quite frankly, have amazed me. If you persist in this kind of business, then I assure you that you will not go home with a smile on your face, because I believe that it is within my discretion to impose appropriate sanctions. I'm going to try as well as I can to have a record that protects me so that my sanctions are upheld.

MR. CZEK: Could I say just a few things?

THE JUDGE: No, let's get on with it. Bring down the jury.

MR. CZEK: I want to make one other comment in my defense. I want to calm things down, too, and I understand your concern, but I am an aggressive, flamboyant lawyer. I mean, that's my style. Now you say, "Try this in a low-key, quiet way." My style is just different. I understand that that style doesn't allow me to do things that are not allowed by the ethics code. I have a different style, and I'm trying to work within the style and still not upset the judge and what he thinks is improper conduct.

THE JUDGE: Well, this issue has got nothing to do with style. This is totally improper. If you want to wave around and bang on the jury rail as part of your final argument, that's fine with me. That's what I call flamboyant. If that's your style, I don't agree that that's a successful style, but if that's your style, that's fine with me. So, I'm telling you now that next time, since I believe that you're able to think on your feet, the next time that you make comments of this sort, I'm definitely applying sanctions on the spot.

MR. CZEK: I ask for a mistrial.

THE JUDGE: Denied.

End of bench conference.

Q. So, where did you go after leaving the Back Bay Lounge?

A. I went to Frank 'N Stein's.

Q. Directly from the Back Bay Lounge?

A. Yes.

Q. And when did you arrive there?

A. Late in the evening.

Q. And how long did you spend there?

A. I'd say about an hour and a half.

Q. What did you do when you got there?

A. I sat at the bar.

Q. And you ordered a drink?

A. Yes.

Q. And what did you order?

A. A beer.

Q. And you proceeded to have a few drinks at the bar?

A. Yes.

Q. And you met Joe Grady at Frank 'N Stein's?

A. Yes.

Q. And what did you do after you met him?

A. I talked to him.

Q. And did you drink while you were with him?

A. Yes.

Q. Did he drink?

A. Yes.

Q. What did he drink?

A. I believe he had a beer.

Q. How many did he have?

A. Only one or two.

Q. Did you watch a movie?

A. Yes.

Q. And what movie did you watch?

A. I don't know the title of it.

Q. Who was in it?

A. I believe Robert Redford.

Q. You weren't wearing your contact lenses that night, were you?

A. Yes, I was.

Q. Yet under hypnosis, you told Detective Ripley you weren't wearing your contacts, didn't you?

A. That's not what I said under hypnosis. I said I did not have the contact lenses on at the time I was hypnotized, but I had them on the evening of October 29.

Q. Under hypnosis, you told them you had them on the night of October 29?

MR. TUESDAY: Objection, that's not what she said.

THE JUDGE: That's not her testimony.

MR. CZEK: She can reject it, if it isn't.

THE JUDGE: Don't say something she didn't say.

MR. CZEK: The transcript of the hypnosis session suggests she did not have her contact lenses on the night of the murder.

THE JUDGE: Mr. Czek, you're inviting a contempt citation if you keep it up!

Red knew it was not worth arguing with Judge Regan, so he did not respond.

Q. So is it your position you had difficulty seeing the imaginary TV during hypnosis because you didn't have your contact lenses on during hypnosis?

A. That's correct.

Q. Can you explain why you had trouble seeing the imaginary TV because you did not have your contact lenses in?

A. Yes, because under hypnosis, you see everything that happened in the past as if it is on a movie screen but in much clearer detail; and I cannot see without my contact lenses very well at all.

Q. You couldn't see the imaginary TV without your contact lenses?

A. I could see, but not very well. It was blurry.

Q. And your eyes were closed during hypnosis?

A. Yes.

Q. You claim you continued during the hypnosis session without putting your contact lenses in?

A. Right.

Q. At any time during the hypnotic session, did you put your contact lenses in?

A. No.

Q. And are you absolutely sure of that?

A. Yes.

Q. And where were your contact lenses at the time?

A. At the YWCA.

Q. You were having trouble seeing what you saw on the thirtieth on this imaginary TV screen?

A. Right.

Q. And at any point, did Detective Ripley say, "Okay, I'll get your contact lenses for you?"

A. No.

Q. Did you ask for your contact lenses during the hypnotic session so you could better see the TV screen?

A. No.

THE JUDGE: You are confusing this witness.

MR. CZEK: Since her eyes were closed during hypnosis, what use would contact lenses be? I am not making a frivolous point in this cross-examination. This is a very relevant issue, and I think there is a strong suggestion that she did not have her contact lenses on October 29. If she had made the statement concerning the contact lenses in reference to her inability to see well the movie through the imaginary TV that night, it would have been logical for Detective Ripley to say, "Well, go put your lenses in." He didn't say that.

MR. TUESDAY: Can I just say one thing in my response to my brother? The hour is getting late. Judge, we have heard testimony that when a witness is under hypnosis, his eyes are closed. Thus, does it matter whether you are wearing your contacts or not under those circumstances?

MR. CZEK: Exactly, that's the whole point!

MR. TUESDAY: Don't have a fit, Mr. Czek.

MR. CZEK: Certainly, if a witness under hypnosis said, "I don't have my contact lenses in," and the hypnotist interpreted that to mean she needed her contacts to profit from the hypnotic session, he would have said, "Okay, fine, Julie, would you like to put them in?" The hypnotic session was taped. We have every comment of Detective Ripley, and he makes absolutely no comment along that line. So, we must assume Detective Ripley made the same assumptions we are, that the witness is talking about not having her contacts on October 29. If we don't make that assumption, then the only other conclusion to draw is that Detective Ripley was not properly conducting this session.

That's why, Your Honor, I believe the only reasonable interpretation that can be made is the one we are making from the facts. It is true that she is saying now that she definitely had her contact lenses in on October 29, but her credibility is at issue on that point, and I am not through with her at all.

MR. TUESDAY: Judge, the witness is booked for a 4:30 p.m. flight out of Logan Airport.

THE JUDGE: She will be on that flight.

MR. CZEK: If you wouldn't object so much, I might get done.

MR. TUESDAY: Don't you tell me how to try my case. You try your own case.

MR. CZEK: You are pulling this witness out of here without a proper chance for me to cross-examine.

MR. TUESDAY: Most respectfully, I would just like to say we have agreed to accommodate Dr. Ox for Mr. Czek, and certain time constraints have been placed on the Commonwealth to accommodate him.

MR. CZEK: But he's willing to come back.

THE JUDGE: Sure, but at a thousand dollars a day!

MR. TUESDAY: That's right, Judge, a thousand dollars a day. Unbelievable.

Q. On October 29, 1979, were you wearing contact lenses on a regular basis?

A. Yes.

Q. Yet it is your position today that you were not wearing them when you were under hypnosis?

A. That's right.

Q. How do you explain that?

A. Because the police gave me a ride home early that morning, and I had only a few hours' sleep. They buzzed up to my room. I wasn't informed of what time they were coming, and I had five minutes to get dressed and go downstairs to meet them and no time to fool with contact lenses.

Q. What time did they come to pick you up?

A. Sometime the next morning.

Q. And you were in your room at that time?

A. Yes.

Q. And the contact lenses were in your room?

A. Yes.

Q. You have great trouble seeing without your contact lenses, don't you?

A. I have trouble seeing distances.

Q. In fact, you couldn't even tell us whether the man sitting at the table was Joe Grady without your contact lenses, could you?

A. That's correct.

Q. And how far would you say it is from where you are to where Joe Grady is sitting?

A. I am no judge of distances. I don't know.

Q. Would it be fair to say approximately twenty feet?

A. Yes.

Q. And so you cannot identify a person twenty feet away?

A. Not that clearly.

Q. You rely completely on your contacts to see?

A. Yes.

Q. And would it be fair to say you have great difficulty seeing without your contact lenses?

A. Yes.

Q. Even near distance?

A. Yes.

Q. So you absolutely need your contact lenses on a regular basis to see in a reasonable manner?

A. Either those or glasses, yes.

Q. And yet when the police called you down that morning, you didn't put in your contact lenses?

A. No, I didn't.

Q. Did you ask the police to wait a minute while you found your glasses?

A. I kept them waiting ten minutes getting dressed and getting washed, and I was buzzed up to my room by the desk clerk, and I got down as fast as I could without bothering with the lenses.

Q. So you characterize your eyesight as poor without some aid?

A. Yes.

Q. How did you get from Father's Five to Joe's apartment?

A. We walked.

Q. Are you sure of that?

A. I am now, yes.

Q. Under hypnosis you said you took a cab, didn't you?

A. I'm not sure.

Q. Would it refresh your memory if you saw the transcript of the hypnotic session on that point?

A. I will take your word for it.

Q. I don't want you to do that. Do you remember what you said under hypnosis on the issue of how you got from Father's Five to Joe's apartment?

A. I am not sure whether I said we took a cab or walked.

Q. You can't remember what you said under hypnosis on that issue?

A. No.

MR. CZEK: May I approach the witness, Your Honor?

THE JUDGE: Yes.

MR. CZEK: I am showing her page nine of the transcript of the hypnotic session.

Q. So have you had a chance to look at page nine of the transcript?

A. Yes.

Q. Does that refresh your memory as to what you said under hypnosis?

A. Yes.

Q. And do you now agree that under hypnosis you said you took a cab from Father's Five to Joe's apartment?

A. Yes.

Q. And is it your position today that you didn't take a cab?

A. Yes.

Q. You had a conversation with another witness?

A. Yes.

Q. In fact, Lynn Clemente told you that she didn't believe you took a cab?

A. Correct.

Q. And now you are changing your position on that point from the story you gave under hypnosis?

A. Yes.

Q. How many people, including yourself, went from Father's Five to Joe's apartment that night?

A. Four.

Q. That's your testimony today?

A. Yes.

Q. Under hypnosis you said three people went to Joe's apartment, didn't you?

A. I'm not sure.

Q. Do you remember being asked this question under hypnosis, "Who is in the room?" and then your answering, "Me and Lynn and Joe?"

A. Yes.

Q. And you didn't mention Ken at all, did you, under hypnosis?

A. I may not have.

Q. In fact, under hypnosis, at no time did you ever mention that Ken went to the apartment or left, isn't that correct?

A. I am not sure.

Q. Would you like to review the transcript?

A. Yes.

Q. Has it refreshed your memory by looking at the transcript as to whether or not you ever said under hypnosis that Ken went to the apartment with you, Lynn, and Joe?

A. Yes, it has.

Q. And now that your memory is refreshed, is it correct that this transcript does not indicate that at any time under hypnosis you stated that Ken went to the apartment?

A. Yes.

Q. Yet your testimony today is that he did go to the apartment?

A. Yes.

Q. Is that based upon your reading the transcript or your memory of what you said?

A. A combination of both.

Q. So the transcript helped you in determining whether or not you made that statement, is that correct?

A. Yes.

Q. Yet your position today is, Ken did go?

A. Yes.

Q. Now, when you were in the apartment that night, did Joe leave at any time?

A. Yes.

Q. And did he leave with anybody?

A. Yes.

Q. Who did he leave with?

A. Ken.

Q. You were asked under hypnosis if Joe left the apartment, weren't you?

A. Yes.

Q. And you said he left the apartment, didn't you?

A. Yes.

Q. And you didn't mention Ken as leaving the apartment at all, did you?

A. No.

Q. Isn't it correct that under hypnosis you never brought up the name Ken on your own?

A. That's true.

Q. At one point, Detective Ripley asked a question with reference to Ken, didn't he?

A. I believe so, yes.

Q. And he asked you whether you knew Ken, didn't he?

A. Yes.

Q. And you said no, isn't that correct?

A. Yes.

Q. How much had you had to drink that night at the time you went to Joe's apartment?

A. Several beers.

Q. What was Joe Grady wearing that night?

A Jeans, short-sleeved shirt, and sneakers.

Q. Are you sure of that?

A. Yes.

Q. He wasn't wearing a sweater?

A. That's right.

Q. But under hypnosis, you told Detective Ripley he was wearing a sweater, didn't you?

A. Yes.

Q. Under hypnosis, you told Detective Ripley, quote, "We are in a cab," didn't you?

A. Yes.

Q. Is it your position today that those statements did not reflect the reality of what actually happened?

A. Yes.

Q. Would it be fair to say when Joe Grady came back to the apartment after being gone, he was covered with blood?

A. Not covered, no.

Q. Have you ever used the expression, "covered with blood"?

A. I don't believe so.

Q. How would you characterize it?

A. He had some spots of blood on him.

Q. What do you mean by spots?

A. Various markings of blood on parts of his body.

Q. Where did he have the blood?

A. Upper and lower arms, neck, and possibly on the hands, I am not sure on that.

Q. You are not sure he had it on his hand?

A. That's right.

Q. Under hypnosis, did you say anything about blood on the upper arm?

A. No.

Q. Can you describe the blood that was on the upper arm?

A. A small area of blood on the upper arm.

Q. On the arm or on the T-shirt?

A. On the arm.

Q. So you are saying he wasn't wearing a sweater now?

A. That's right.

Q. He was wearing a T-shirt?

A. Yes, a short-sleeved shirt.

Q. And the blood was below the bottom of the arm on the short-sleeved shirt?

A. Yes.

Q. And can you describe the size of the blood spot?

A. A streak approximately that big or so.

Q. You are saying it is a streak rather than a spot now?

A. It was an area—

MR. CZEK: Hold it, now. The district attorney has something to say.

MR. TUESDAY: Thank you, Mr. Czek. I was just wondering if perhaps, so that the record is clear, Mr. Czek could have the witness describe how wide apart she is holding her fingers so that we know what amount of blood she is describing.

MR. CZEK: If you allow me the opportunity to do so, I will.

THE JUDGE: As you raise that point of whether it was a streak, as distinguished from a spot, would you explore that?

Q. You said you saw blood spots on Joe Grady, is that not correct?

A. Yes.

Q. Now you say that in further defining the blood spot on the upper arm, it was a streak about an inch and a half long?

A. Yes.

Q. Could you describe the width of the streak?

A. About a quarter of an inch.

Q. So would you say now it was a streak, rather than a spot?

A. A spot is just a marking of blood. It doesn't mean it is a round circle. It is a marking of blood somewhere.

Q. So would you say it is better to characterize it now as a streak?

A. It is still a spot.

Q. You say that you have taken heroin, Julie?

A. Yes.

Q. And have you shot that heroin?

A. Yes.

Q. Where have you shot it?

A. In my arm.

Q. Where on your arm?

A. Right in the vein, here.

Q. And have you shot it anyplace else?

A. No.

Q. When you shot it, have you ever gotten blood?

A. Yes.

Q. And you shot cocaine that night?

A. Yes.

Q. Where was that shot?

A. In the right arm.

Q. Did you get blood from the shooting of the cocaine?

A. I am not sure.

Q. But many times when you have shot heroin, you have gotten blood?

A. Yes.

Q. And did you shoot cocaine after that night?

A. Yes.

Q. Was that the first time you shot cocaine?

A. Yes.

Q. Since that time, have you shot cocaine regularly?

A. Yes.

Q. Was that because it gave you a better high?

A. Yes.

Q. You say there was blood on the upper arm?

A. Yes.

Q. Which arm?

A. On the left.

Q. And did Joe shoot up that night when he came back?

A. Yes.

Q. Which arm did he shoot?

A. I'm not sure.

Q. Was there blood elsewhere?

A. Yes.

Q. Where was that?

A. The left neck.

Q. Could you describe the nature of it there?

A. A very small spot on the left neck.

Q. Was it a spot, a classic round spot?

A. No, not a classic round spot. It was a marking of blood.

Q. Can you describe it any better than that?

A. It wasn't exactly circular, and it wasn't in a streak as on the arms.

Q. How wide was it, approximately?

A. It wasn't very wide. Like half an inch.

Q. How long?

A. Probably about the same.

Q. So you did shoot up on coke?

A. Yes.

Q. And did you get high on it?

A. Yes.

Q. Was it a good high?

A. Yes.

Q. Are you sure of that?

A. Yes.

Q. Under hypnosis, you told Detective Ripley you didn't get that high off coke, didn't you?

A. I didn't say how high. I said I got high off of it.

Q. Didn't you tell him, "I didn't get high"?

A. I wasn't running around the room jumping. It was the first time I had taken anything intravenously, and I expected it to feel much stronger than it did.

Q. Once again, my question is, do you remember telling him, "I didn't get high"?

A. Yes, I do.

Q. But you told me a minute ago your present recollection is you did get a good high.

A. I got high, yes.

Q. And you told me a good high, didn't you?

A. Yes.

Q. Didn't you testify on direct examination by Mr. Tuesday that you didn't go to sleep the night you were with Joe Grady?

A. Yes.

Q. But under hypnosis, you told Detective Ripley you went to sleep.

A. No, I didn't.

Q. Do you remember Detective Ripley saying to you under hypnosis, "Now, I'll fast-forward this film until the time that you're awaking?"

A. Yes.

Q. And do you remember your answer?

A. Can you—

Q. Am I putting you under hypnosis?

A. No, you are not. Can you please repeat that?

Q. Do you remember under hypnosis Detective Ripley asking you this question, and I'll try not to be quite as dramatic: "Now, I'll fast-forward this film until the time that you're awaking. You're waking up now."

A. Yes.

Q. And do you remember your answer?

A. No, I don't.

Q. Does it refresh your memory if I told you your answer was "still sleeping"?

A. That's in reference to my still being in a hypnotic state.

Q. Well, weren't you in a hypnotic state throughout the questioning by Detective Ripley?

A. Yes. But Detective Ripley was slowly bringing me out of the hypnotic trance. That's what he was saying there. He was not referring to me asleep or awake on the floor in Mr. Grady's apartment.

Mr. Czek: Your Honor, may I approach the witness?

The Judge: Yes.

Q. Let me show you page thirteen. Would you look at that, please? He is not bringing you out of any trance, is he, at that point?

A. No.

Q. And when he continued the film and stated, "You're waking up now," your response was, "still sleeping," isn't it?

A. Yes.

Q. So, in effect, you told him that you were sleeping in Joe Grady's apartment, didn't you?

A. Yes.

Q. But your testimony today is you didn't sleep?

A. Yes.

Q. When he left, did he say he was going to get drugs?

A. Yes.

Q. Did he say he was going to get cocaine?

A. Yes.

Q. Was he gone some time?

A. Yes.

Q. When he came back, did he have cocaine?

A. Yes.

Q. To your knowledge, do you know whether or not he shot up any cocaine while he was gone?

A. I have no idea.

Q. For all you know, he might have?

A. He might have, yes.

Q. Do you remember the last question Detective Ripley asked you under hypnosis?

A. No.

Q. Do you remember what the subject matter of the last question was?

A. No. He asked me so many questions. No, I don't remember.

Q. Did you look carefully at the transcript of the hypnotic session?

A. Yes.

Q. And did you notice that the transcript seemed to end abruptly?

A. Yes.

Q. Can you explain why it so ends?

A. No.

Q. What did Detective Ripley say to you after you were brought out of the hypnotic trance?

A. "How do you feel?"

Q. What did you say?

A. Fine.

Q. Did he say anything else to you?

A. No, not really, but I asked him if I said anything important.

Q. What was his response?

A. He said that I did really well, and that I would be an important witness.

Q. Did Sergeant Grazzi tell you why you were being put under hypnosis after you talked to him at headquarters?

A. Yes.

Q. What reason did he give?

A. He said it was being done to give me a more vivid memory so I would remember some details I couldn't seem to recall.

Q. Did he tell you what he was after in particular?

A. No.

Q. He didn't tell you what details he was after?

A. No.

Q. Did you have any idea as to what he was after?

A. Just more details.

Q. What was the defendant, Joe Grady, wearing on his feet the night of October 29, 1979?

A. I believe he was wearing sneakers.

Q. Are you saying he was or was not?

A. Yes, he was.

Q. Didn't you state earlier that you assume he was wearing sneakers because that's what one would wear when they're wearing a T-shirt and jeans?

A. Yes, I did.

Q. So you were not sure he was wearing sneakers?

A. At the moment I am, but at the probable cause hearing I was not positive.

Q. At that time you said, "I can't say he was, I just assume he was?"

A. Yes.

Q. Now you are saying you are certain he was wearing sneakers?

A. Yes.

Q. So your testimony today is different than at the probable cause hearing?

A. No, just more certain.

Q. It is more certain today than at the probable cause hearing?

A. Yes.

Q. Yet the probable cause hearing was nearer to the time of the crime?

A. Yes.

Q. Why are you more certain of your testimony today?

A. My memory is clearer, and I am less nervous than I was at the probable cause hearing.

Q. You are less nervous today, so you remember better?

A. That's right.

Q. And you had intercourse with Joe Grady?

A. Yes.

Q. Did he climax at intercourse?

A. I think so. I am not sure.

Q. Did you?

A. I am not sure.

Q. Was there any other sexual activity outside of intercourse?

A. No.

Q. Did you have intercourse only once?

A. Yes.

Q. You say Joe left the apartment during the early morning hours?

A. Yes.

Q. When did he leave?

A. At approximately quarter of three.

Q. Was a radio on when you were there?

A. No.

Q. Did you listen to the late news while you were waiting?

A. No.

Q. Was the TV set on?

A. No.

Q. Was there any clock there?

A. No.

Q. Was there any watch there?

A. No.

Q. Did Joe come back with Ken before he left the second time?

A. Excuse me?

Q. You say Joe left around quarter of three?

A. Yes.

Q. Are you sure of that?

A. Yes.

Q. Did he come back again before he came back around five o'clock?

A. No.

Q. Are you sure of that?

A. Yes.

Q. Did Ken come back again?

A. No.

Q. Of course, you never mentioned Ken coming to the apartment at all in your statement under hypnosis, did you?

A. No.

MR. CZEK: I am moving to dismiss the charges. That pre-hypnosis statement of Julie's was not turned over to us until today. Hiding of evidence by the government is highly improper.

THE JUDGE: I think Mr. Tuesday should have the opportunity to respond.

MR. CZEK: They have been playing games with statements all along. They never told us about hypnosis. Eventually they give us only typed-up notes, and then we learn someone was in the room taking down her verbatim statement and there is a transcript of the hypnosis.

Q. Is it your memory you told the police before you were put under hypnosis that Ken was with you in the taxicab on the way to Joe's?

A. Yes.

Q. Are you sure about that?

A. Yes.

Q. Yet isn't it correct that this statement of what you said before you were placed under hypnosis describes you as saying that "three of us took a cab"?

A. Yes.

Q. And have you seen any statement that you made prior to the hypnotic session where you said Ken was in the taxicab with Lynn, Joe, and you?

A. No, because that's the only statement I have seen.

Q. You haven't seen any other statement?

A. That's right.

Q. But you are saying this statement is apparently wrong in that you specifically remember telling Detective Grazzi that Ken was in the taxicab?

A. Yes, I am saying I specifically remember telling the officer that Ken was with us that evening.

Q. This statement doesn't say anything about Ken being with you or leaving?

A. No.

Q. Are you saying Detective Grazzi didn't correctly take down what you told him?

A. Possibly, yes.

Q. Are you absolutely positive you told Detective Grazzi that Ken was in the taxicab and the apartment?

A. Yes.

Q. And yet it is not in this statement?

A. That's right.

Q. So your position is this statement is inaccurate?

A. Correct.

Mr. Czek: I have nothing further.

17

The Hypnosis Expert

TUESDAY FOLLOWED UP THE TESTIMONY OF JULIE CONNORS WITH THAT of Dr. Richmond, the medical examiner. He was tall with a crew cut and dressed in a cheap, three-piece suit that didn't fit and was missing a button on the vest. He held his back straight as a ramrod. He recited his background and experience in a low monotone. He had conducted over eight thousand autopsies and testified in court hundreds of times. After describing the injuries received by the victim and giving his opinion as to the cause of death, Tuesday inquired of him as to how he had determined the time of death. Dr. Richmond testified that he took the temperature of the liver at 11:20 a.m., and that, based on a temperature of eighty-four degrees at the time, and also upon the state of rigor mortis of the body, he concluded that death had occurred between five and a half and seven hours previously. Upon further probing by Tuesday, he placed the time of death as closer to 4:15 a.m. than 6:55 a.m., when the body was found.

He further testified to the taking of smears from the vagina and rectum and making slides. These stains, under later examination by him, revealed the presence of semen in both places. The material he had collected from the anal area, he now claimed, was actually taken more accurately from the perineum, or the area between the anus and vagina. Thus, it could be concluded that there was no finding of semen in the anus, and Joe could not be eliminated as the murderer. He blood-typed the victim as O.

Red Czek could hardly wait to get this pompous ass on cross-examination. When he was confronted with the police report stating that he had called into police headquarters the day of the murder, after he had conducted the autopsy, and given the time of death as "no later than four a.m.," he flatly denied giving any such opinion. Red didn't mind the answer, for he planned to impeach him with Gus's testimony. Gus could hardly deny what was in his own police report.

Dr. Richmond would not give Red a straight answer to any question. He held firm to his position on direct examination that the material he had collected from the anal area came actually from the area in between the anus and the vagina, in spite of the fact that he was confronted with the label he personally placed on the jar containing the material which stated: "Material collected from the anal area." Nor would Dr. Richmond concede that he should have taken a sample of the victim's saliva in order to determine her secretor status. Red realized fully the importance of isolating the material in the sample in the area of the anus, so that Tuesday could not effectively argue that the semen sample of type A, which was not Joe's type, was simply a result of Jonathan Williams's vaginal intercourse with Sasha.

The next witness called by the DA was the police hypnotist.

DIRECT EXAMINATION OF DETECTIVE
BEN RIPLEY

Q. Would you state your name, sir, for the record?

A. Benjamin Ripley.

Q. What is your occupation?

A. Police officer, city of Boston.

Q. How long have you been a police officer?

A. Twenty years, sir.

Q. And what is your present duty assignment in the police department?

A. I am the director of the Hypno-Investigative Unit.

Q. Would you state what training you actually received in the use of hypnosis in law enforcement police work?

A. I attended the training seminar put on by the Criminal Justice Council, and I also attended a three-day Law Enforcement Hypnosis Institute symposium entitled "Investigative Hypnosis" in San Francisco, California.

Q. When was the Boston Police Hypno-Investigative Unit formed?

A. January of 1980.

Q. On or around February 1, 1980, were you contacted by homicide detective Gus Grazzi?

A. Yes, sir, I was.

Q. As it relates to a particular investigation then ongoing into a first-degree murder?

A. That is correct.

Q. Would you state, sir, your memory of that initial contact, how it occurred, and what was said?

A. Yes, sir. Detective Grazzi contacted me regarding this particular case and said that he had a witness, and he asked what my availability might be to utilize hypnosis in this particular case.

Q. What did he tell you about the witness?

A. He told me that he had a witness who he believed at that time spent some time in an apartment with a suspect and also, at a later date, was witness to an admission from him.

Q. Did he state any particular reason he felt hypnosis was appropriate?

A. No, he simply felt she knew more than he was getting out of her.

Q. Given your training in the methodology of hypnosis as it relates to your work as a police officer, what is a case, in your opinion, that is appropriate for hypnosis?

A. On a serious case of this nature, if a person, for whatever reason, is having a problem recalling facts, then hypnosis many times can be helpful.

Q. After being contacted, and after, in your opinion, deciding that hypnosis in this instance was appropriate, would you describe what procedures were then followed, step by step?

A. Yes, sir. I asked Detective Grazzi to bring that young lady to District Fourteen. He asked if I had any objection if a district attorney came to the induction. I stated I had no objection. Detective Grazzi was also there, as well as a young lady, who was a police cadet. I thought that it would be important to have a woman there, since we would be dealing with a woman.

Q. Other than the initial information needed to decide whether hypnosis was appropriate, as you decided it was in this case, did you ask for any further information?

A. No, sir. It is my standard procedure, because of my training, to know as little as possible about the case. The reason I do this is so that no leading statements, to the best of my ability, will be given to the subject.

Q. What facts did you know about the case from Detective Grazzi, either by the telephone contact or by the contact you had with him when he arrived at District Fourteen?

A. I knew that a person had been murdered. He also told me that the subject had been with a suspect in the evening preceding the murder, and that at some particular time the suspect had left the apartment and returned. I also knew that a potentially incriminating statement had been made in a bar a few weeks later.

Q. Would you describe in as much detail as you can the exact contact you had with Julie Connors from the moment you first met her?

A. When Julie Connors came to my office, I introduced myself to her. I sat with her and asked her what she knew about hypnosis. My purpose was to dispel any misconceptions she might have concerning it. I asked her if she was nervous. She said she was, a little. I asked her what she knew about hypnosis. She said basically not much. I asked her if she thought she would be asleep during an induction. She said she didn't know. I gave her a definition of hypnosis and asked her if she understood it.

Q. State what you said.

A. I explained to her that hypnosis was nothing more than an altered state of consciousness involving focused attention, heightened awareness, and concentration, and she would be in a very relaxed situation and, with this focused attention, able to recall quite vividly the incidents of that night.

Q. Had you ascertained, at this point, by the way, whether Julie Connors was willing to undergo hypnosis?

A. Yes, sir. I asked Sergeant Grazzi. He said she would be willing. It's also part of my procedure to make sure that the person is willing and has the correct attitude and motivation.

Q. After you explained what hypnosis was, did you ask her if she was willing to undergo it?

A. Yes, I did.

Q. You say you described the process as one of relaxation?

A. That is correct.

Q. Did you explain the techniques that you would use in inducing hypnosis and during the hypnotic state itself?

A. Yes. I gave her a basic idea of exactly what we'd be doing. I told her we wouldn't be going into anything in her past, that she wouldn't be exposing a dark, deep secret, that she would be in control, and that she would answer the questions that she wanted to answer.

THE JUDGE: What did you mean, "she would be in control"?

DETECTIVE RIPLEY: She would hear every question that I asked her, as opposed to being asleep and not knowing what was going on. I told her she would be fully aware of what was going on.

Q. Did you describe what has been referred to in these proceedings by another witness as the TV technique?

A. Yes, I did.

Q. Will you tell us what you told her about the technique you would use?

A. I told her that she would be in a very relaxed state, and that she would be able to watch this incident on a television set in a relaxed and secure manner.

Q. Explain just exactly what you told her you would be doing.

A. I told her she would be very comfortable and relaxed. "You will simply be watching this TV as you might a documentary, and you will be telling me what you are seeing on this TV regarding the incidents of that particular night."

Q. Did you tell her at any point in the pre-induction ceremony that what she would be seeing under the hypnotic state using this technique was an actual presentation of what she had observed?

A. No, sir.

MR. CZEK: Objection. If that is not a leading question, I don't know what it is. May the answer be stricken.

THE JUDGE: I am going to let it stand.

MR. CZEK: Note my objection, Your Honor.

Q. In your area of expertise and learning techniques of hypnosis, is it an important consideration that you not have said that?

MR. CZEK: Objection.

THE JUDGE: I'm going to sustain that. He indicated what he did. What we are trying to do is to see what procedural safeguards were followed during the hypnosis.

Mr. Czek: That's fine with me. I just don't want leading questions.

The Judge: I am going to allow everything that he did, if questioned properly, to go into evidence. I want to know what it was that Detective Ripley did prior to his actually engaging in the hypnotic session with this woman.

Mr. Czek: I am in full agreement with Your Honor. I objected only to the way the question was framed.

Q. I believe we had you at the point where you were relaxing Julie and explaining to her the TV technique and that you had made the suggestion that she would remember everything that occurred under hypnosis.

A. Yes, sir.

Q. Is there anything else in the pre-induction phase that is not on the tape-recorded transcript we have that you can recall you said?

A. Yes, sir.

Q. If so, state that.

A. Yes, sir. I explained to her that she was not going to be hypnotized at this time, but that we were going to give her some suggestibility tests. I administered three suggestibility tests.

Q. State what you did.

A. The first test I gave her was the Spiegel Eye-Roll Test.

Q. Explain the Spiegel Eye-Roll Test.

A. The Spiegel Eye-Roll is used as a standard procedure prior to a hypnotic induction. The method is that I place my hand on her head, and then I take it away and ask her if she would roll her eyes up as if she were looking through the top of her head, to where I placed my hand.

Q. Using your own head and without hypnotizing yourself, show us how you did it.

Mr. Czek: Or anyone else in the room.

Laughter from the jury.

A. I simply placed my hand on the head in this fashion (*indicating*). I told her when I removed my hand, she would still feel the pressure, and I asked if she would roll her eyes up to it, and then I would observe how much white was showing. I also asked if she could close her eyes halfway, and she did. Depending on how much eye white shows, she is ranked from one to four, one being the least suggestible subject to suggestion, and four being the most amenable to suggestion.

Q. How did she do in the Spiegel Eye-Roll Test?

A. She was, in my opinion, a four.

Q. What other tests did you conduct?

A. Another standard test I did with her is I had her stand up and close her eyes and extend both hands, palms upward, in front of her. I had her place one thumb in an upward direction, keeping the other palm straight out. I suggested to her that on her left thumb I was tying a string and on the other end of the string there was a large balloon filled with helium gas, and that she would get a sensation of it being pulled up toward the sky. In her right hand I would place a dictionary weighing twenty-five pounds, and I asked her to feel the difference in sensation where one is being pulled up toward the sky and one is getting heavier and heavier.

Q. And this is a suggestibility test?

A. That is correct.

Q. What results did you see in this subject?

A. Her left hand rose toward the ceiling. Her right hand went down.

Q. What is that meant to demonstrate?

A. First of all, whether or not they are carrying out directions sufficiently, and second, whether or not they have the intelligence and imagination to get these responses.

Q. After administering the two standardized suggestibility tests, did you come to an opinion as to whether or not Julie Connors was a good hypnotic subject?

A. Yes. It was my opinion that she would be a good subject.

Q. Did you decide at that point to go ahead with an induction ritual?

A. Yes. I made that decision.

Q. And in making that decision, sir, did you then do something with a recording device?

A. Yes, sir. I did.

Q. What was that?

A. I turned the recording device on.

Q. Before we get into the actual recording session, describe the surroundings in which this pre-induction phase was going on.

A. I was on the second floor in my office of the Hypno-Investigative Unit.

Q. Describe your office.

A. My office is different, perhaps, than a standard office in any police department. The walls are painted light blue. I have a lowered ceiling with track lights and wall-to-wall carpeting. This is done to give the person comfort and help them to relax.

Q. Do you have hard, wooden benches or plush, soft chairs?

A. We have very nice chairs.

Q. Was she sitting in a nice chair?

A. Yes, she was.

Q. Were there other people in the room?

A. Yes, there were.

Q. Who were they, and where were they seated in the room in relation to you and Julie Connors?

A. There was Detective Gus Grazzi of the Homicide Unit; Detective Lou Levitt, Homicide Unit; attorney Rick Baxter, assistant district attorney; and Cadet Trudy Jones.

Q. Where were they sitting in relation to where you and Julie Connors were seated?

A. They were seated in front of my desk. Julie Connors was to my left, facing me.

Q. Would it be fair to say that you are, first and foremost, an investigative police officer?

A. Yes, sir.

Q. And that in your police work you use a technique which you have learned and follow protocols which you have learned to induce hypnosis in certain cases to aid police work?

A. Yes, sir.

Q. Please explain the progressive relation technique.

A. The technique is to relax the body and, in doing so, relax the mind. I start off by eye fixation and, in this particular case, I used a ring for eye fixation, which causes muscular relaxation of the eyes by following the ring, and eventually the eyes close. Then, from that point, what I do is I relax the body from the top of the head to the soles of the feet, including both arms, watching the person and how they respond to my suggestions, which gives me some type of indication of where they are and how they are entering hypnosis. That is coupled with deepening techniques to put a person to an acceptable level to achieve our objectives.

Q. The transcript indicates that you talk about elevators and going down stairs. Is that part of the deepening technique?

A. Yes. Those are the techniques I was taught.

Q. As you progressively relax the person and go through this ritual of relaxation, what are the symptoms, externally, that manifest themselves on a subject and, indeed, what manifested themselves in this particular case on Julie Connors?

A. The observations that I made with Julie Connors were that after a very short time, her eyes did close; her breathing began to slow down and went from the upper chest to the lower part of the stomach; her head tilted forward and slightly to the left; her mouth opened slightly; and she appeared to be in a very relaxed condition.

Q. Are those all characteristics you have come to recognize as those of a person in a hypnotic condition?

A. Yes, sir.

Q. What is a positive hallucination?

A. A positive hallucination is when you can see something in your inner mind's eye that isn't there.

Q. Are you asking that Julie Connors positively hallucinate at this point?

A. I am suggesting to Julie Connors that she sees her television set, and I also ask additional questions to make sure that she sees it.

Q. Is that, in your understanding and expertise, a suggestion of a positive hallucination?

A. She is observing what I'm asking her to do.

Q. Is that ability, while under hypnosis, a characteristic of the hypnotic state?

A. Yes, it is. It is one of the many characteristics.

Q. What did you ask her to do after she had turned that television set on, and why did you ask her to do that?

A. I asked her to see something on the screen. I suggested what that would be, and she saw that.

Q. What did two kittens have to do with the case in question?

A. It showed me she was getting mental images for that screen.

Q. Did she indicate by a response that, indeed, she was adopting the suggestion and able to hallucinate two kittens doing something?

A. Yes.

Q. At that point, was it your opinion that you were able to proceed with further use, as you have learned to do it, of this TV technique?

A. Yes.

Q. What was your next step?

A. My next step was to instruct her that, on the count of three, I was going to change the channel, and the documentary of the particular night in question would begin.

Q. Now, looking at page five of the transcript of the hypnotic session, you say, "Fine, fine, so good. And now, at the count of three again, I will turn the channel to another channel, and we will begin by watching a documentary of what took place early in the evening of October 29, and you will see this and tell me what is happening, adding nothing or detracting nothing, just as you watch it on the screen." What was your purpose in saying that?

A. Well, what I wanted her to do is to relate to me the observations that she was making, and I wanted her to add nothing or detract nothing, but merely tell me what she was observing on the screen.

Q. Before the hypnosis commenced, did you tell Julie Connors anything concerning what she would remember after hypnosis?

A. Yes. I told her she would remember everything that she stated under hypnosis.

Q. Was Julie Connors wearing contact lenses when she came to your office to be hypnotized?

A. I believe she wore contact lenses to my office and that she removed them there.

Q. Why isn't all of the hypnotic session on the tape?

A. Because the plug came out.

Q. Where did the plug come out of?

A. The plug came out of the tape recorder and remained in the wall.

Q. When did you discover the fact that some questions and perhaps answers were not on your tape recording?

A. After the induction, I put it in reverse to see how the sound quality was and discovered the end was missing.

CROSS-EXAMINATION OF DETECTIVE BEN RIPLEY BY MR. CZEK

Q. Detective Ripley, you state that in your opinion, your main function and your role as a hypnotist is to get information for a criminal investigation, is that correct?

A. Yes, sir.

Q. You stated you have only testified in one other case before your testimony in this case?

A. That is correct.

Q. And your first contact with hypnosis was in 1964?

A. Yes, sir.

Q. So, you heard one lecture on hypnosis back in '64?

A. And that stimulated my interest, yes.

Q. Based upon that stimulation of interest, when was the next time you had any experience with hypnosis?

A. Oh, since that time, I have been on my own, reading different books about it.

Q. When was the first time after '64 you read a book on it, if you can remember?

A. A short time afterward.

Q. What was the name of the book?

A. I believe it was by LeCron, and it was a book on self-hypnosis?

Q. Did that book deal with how to hypnotize yourself?

A. That's correct.

Q. My question is, in your role as a Boston police officer in charge of the Hypno Unit, do you do any self-hypnosis?

A. On whom, sir?

The jurors smile, and a few of them softly chuckle.

Q. Well, isn't that fairly clear? I said self-hypnosis.

A. Yes, I do, on occasion, yes.

Q. On yourself?

A. Correct.

Q. You hypnotize yourself?

A. Certainly.

Red was enjoying himself with this witness, so he continued this line of questioning.

Q. For what purpose do you hypnotize yourself?

A. For many purposes.

Q. Can you describe them?

A. Certainly. To relax, to relieve stress.

Q. So you do that at home, as an extracurricular activity, so to speak?

A. On my lunch hour, coffee breaks.

Q. So you say sometime after '64 you read that book. Did you read any other books in the sixties?

A. Yes.

Q. What books were those?

A. I don't know.

Q. Is it now the policy of the Hypno-Investigative Unit to videotape each witness hypnosis incident?

A. We will be doing that, sir.

Q. Well, is it your feeling that it is a good policy to have the hypnosis session videotaped?

A. Yes. I think it is an excellent policy.

Q. And why is that?

A. My policy now with videotaping will be that the moment I have any contact at all with the person and they walk into the room, they will be on videotape.

Q. Until the time they leave the room?

A. Yes.

Q. You state that you are now tape-recording the full interview from the time the witness comes in to the time the witness leaves?

A. Yes, sir.

Q. And what is the reason you would tape what goes on from the time the witness comes in until the time you actually start the induction?

A. Perhaps even two tape recorders would be good in case you had a malfunction on one.

Q. But you didn't have a malfunction problem in the taping of the pre-induction period of Julie Connors, did you?

A. A malfunction problem?

Q. Yes.

A. No, sir.

Q. In fact, you didn't have any tape recorder on her at all during that period, did you?

A. That is correct, sir.

Q. But now you always have a tape or video recorder on for that?

A. I will in the future, yes.

Q. Could you explain to the court why you think that it's important to videotape everything?

A. Because of nonverbal communication that goes on between people.

Q. Officer, is it your testimony that you took no statement from the witness, Julie Connors, as to her version of what happened before you started the induction?

A. That is correct, sir.

Q. Is it your testimony that even now, when you put witnesses under hypnosis, you still don't take a full statement from them before the hypnosis, as to exactly what they remember?

A. That's correct, sir.

Q. Why don't you?

A. It is my standard procedure, because of my training, to know as little as possible about the case. The reason I do this is so that no leading statements, to the best of my ability, will be given to the subject.

Q. But you don't think it's important that you get her story down as to what she remembers without hypnosis before she goes into hypnosis?

A. Yes, but the officer on the case should do it, and I will compare what she said before the hypnosis with what she said during hypnosis to determine what she "remembered" under hypnosis.

Q. And you don't determine yourself what the witness knows before?

A. No.

Q. You just have the investigating officer tell you some very bare facts concerning the case?

A. That is correct.

Q. And then you go right into the session?

A. Yes, sir.

Q. It is a fact, is it not, that we don't even have the full transcription of the actual induction?

A. For a few minutes or so at the end of it, yes, that's correct.

Q. And what was your explanation as to why, once again, we don't have a full tape?

A. My explanation, again, is that the plug that goes from the wall to the recorder fell out or loosened.

Q. Previously you said it pulled out, didn't you?

A. It fell out or loosened.

Q. But previously you said it pulled out, didn't you?

A. Pulled out, fell out, yes.

Q. So it actually fell out?

A. Yes.

Q. You start by asking the witness to describe the glass she is drinking from, don't you?

A. Yes.

Q. And then describe whether the ice is crushed or cubed?

A. Yes.

Q. And whether the drink tasted good?

A. Yes.

Q. What was the purpose at the point of asking those questions?

A. The purpose of that at that time was to see what her memory was at that time under the induction.

Q. Well, you certainly weren't interested in whether the ice was crushed or cubed, or some of the specific questions being asked at that time, were you?

A. No, sir.

Q. So, in other words, at that time, you were, in effect, setting her up for going into areas of importance, were you not?

A. Yes.

Q. You weren't really interested in her answers to those questions, were you?

A. No, sir.

Q. In reference to this point concerning whether the contact lenses were on during hypnosis, aren't there two ways of looking at it?

A. There are two ways of looking at it.

Q. Under one interpretation, she was talking about the night of the murder, and under the other she was talking about the day she was under hypnosis. Isn't that true?

A. Yes.

Q. Did she ever come out of hypnosis during the session?

A. No.

Q. Then when she said she did not have her contacts in she was with Joe on the night of the murder?

A. I guess so.

Q. Did you tell Julie Connors that she would be able to recall quite vividly the events of the night of the incident?

A. Yes, sir.

Q. When did you tell her that?

A. In the pre-induction phase.

Q. You used the words "quite vividly"?

A. Yes, I believe those were my words.

Q. What did you tell her before the tape recorder was turned on?

A. I told her she would be very relaxed, and I asked her what she thought of hypnosis. I explained what the process would be.

Q. Did you discuss the TV technique approach you would take?

A. Yes. I told her that she would be able to watch the TV, very comfortably and relaxed.

Q. Watch on the TV?

A. The events in question.

Q. Did she turn out to be a suggestible witness?

A. She turned out to be a good subject, in my opinion.

Q. And you told her, did you not, that the TV was like a documentary?

A. That's right.

Q. What is the purpose of asking the witness to relive the event?

A. So that we can hopefully get as much information as the witness might have.

Q. So, it is certainly not your position that just because she was under hypnosis everything she told you when she was under is true. Is it?

A. Well, there is no way of telling at that particular time that everything she was saying was true.

Q. Now, you state that Detective Grazzi passed you some notes during the session?

A. Yes, sir.

Q. Do you have those notes with you?

A. No, sir.

Q. Do you know where those notes are?

A. No, sir, I don't.

Q. You told her there were some kittens on the screen, didn't you?

A. Two little kittens playing with a ball of string.

Q. You asked her if she saw those kittens, didn't you?

A. That is correct.

Q. She told you she did see them, didn't she?

A. Yes, sir.

Q. So, you got her to see what you wanted her to see at that point. Isn't that correct?

A. I got her to visualize in her inner mind's eye some of what I was expecting her to see.

Q. But those kittens had no basis in reality at all, did they?

A. No.

Q. Would you agree with the statement, "The mind is constantly taking pictures. It has a great storage capacity but a weak retrieval system. This is what hypnosis attempts to call up"?

MR. TUESDAY: Your Honor, objection. I have not offered this man as an expert on the nature of hypnosis.

THE JUDGE: I will allow it, for what it is worth.

A. I don't believe I would.

Q. Did you have a discussion with Maria Moby of the *Globe* staff?

A. Yes, I did.

Q. Was that relative to your hypnosis unit?

A. Yes.

Q. Do you remember at that time talking with her about hypnotism and the mind and what hypnotism is and questions along that line?

A. Well, we spoke about hypnosis in general.

Q. Do you remember at that time stating, "The mind is constantly taking pictures. It has a great storage capacity but a weak retrieval system"?

A. I said it had a great storage capacity. I remember saying that.

Q. Do you remember saying, "The mind is constantly taking pictures"?

A. I don't know if I used the words "constantly taking pictures." I might have said, "constantly making observations."

Q. Would it refresh your memory if you saw the article as to what you told her?

A. I don't recall saying "pictures."

Q. She might have written it down wrong?

A. Very possibly. This happens.

THE JUDGE: Anything more of this witness, Mr. Czek, with reference to how he conducted the hypnotic session of Julie Connors on February 5, 1980?

MR. CZEK: No, Your Honor. I think that pretty well covers the field.

THE JUDGE: Very well. Any questions, Mr. Tuesday?

MR. TUESDAY: No further questions, Your Honor.

THE JUDGE: You are excused.

18

The Defendant's Ex-Friend Testifies Against Him

RICHARD RAYMOND, THE BOYFRIEND OF THE VICTIM, SASHA LEWIS, WAS called by the prosecution. He testified to last seeing Sasha alive at about one o'clock on the morning of the murder when he claimed to have left her at the Beacon Hill Pub and gone home alone. He described the incident wherein a man who, a year earlier, had knocked down Sasha's door, had made some wisecracks to him that evening at the pub. He stated that Sasha drank heavily at times and that she almost invariably traveled by taxis, particularly at night.

On cross-examination, he denied having quarreled with Sasha Lewis shortly before her death over an incident where he was alleged by one of Sasha's girlfriends to have pulled up her blouse in public. He also denied threatening Donna Cressey and telling her to leave his name out of the murder investigation, as he knew nothing about it. He further testified that he was never requested to give a sample of his blood or saliva by the district attorney.

Dick Brown, Joe's foreman on the construction job, testified that two or three days after the murder, he ran into Joe coming out of his apartment at the construction site, and that he had a rolled-up tan shirt with blood on it in his hands. Before Brown could make any response, Joe volunteered that he had been in a fight and that it was the source of the blood.

Sidney Goldberg, the taxi driver, related to the jury how he was sent by his dispatcher to pick up a fare at 4:05 a.m. at 486 Beacon Street, Joe's address, on the morning of the murder. He took two young men, neither of whom he could now identify, to 31 Peterborough Street, which was but a couple of minutes away. He waited for one of the men to come back to the taxi, and he returned him to the corner of Beacon Street and Massachusetts Avenue a few minutes later. He noticed nothing unusual about the behavior of the men, who presented no problem to him. He described them as pleasant.

Mr. Block, the state chemist, testified that he received and examined the materials forwarded to him by Dr. Richmond, the medical examiner. He testified that blood types A and O were found in the semen from the anus of the victim. District Attorney Tuesday was forced to bring out on direct examination through Mr. Block that Joe was an AB secretor, and thus was excluded as the depositor, since his B type would have shown up if he were the depositor.

He also agreed it was a mistake not to have retained the blood sample of the victim in order to determine her secretor status, for if she was a nonsecretor, then the A and O substances found could have been attributed to the semen depositor. The evidence that Williams was the depositor of the semen would have been strange, since he and the victim both had type O blood. He also stated that

Dr. Raymond should have taken a saliva sample of the victim, as another means of determining secretor status.

Ed Lovett was ushered into the courtroom in the custody of two plainclothes policemen. He was wearing a tattered Jethro Tull shirt, dirty and ripped dungarees, and work boots. He looked as though he hadn't shaved in a week. Red chuckled to himself, realizing the government had had such a hard time getting their own key witness into court, they didn't even have time to give him the customary new suit of clothes.

DIRECT EXAMINATION OF ED LOVETT

Q. Please state your name.
A. Ed Lovett.
Q. How old are you, Ed?
A. Nineteen.
Q. Are you employed?
A. Yes.
Q. Where?
A. For the circus.
Q. Do you know a Joe Grady?
A. Yes, I do.
Q. How long have you known him?
A. About five years.
Q. Would you describe your relationship with him?
A. We were good friends.
Q. How often in the course of the week would you see Mr. Grady in the fall of 1979?
A. Twice a week, maybe, if that. I would not see him for about a month, and then I'd hang out with him three months at a time, off and on, for several days.
Q. Did you have any particular establishment you would frequent together?

A. Father's Five.

Q. Any other places?

A. Lots of bars.

Q. Were you familiar with the young lady by the name of Sasha Lewis?

A. I'm familiar with the name.

Q. Did you know her before she met her death?

A. Not personally.

Q. Had you ever seen her before then?

A. Yes.

Q. Where did you see her?

A. At Father's Five.

Q. Do you recall when it was that you saw her?

A. No, but I saw her playing *Space Invaders* with Joe.

Q. Playing what?

A. *Space Invaders*.

Q. Is that a pinball machine?

A. No, it's a video game.

Q. And she was playing that particular game with Joe?

A. Yes.

Q. Do you know whether or not Joe had a conversation with her on that night?

A. No, not really.

Q. Did you see her at any other time?

A. I've seen her once down the bar before.

Q. The same place?

A. Yes, at Father's Five.

Q. Was Joe with her at that time?

A. No, I don't think he was.

Q. Did Joe ever mention Sasha Lewis?

A. Yes, once.

Q. When was that?

A. It was about ten days before she died.

Q. What exactly did he say?

A. He said, "That fucking cunt wouldn't go home with me. She's an asshole. She thinks she's too good for me."

Q. Where were you when he said that?

A. In the back of the bar at Father's Five.

Q. At some time in late February 1980, were you in a 1978 red Mustang with Joe Grady?

A. Yes, I was.

Q. Where were you coming from?

A. The Hilltop Steak House in Saugus.

Q. And had you had lunch with Joe there?

A. Right.

Q. And where were you headed?

A. Back to Boston.

Q. Did you have a conversation with Joe during the ride?

A. Yes, I did.

Q. Would you relate that conversation to the court?

A. When we left Boston, I told Joe I was only going to drive for twenty minutes. But I drove all the way up to Danvers. And I was driving back, too, and we smoked a joint. Then Joe said, "District Four. Quick."

Q. What did that mean to you?

A. Just a goof.

Q. Had he ever said this before?

A. A few times. We both have.

Q. Would you say it in any particular circumstance?

A. If we were doing something wrong. District Four referred to a police station.

Q. And what did he say after that?

A. Nothing right away. But I told him, "By the way, they are looking for you, Joe, for, you know, Sasha Lewis." And he said, "So what?" Then, as I was driving, he put his hand on the stick shift of the car and he put it in neutral when I was in the middle lane of the highway, and he said, "Pull the car over, or I'm going to pull a Sasha Lewis on you." And I said, "You probably did kill that girl." He responded, "Yes, I did, but so what? They are going to hang me on the seventeenth anyway." And that was it.

Q. And thereafter, did you talk with the Boston Police Department?

A. Yes, I did.

Red Czek had been anxiously awaiting the opportunity to cross-examine Ed Lovett. He got up from his chair and slowly approached the witness until he stood but ten feet in front of him.

CROSS-EXAMINATION OF ED LOVETT

Q. Mr. Lovett, would you please tell this jury how many criminal cases you have pending against you in other courts?

A. I don't know.

Q. Well, do you have cases pending?

A. I'm not sure.

Q. Would it refresh your memory, Mr. Lovett, if I show you certified copies of these convictions?

MR. CZEK: Your Honor, may I approach the witness?

THE JUDGE: You may.

Red Czek approached the witness with a handful of certified criminal convictions and handed the documents to the witness. Before looking at them, Lovett volunteered an answer.

A. Now I remember. I have minor violations pending in Boston, Somerville, and Lynn.

Q. And did you have them pending when you made your original statement to Detective Grazzi?

A. Yes, I believe I did.

Q. What are these "minor" charges?

A. B and E and extortion.

Q. And you consider those minor matters?

A. I won't be going away for them.

Q. How do you know that?

A. Gus told me the courts where the charges are pending would be informed of the cooperation I am giving the investigation.

Q. So you're on a first-name basis with Detective Grazzi?

A. Yes, he's a nice guy. He's been fair to me. He's never done me wrong.

Q. When did Gus tell you the courts would be informed of your cooperation?

A. I believe he told me when I first talked to him.

Q. And that was when you were under arrest at the police station?

A. Right.

Q. By the way, at that time, you never told the police about what Joe already said to you in Father's Five concerning Sasha Lewis, did you?

A. No.

Q. And you were on default in several of those cases that were pending at that time, weren't you?

A. Yeah.

Q. And Gus at that time took you around to the various courts to clean up the defaults, didn't he?

A. I can't remember.

Q. Well, they got cleared up, didn't they?

A. I believe so.

Q. But now you're on default again in those courts, aren't you?

A. If you say so.

Q. I'm not saying anything. I'm asking you for an answer.

A. I might be.

Q. You've been on the run for the last few months, haven't you?

A. I've been in Florida.

Q. Why did you default in those pending cases?

A. Because I'm afraid of one of the judges. He doesn't like me.

Q. What were you doing in Florida?

A. Northing much, just living in a motel.

Q. Under an alias?

A. No, that's a lie.

Lovett looked at Tuesday as if to plead for help.

Q. But when your friend Gus finally tracked you down to your motel, you greeted him with a phony name.

A. But that was the only time. If I had used my own name, they would have sent the cops down to get me.

Q. If Gus is such a friend of yours, why didn't you call him when you returned to Boston?

A. I tried.

Q. How?

A. I don't remember.

Q. In fact, the only way he could get you in here was to arrest you, wasn't it?

A. No.

Q. You were arrested last night at a Cambridge motel, weren't you?

A. Yeah.

Q. And you were in jail overnight?

A. Yeah.

Q. This morning you had a long talk with your friend Gus and District Attorney Tuesday, didn't you?

A. I wouldn't say it was a long talk.

Q. You called me at home last night, didn't you, Lovett?

A. Yes.

Q. And why in the world were you calling me, the defense lawyer?

A. Because I heard you wanted to talk to me.

Q. You've been difficult to locate recently, haven't you?

A. You might say that.

Q. And what did you talk to me about last night?

Red realized it was dangerous to ask such an open-ended question, but he thought he would get the best of Lovett.

A. I didn't want any bad feeling between Joe and me.

Q. I asked you if you were going to testify, didn't I?

A. No, you told me not to testify.

Q. You lie, Lovett.

MR. TUESDAY: Objection.

THE JUDGE: Sustained.

Red didn't want to get into a pissing contest with the state's key witness, but he had little choice left but to continue.

Q. The truth is, I told you it was up to you to decide what you wanted to do, didn't I?

A. No, you didn't.

MR. TUESDAY: Objection, Your Honor. Mr. Czek is testifying.

MR. CZEK: I have a right to defend myself against scurrilous attacks.

THE JUDGE: Objection sustained.

Q. What else did I tell you, Lovett?

Again, Red was treading in perilous waters.

A. You said Gus and the district attorney would be real nice to me, and after I testified, they would throw my ass in the slammer.

Q. I told you I was taking notes on what you were saying, didn't I?

A. Yeah, you said you were not stupid.

Red picked up a piece of paper that he had been referring to during the cross-examination. He read the next question directly from it, to convince the jury he was not making up Lovett's responses.

Q. When I asked you if you were going to testify, you responded, "Boston Police would bury me if I don't. I would have to leave the country." Didn't you?

Before the question was hardly completed, Lovett rose out of the witness chair, pointed at Red Czek, and leaned forward, screaming: "You liar, you liar! I'll get you!"

The court officers moved in and settled the witness back in his seat. Red decided to change the subject, as he had gotten all the mileage he could out of that issue and showed the jury how unstable Lovett was.

Q. Joe doesn't smoke, does he?

A. No, he feels uncomfortable around smokers.

Q. You never asked Joe for details about the murder when he allegedly made that statement to you in the car, did you?

A. No, I didn't have to. It was as serious as a heart attack, what he told me.

Q. Joe never gave you your share of the $200 he received for doing away with that automobile you were riding in when he allegedly made the incriminating statement, did he?

A. No.

Q. That made you angry, didn't it?

A. Yes.

Q. You were busted when you were in Florida, weren't you?

A. But only for carrying a double-edged blade and some pot. I'm no angel, I admit.

Q. Joe didn't have any problem getting dates with girls, did he?

A. No, he was popular with them.

Q. You went to Father's Five on your return to Boston last Saturday, didn't you?

A. I might have.

Q. And you ran into Mary Katz, didn't you?

A. Yeah, she was there with some girlfriends.

Q. And you told her to tell Joe not to worry, as you had lied when you implicated him in the murder, didn't you?

A. Yeah, but I was afraid of her and her friends.

Q. They never did anything to you, did they?

A. No.

Q. And you voluntarily returned to Father's Five, didn't you?

A. Yeah.

Q. Even though you knew word was out you were testifying against Joe?

A. Yeah.

Q. The police had to arrest you last night to get you in here, didn't they?

A. I would have come anyway.

Q. Well, you didn't show up on your own, did you?

A. I guess not.

Q. And, finally, Lovett, didn't you tell me over the phone you thought District Attorney Tuesday was an asshole?

A. Yeah, and you're one too!

Red terminated his cross at that point. He believed Lovett's credibility had been destroyed and that the jury thought little of him.

The final witness called by District Attorney Tuesday was the chief investigating officer on the case, Gus Grazzi. He traced the investigation of the case from its inception and described how Joe Grady finally became the chief suspect. He related to the jury the statement that Joe had given when he was interviewed at his construction job in November. Red could hardly hide his pleasure with the decision of Tuesday to bring out Joe's statement through Gus's testimony. For although there were perhaps slight inconsistencies on the question of times, it was basically exculpatory in nature. Red was now in a position to seriously consider not putting Joe on the stand, as he already had his story through Gus. The central problem with his testifying was that it would allow Tuesday to use his prior criminal record to impeach him. The risk was that the jurors would convict him because they believed him to be a bad person or not believable, rather than because they were convinced that the government had proven its case.

Gus could not explain how he could talk to Joe for about forty-five minutes, yet have only a one-page statement to show for it. It was a product of his now-destroyed notes and his memory of what he had said. Further probing on cross-examination revealed that Gus had typed up the one-page statement of Julie Connors on the day after her initial interview and after he had sat through her statement under hypnosis. Gus finally conceded that the one-page statement was a comingling of what she said both before hypnosis and during hypnosis, and that nothing in the written statement indicated the portion of it that was a product of the hypnotic session.

As Tim Tuesday announced to the jury, "the Commonwealth rests," all eyes focused on the defense table. Red Czek rose and addressed the court: "The defense calls Dr. Otto Ox to the stand."

19

The Defense Begins

DR. OX WAS AN IMPOSING FIGURE. HE AMBLED TOWARD THE WITNESS chair with the aid of a walking stick. He was short and fat and wore an old-fashioned suit that looked like he had slept in it for the past several weeks. His bright red suspenders were not mere ornaments, as they served the vital purpose of holding up his pants. A gold watch chain looped down from his waist. His old-fashioned spectacles sat on his nose as he peered over them.

DIRECT EXAMINATION OF OTTO OX

Q. Will you tell us your name, please?
A. Dr. Otto Ox.
Q. And where are you presently employed, Dr. Ox?

A. I am a professor of psychiatry at Harvard University.

Q. And what actually are your responsibilities in that position?

A. I teach both the medical students and residents, and I am director of the Unit for Experimental Psychiatry at Massachusetts General Hospital. I also am a senior attending psychiatrist.

Q. So you have an MD degree?

A. Yes, I do.

Q. And you are a psychiatrist?

A. Yes, I am.

Q. And you are also a psychologist, is that correct?

A. Yes, I am.

Q. And you have a PhD in psychology?

A. Yes, I have a PhD from Harvard.

Q. Doctor, does your work have anything to do with hypnosis at this time?

A. Yes. Our laboratory has done research on the nature of hypnosis. My own research in hypnosis dates back to the late forties.

Q. Can you explain to the court what your work is presently?

A. I'm the director of a major research lab that's been supported for many years by the National Institute of Mental Health, the Office of Naval Research, the Air Force Office of Scientific Research, and other agencies interested in supporting basic research on the nature of hypnosis, basic psychophysiology, and related phenomena relevant to an understanding of mental processes that underlie psychiatric issues. We are studying primarily normal individuals.

Q. Dr. Ox, could you please describe to His Honor and the rest of us the nature of hypnosis?

A. It is a state or condition where the individual focuses his mind onto the ideas presented to him by the hypnotist and where the subject, as he focuses his mind, becomes responsive to suggestion, on one hand, and lowers his critical judgment on the other.

Q. Could you describe what you do with your students on the first day of class?

A. I ask one for his right shoe, another one for his glasses, a third one for his wallet, a fourth one for his watch. Everybody does these kinds of somewhat foolish things. Then I ask them, "Were you hypnotized?" And they say, "No, of course not." And I say, "Good. Now, if I first hypnotized you and told you to do every one of these things, everybody would have said ooh and aah, he controls their behavior." In point of fact, they will do these things without hypnosis, simply because of the relationship between the student and the teacher. They take for granted that there is a legitimate reason. This is an example of precisely what hypnosis is not. In other words, it's not a way to increase the control you have over individuals, because you do not practice hypnosis in a vacuum. You have to compare the control you have with hypnosis over the control that you have without hypnosis in the identical context.

Q. Does the hypnotist require any particular training?

A. In terms of inducing a trance state, it requires very little skill. However, it does require that the subject has the right attitude. The thing that is important is how you set up the relationship before you start the induction procedure, because at that point, most of what is called induction takes place.

Q. And would it be fair to say that you have really three stages of the process: you have a pre-hypnotic state, where there is discussion with the subject as to what is going to happen; you have the actual hypnosis; and then you have a post-hypnotic stage, where there is a discussion after the patient is out of hypnosis?

A. Right.

Q. Dr. Ox, so I can get this clear in my mind: As I understand your testimony, there are three important and rather central characteristics of the hypnotic state. One is that the subject is more amenable to suggestion. Two, that the hypnotic state lowers the critical judgment. And three, that there is increased concentration on the part of the subject.

A. Yes.

Q. Would you briefly touch on the suggestibility aspect?

A. Yes. It is the capacity to distort perception or memory in accordance with cues from the hypnotist.

Q. So, it would be fair to say that when a subject has been hypnotized, he may very well, because of that process, accurately recall what he had not been able to recall before.

A. Oh, yes.

Q. Yes. But isn't it also possible that he may create something that doesn't accurately reflect the real world?

A. Yes.

Q. Could you briefly comment, Doctor, on the phenomena of decrease of critical judgment during the hypnotic session?

A. The individual who is hypnotized tends to be willing to accept something which he might not otherwise be willing to accept. And the problem you have is that you are dealing with a state where an individual is a) hyper-suggestible and b) has lower critical judgment, and that combination is what causes people to be much more vulnerable to creating recall. The danger in hypnosis is that capacity to check "doesn't fit" is altered.

Q. What do you mean by the expression "created recall" under hypnosis?

A. There is a very nice illustration of it in this case, where the witness, Julie Connors, made a statement that the defendant was wearing sneakers. When challenged on that point, she says, "I can't say for sure, but he was wearing dungarees, so I assume he wore sneakers since most people do with dungarees." This is a classic example of how you create recall. I mean, it's plausible, it fits, and it is incorporated into memory. In the awake state, you have the same process going, but you have much more of the critical judgment present than in hypnosis, and that's the big difference.

Q. Does hypnosis play a legitimate role in the investigation of crimes?

A. Hypnosis causes you to recall more things, which makes it much better for investigative purposes, because you will say things that you aren't willing to hazard a guess on. Now, if you're investigating, you want as much data as possible, even if it's inaccurate, because it can be later checked for accuracy. It's another thing if you assume that that statement is correct because it came under hypnosis, or is likely to be correct because it came under hypnosis, because these are misconceptions. It's actually less likely to be correct, but you get more information.

Q. Dr. Ox, what are the techniques that have been traditionally used to increase recall?

A. There are two procedures that have been used widely. One is the technique of hypnotic age regression, and the other is suggestive hypermnesia. In hypnotic age regression, which is the technique that comes from therapeutic practice, you suggest to somebody that he return to an earlier period of development.

Q. And what's the purpose of doing that?

A. It's an attempt to reinstate that earlier period of development, so you may have an adult recall things that happened when he was a child. You may also have him recall things that happened last week. There is no difference in process, whether it's last week or twenty years ago. Freud observed that if he took his patients who had hysterical symptoms and regressed them back to the point where these symptoms seemed to have come from, the individuals would relive these events with tremendous feeling. They would describe in exquisite detail all kinds of things, like a scratch on the furniture, a spot on the tapestry, a curtain that was a little crooked, a picture that wasn't just straight or had a smudge on it—all kinds of details you couldn't possibly know if you weren't there. That's what made it so compelling.

And finally, when they woke up after this experience, they would be without symptoms. They would lose the symptoms that seemed related to this. Now, these three things—the intense effect, the tremendous detail of recall, and the fact that they lost their symptoms—convinced Freud that these memories were real memories and that they were really living past events.

Now, it took Freud some years before he realized that these memories were not in fact accurate, even though they were given with great feeling and in great detail. They represented fantasies of the child more often than they represented actual experiences. But they were representing intensely felt fantasies, and from a psychiatric viewpoint that was every bit as important as if they had actually happened. So it didn't really matter to him, ultimately, whether these things happened or whether they were fantasies of the child that were being re-experienced. It mattered that the people were able to think about them and eventually no longer had the symptoms.

Q. So that truth of what was remembered was not critical to the therapy?

A. Correct. And there's a lot of evidence that you don't need accurate recall for treatment purposes. You may recall things that are a mixture of many things and may not be accurate and yet get very good therapeutic results.

However, consider what would have happened if Freud had gone to the police and accused some poor parent of incest—which is what many of these fantasies were about. It would have been a catastrophe, since the man was perfectly innocent. It was fantasies that were being remembered.

Q. Can you describe experiments you have done on age regression?

A. I asked a student to age-regress to his first grade of school. I said to him, "Look, you see your teacher." He couldn't see her. So I said, "You're seeing her," and he says, "I can't make her out." So I suggested, "As your right hand floats up, ask the teacher to help. You will recognize your teacher." That's a technique that's often done—you change one suggestion to another. It's a very powerful suggestive statement. "As your hand goes up, you will recognize her." So the hand slowly floats up, and you can see the smile of recognition when suddenly you have the insight. He sees her. "Miss Jones." He begins to talk to her, sees her very clearly. It's obvious he recognizes her. Everything is fine. And my colleague who was with me was absolutely convinced that was it.

Well, being somewhat skeptical, when it was all over I said, "By the way, who was your first-grade teacher?" And he said, "I don't remember." "Who was your second-grade teacher?" "I don't remember." So I asked him, "Did you have a schoolteacher by the name of Miss Jones?" "Oh, yes, I liked her, very nice." He described her. "That was my third-grade schoolteacher." What happened was, I put pressure on him to remember. He confabulated the next available teacher into the first grade. Now, mind you, he didn't do that until I had kind of pushed him to remember. When I pushed him to remember, he took that memory from one place and put it into the wrong place. It's important to recognize that in that particular procedure, I was careful to separate the things that came from the hypnosis from the things that came from waking recall, something that is not normally done.

Q. Doctor, you mentioned confabulation in discussing age regression. What do you mean by that term?

A. Confabulation is a process that occurs whenever you're trying to fill in a gap in memory, where you're aware that you have some kind of gap but feel you should know something. It happens to us all the time when we have some detail we don't remember fully. We make up what seems plausible. That is normal memory process.

However, there is normally a quality control. We have a critical judgment, and we don't allow the thing to be a very poor fit. It has to be quite reasonable. In hypnosis, it's easier to confabulate, because you have a lower critical judgment.

Q. I see.

A. And that is why it becomes much more of a problem.

Q. Did you examine the transcript of the hypnotic session of Julie Connors conducted by Detective Ripley?

A. Yes.

Q. And did you note the type of approach he was using relative to this theory of hypnosis?

A. Well, if I could, before going into that, just explain the data for or against this theory, because it's kind of a key issue whether the theory is right or not.

Q. You have made clear that you don't subscribe to the theory. Isn't that correct?

A. It's not a matter of opinion. I'd like to present the facts to you, the data, so that you don't have to accept it because I said so, but rather evaluate the same evidence that I have.

Q. In other words, you're saying that in your opinion, the facts don't support that theory of the nature of hypnosis?

A. In my opinion, they do not, but I'd like to share the facts with you.

Q. Okay. Explain why you hold that view.

A. Yes, sir. Thank you.

The notion that we can remember something from a time when we did not understand language would imply that we remember by echoic memory—in other words, memory like a phonograph memory. If it could be done, then you would have to be able to show an increase of memory with nonsense syllables, because to a tape recorder it doesn't matter whether they are nonsense syllables or whether they are meaningful words. But the data is unequivocal. There is no increase of memory for nonsense syllables. Therefore, we cannot have some kind of mechanism that doesn't care about meaning. I could go on at length about other data which would show that it doesn't make sense, but suffice it to say, these are solid bits of evidence which show that that kind of theory just won't hold water.

Q. What is the most common technique employed in an attempt to encourage an individual under hypnosis who is a potential witness at a trial to bring forth information?

A. The most common technique used is a modification of the television procedure that was originally developed by Milton Ericson, where you essentially tell the subject to visualize a television screen and imagine that you see things happening on the screen, and you suggest to the subject that they will be able to see events going on on that screen. Instead of asking a witness to relive the event directly, they are told that things will appear there on the screen, and they will be able to observe them and describe them. It's sometimes described, as it was in this instance, as, "You will be seeing a documentary," which implies that there will be an accurate portrayal of the events that happened at some time in the past.

Q. Why would cross-examination not reveal the historical inaccuracies of what a witness is saying on the stand at trial that were the result of misuse of the hypnotic process?

A. Consider the experience of the hypnotized subject who is told to look at the television screen and see the thing happening. He experiences himself looking at a television he believes is real, so he gives it an entirely different level of certitude, even though all the errors of memory, plus all of the errors that have been induced by compliance and as a result of suggestion, are still there. From the subject's point of view, it's like truth, like a videotape of actual events.

The problem is that it alters the witness's belief about truth without affecting the accuracy of his statements. The problem arises because the whole technique that has been developed to ascertain truth is based upon the usual circumstances where cross-examination can shake a witness, where a witness doesn't have this very special way of having created certainty, and where you normally can say to a person, "Look, I want you to think hard. Is it really your memory?"

When somebody has seen the pseudo-videotape and he says in his mind, "I've seen that, I know it happened," that is something very different from an individual who hasn't had that pseudo-memory aid. It does not necessarily alter accuracy, but it can.

It does, however, alter certitude, and these are two different things. And to the extent that it alters certitude, it totally alters the way in which people think about their experiences, making cross-examination ineffective.

Q. And were you given the tape of the hypnosis session by Detective Ripley of Julie Connors?

A. Yes.

Q. Were you given a transcript of the tape?

A. Yes, I have a transcript.

Q. And you have listened to the tape and read the transcript?

A. Yes, repeatedly.

MR. CZEK: Could we mark as an exhibit, Your Honor, the transcript of the tape?

MR. TUESDAY: No objection, Your Honor.

THE JUDGE: All right.

Transcript of the tape of examination under hypnosis of Julie Connors received in evidence and marked EXHIBIT ONE for the defense.

Q. From reading the transcript and listening to the tape, do you get any indication as to whether or not anything transpired between the witness Connors and Detective Ripley before the tape recorder was apparently turned on?

A. Yes, sir. On page 1, Detective Ripley says: "Excuse me, Julie, if you have other questions at all other than what we talked about up to this time, ask me. We've talked a little bit about what hypnosis is. Do you feel comfortable with hypnosis?" Now, I'd like to know what this "little bit about hypnosis" is. It isn't on the tape. That little bit is a key issue of what is going to happen afterward.

Q. And why is that?

A. Because that sets up the expectations and beliefs which will then cause the hypnotic subject to behave in a certain way. Without knowing that, you simply don't know what the hypnotized subject is going to believe.

Q. What other problems were there with the procedure employed by Detective Ripley?

A. There is no evidence at all that the officer made any effort to get at what this girl remembered before hypnosis took place.

Q. You mean before he starts the hypnotic session he should ask her what she remembers about the incident?

A. That's correct, so that the witness's original memory can be isolated from the influence of the hypnotic experience. For if the hypnotic procedure is defective and polluted, the memory you still have is the uninfluenced original statement.

Q. What is the significance of the fact that there are apparently several people, including the chief investigating police officer, in the room at the time that the witness was hypnotized in this case?

A. Ideally, only the individual doing the hypnosis ought to be in the room with the subject, simply because the more people present, the more there is a tendency for people to make comments, and I don't mean audible comments, but simply drawing in one's breath as things get exciting when you get close to something. We tend to be very sensitive to all kinds of cues from each other, and the less opportunity there is for this kind of subtle nonverbal communication, the better. So, I would rather have everybody outside of the room, and then, when somebody wants a question asked, instead of whispering it to the hypnotist, you make a little note and you slip it under the door, so that you then have a permanent record and know what information was given. The issue of how much information the hypnotist has at the time he does the hypnosis is very important, since we know that if the hypnotist has a lot of information, he may very well unwittingly communicate it to the subject. It is essential to know, therefore, how much information he had and where he got it from, and you don't know that unless you can separate it.

Q. By the way, Doctor, have you testified for the prosecution in some cases?

A. Yes. About as often as I have for the defense.

MR. CZEK: Your Honor, this would be an appropriate place to take the recess right now.

THE JUDGE: I think we'll take this opportunity to take the morning recess.

Recess.

After the recess.

THE JUDGE: You may proceed, Mr. Czek.

Q. Doctor, can you give an example of a case in which the witness recalled something in hypnosis that later turned out not to be so?

A. Yes, sir. Probably one of the best examples was a court-martial in 1973 in Philadelphia. The facts of the case were that two sailors were sitting in the Philadelphia Naval Hospital recuperating, and somebody came by, pulled a gun, and shot at one of them. He fortunately dived and was only grazed. A witness identified one individual as the shooter. The victim failed to identify this individual, and in fact when he was shown the picture said, "No, this man looks like him, but he is not the man."

There was then a hearing, and at the hearing the witness again identified this individual as the person who did the shooting. The victim again said, "No, that is not the man. He looks like him, but it isn't him." And after that he was hypnotized to help him remember who the man was who shot him, because he couldn't remember it. And during the first hypnosis, he failed to identify him. He was hypnotized a second time, and during the second hypnosis, he then identified the man who was the same man who had been identified by the witness. When he came out of the hypnosis, he was convinced it was that man.

At the court-martial, I was asked to testify about this particular event, and I pointed out that he had made a negative identification twice before hypnosis, and that after hypnosis, he had changed his view. I pointed out how unreliable the hypnotic procedure was.

The judge advocate's representative at this court-martial ruled as a matter of law against the testimony being introduced, and in fact, for that reason, the accused was judged to be innocent.

There are two things that are important about the case and very interesting. One is that some week or two after the case was finished, some people returned from overseas who were alibi witnesses for the accused seaman, and they conclusively documented that he could not have been the person who was responsible for the shooting.

The other equally interesting point is that the victim became progressively disillusioned with the navy, and about a year after wrote a letter to *The Stars and Stripes* in which he alleged, "Somebody nearly killed me by shooting me, and they let the man go," indicating that his conviction, which had been established by hypnosis, remained with him. In other words, it wasn't as though it was a transient thing. It was a permanent change in his memory, and it illustrates in an actual case how, in a very real sense, hypnosis can alter the information inside a man's mind.

Q. Now, Doctor, you stated that you have examined the transcript of the tape recording of the hypnotic session with Julie Connors?

A. Yes, sir.

Q. What is the significance, Doctor, of the hypnotist saying, "Let's press the button and backtrack on the screen?"

A. Well, his pressing the button says: "Okay, I'm not so interested in what's happening now. Let's go to more interesting things." I mean, that's the way you tell people how to focus in.

Q. But is it clear that he is using a certain technique in his approach to the witness?

A. Oh, yes.

Q. And what is that technique?

A. That is the television procedure, where he is telling the victim or witness, "It's out there, and you can see it out there, and I'm going to press the button, and you will tell me what you see."

Q. Do you see evidence that it was used right from the beginning?

A. Yes. He is suggesting that she should see a television screen right in the beginning, as soon as hypnosis is induced.

Q. And was there evidence throughout the hypnotic session that he was continuing to use that same technique?

A. Yes, throughout. And by the way, it should be emphasized that this technique, like all aspects of hypnosis, inevitably communicates what is wanted to the subject, because when you tell the subject, "We're going to fast forward," you are really saying, "Move along. I'm not interested so much in where you are now. Go to something else."

When the hypnotist says, "Let's go back over that; we'll do instant replay," he is, in effect, saying, "Hey, this is very interesting; we'll go over it some more. There are more details I want." So there are suggestions that take place without necessarily saying something explicitly.

Q. Did you detect any seemingly incorrect statement of the witness under hypnosis?

A. Yes, she had some incorrect memories during hypnosis, which are clearly incorrect, as I understand the facts, based upon my reading of the probable cause hearing transcript.

Q. During the hypnotic session, does she mention any Ken as being in the defendant's apartment with her and Lynn?

A. No, absolutely not. In fact, she says she doesn't know any Ken.

Q. And you have read some of the other material in this case, where other witnesses clearly place Ken at that apartment?

A. That's what I find interesting, yes.

Q. And in regard to the taxicab, she states in the hypnotic session that she took a taxicab?

A. That's correct.

Q. And from reading the other materials, was there evidence from other witnesses that there was absolutely no cab taken?

A. It would appear that there was no cab taken.

THE JUDGE: The thrust of this line of questioning, I gather, is to further support the doctor's contention as to why hypnosis testimony is unreliable.

Q. Do you have other comments on the transcript of the hypnotic session?

A. Yes. The hypnotist says, "All right. Okay, you're doing so good, so good, so relaxed. Your body is so relaxed, so comfortable, peaceful, and secure. So comfortable, so peaceful." This is the kind of reinforcement I'm talking about, which is quite characteristic of a suggestive hypnotic experience.

And then out of left field comes the question: "Did she mention Peterborough Street?" Now, again, the hypnotist is being suggestive by the use of a leading question.

THE JUDGE: Here's some water; you may be a little dry.

DR. OX: Thank you very much.

Q. Now, what is the significance on page twenty, at the bottom of the discussion about the ice and the drink, and whether it's weak or strong, in relation to the fact that the script ends on page twenty-one at the top?

A. Well, you would tend to do this if you wanted to increase depth, as you get the person talking about their experience.

Q. But normally, you'd be going into a new major area, as opposed to coming to an end?

A. Correct. The procedure here is not what you would be doing to come to an end. One would expect that there was a good deal more material elicited. It's just missing.

Q. Now, if you were informed that the plug was accidentally pulled at that point, what would be your reaction?

A. I would find it difficult to understand how this can happen without one becoming aware of it. Tape recorders make noise, and the absence of noise is something we're trained to pick up.

Q. Have you ever heard of this happening before?

MR. TUESDAY: Objection, Your Honor.

THE JUDGE: Sustained.

Q. Should the post-hypnotic discussion be on tape?

A. Yes. Not only would I want to know what happened during hypnosis, but I would also want to be able to listen to the discussion after hypnosis, where the one being hypnotized would typically say, "Well, you know, it was like—different from what I expected." And then you'd say, "What do you mean?" And then you'd gradually get an idea of what this experience was like. You'd need that to make a true assessment of the reliability of what had happened. You simply don't have the data here.

Q. Doctor, what is your opinion as to the reliability of the testimony of Julie Connors?

A. I believe you cannot trust any of the testimony that this witness gives at this point, as we don't have even a complete transcript of the hypnotic session, or anything of it after the induction and not all of it before. We simply do not know how deeply the hypnosis polluted her memory.

Q. Doctor, finally, based upon your experience and the writing you've done and the societies to which you belong, could you tell the court what the attitude of the scientific community is relative to the validity of hypnotism in forensic matters?

A. With very few exceptions, it is the view of members of the scientific community that hypnosis is a state that leads to increased suggestibility and a decrease in critical judgment. Where hypnosis is used to help people recall, it may increase memory, may alter memory, and may create memory, and you cannot tell which is which. And since there is no way of determining whether the memory that follows from hypnosis represents correct recall or confabulation, these memories are such that they should not be introduced into a court of law, though they may be very useful for the purpose of criminal investigation.

CROSS-EXAMINATION OF DR. OTTO OX

Q. Is there really any difference between the suggestiveness inherent in ordinary police interrogation and that in the hypnotic setting?

A. There are real differences between these two, and to say they are similar really obfuscates the major differences. In one case, you have an individual who is much less suggestible, though the situation makes him suggestible to some degree. Certainly, the context of a police station is one which makes people willing to go along with things more, but there is this critical judgment, which is preserved. He is much less likely to accept something that doesn't quite fit his preconception.

Q. But wouldn't you agree that, given the contextual situation that he's in, of wanting to be a good citizen and helping the police, that a police suggestion of, "Didn't you see the raincoat?" could suddenly be adopted even with this waking witness?

A. This is entirely possible. That is the problem of all eyewitness identification, and everybody knows that, but that is not the same level of problem that you have with hypnosis.

Q. Aren't we talking about testimony in this case from a witness who, prior to her testimony, perhaps was hypnotized, but is now stating, "I have a memory of what happened on a particular date."

A. That testimony is just as much from hypnosis as if you were hypnotizing the witness in court, because she is basing her memory not on her memory traces dating back to the original event, but what happened in hypnosis. Therefore, she is erroneously attributing it to other time periods.

Q. And what makes you make that vast assumption about the witness's testimony?

A. Simply because that is what happens following hypnosis.

Q. Well, Doctor, are you testifying—and surely I don't think you are—that the fact that a witness undergoes hypnosis destroyed the critical judgment in the post-hypnotic, waking state?

A. It certainly interferes with the critical judgment in the post-hypnotic, waking state. This is precisely what I'm testifying to. If you consider the case of the court-martial, where the individual before hypnosis twice said, "This man was not the one who shot at me," and after being hypnotized, he said, "This is the man who shot at me," and then was given a great deal of evidence to the contrary and still insisted, "That was the man who shot at me." Clearly, the hypnosis altered the post-hypnotic judgment.

Q. In other words, the devilishly clever hypnotist can clearly confound if he works at it?

A. I beg your pardon. It's not a purposeful thing, if you use the standard procedures which are recommended by people for use by police hypnotists.

Q. Don't go any further, Doctor.

MR. CZEK: May he be allowed to answer the question? He breaks in on the witness, and the witness doesn't do it to him. What's good for the goose is good for the gander.

THE JUDGE: I'll set the rules, Mr. Czek. Just stand up and object, and I'll rule on the objection. The objection is overruled.

Q. What is, in your assumption, the standard pre-hypnotic customary formulation that would lead to the devilish result?

A. I object to the notion of a devilish result. I believe that the people who are doing this are doing it in good faith. I believe that the police hypnotists are doing it thinking that they're doing the right thing, but they are misinformed.

Q. Doctor, assume the witness has made certain observations. Assume further that, given the normal delay and all the business we've gone through about leveling and sharpening, nevertheless, there are strong memories of what happened. In the articulation of what happened, some of these memories may not be mentioned. It doesn't mean you would agree they are not there. It's just that he didn't or she didn't mention them in that particular interview.

Hypnotically, in a question-and-answer form, whereas on A and B had been mentioned, A, B, C, D were mentioned in hypnosis, but indeed in the mind there was memory of A, B, C, D.

MR. CZEK: Is he testifying or asking a question?

THE JUDGE: It's a form of hypothetical. The court will allow him to continue. You make an objection that he makes the question as not being based on facts that are in evidence, but I'm going to allow him to ask that hypothetical question. Go ahead.

Q. A witness has seen A, B, C, D, E. That would be five factors. In articulating his or her memory to the police officer in the first statement, only A, B, and C are mentioned.

A. Prior to hypnosis?

Q. Prior to hypnosis. Under hypnosis, all five factors come out, so that for the first time we have D and E. But also, we have factors you would say were confabulated. Would it be fair to say that the confabulations would be consistent and not irrationally related to the true memories of the event?

A. They would be indistinguishable by either the witness himself or the observers, unless you had independent data.

Q. But would you agree that they wouldn't be irrationally related and would fit into a total picture?

A. They would make sense to the subject.

Q. Would the witness's memory defy the normal expectations of someone recalling an event?

A. He would not tend to remember something that defies common sense. He would not remember an elephant on Tremont Street, for example, if there had not been an elephant. He would probably confabulate things which are somehow plausible in his mind. Now, if he had happened to have been at a circus that day, he might indeed remember an elephant.

Q. But in a discussion of normal memory, doesn't that same filling-in with expected results happen constantly?

A. The process is similar, but the extent to which critical judgment is lowered under hypnosis is so much greater as to make it a qualitatively different thing, and it really doesn't make sense to say it is no different than the normal memory process.

Mr. Tuesday: Thank you, Doctor. No further questions.

20

The Defense Case Continues

THE NEXT DEFENSE WITNESS WAS WILLIAM WISE, THE CHEMIST WHO testified that he had examined the same specimens as the state chemist, Brandon Block. He disclosed the more elaborate tests that he was asked to perform on the substance in his specialized lab. He was an important witness for the defense, since he would differ from Block in his analysis of the material taken from the anus. He testified that although he found much semen, he uncovered no blood types. Thus, he concluded that a nonsecretor was the depositor of the semen. As Joe was a secretor, he could be eliminated as the murderer. Block had testified to finding type O blood in the semen, and thus concluded that Jonathan Williams, since he had type O blood and was a secretor, could not be eliminated as the depositor of the semen in the rectum, in spite of his claim that he did not have anal intercourse with the victim.

Mr. Wise also contradicted chemist Block in testifying that even if there were more than one depositor of semen, there were sufficient amounts of the substance that Joe, having type AB blood, could positively be eliminated as the depositor, since absolutely no B type blood substance was detected.

The defense had difficulty locating Lynn Clemente. But once they did, she was reluctant to come testify, so Red was forced to subpoena her. When she arrived at the courthouse, she reported to the district attorney. Red was not certain as to how her testimony would turn out, but she was a critical witness in order to reveal the demeanor of Julie Connors on the night in question. Red got only a brief opportunity to discuss her testimony before it was time to call her to the stand. As she passed the defense table in her ultratight Calvin Klein dungarees on her way to testify, Red leaned over to Joe and remarked, "Did you see the ass on her?" Joe smiled slightly, as he hardly expected such a comment from his lawyer.

DIRECT EXAMINATION OF LYNN CLEMENTE

Q. Do you know the defendant, Joe Grady?

A. Yes.

Q. And did you see him one night in late October of 1979 outside of Father's Five?

A. Yes.

Q. And was he with anyone when you saw him?

A. Yes, Julie Connors.

Q. And at that time did you know the name of the lady he was with?

A. No.

Q. And were you with someone that night?

A. Yes.

Q. Who were you with?

A. My boyfriend Ken.

Q. Where had you been earlier that evening prior to seeing Joe Grady?

A. In Father's Five.

Q. Had Ken been in Father's Five?

A. Yes.

Q. And what time did you leave Father's Five that night?

A. About two o'clock.

Q. And when after leaving Father's Five did you see Joe Grady?

A. He was right outside.

Q. And was this young lady with him at that time?

A. Yes.

Q. Did you proceed to go anyplace from Father's Five?

A. Yes, over to Joe's apartment.

Q. Who went over to Joe's apartment with you?

A. Ken, Julie Connors, and Joe.

Q. There were how many of you?

A. Four.

Q. Are you absolutely certain of that?

A. Yes.

Q. How did you get to Joe's apartment from Father's Five?

A. We walked.

Q. Are you absolutely certain of that?

A. Yes.

Q. Could you have taken a taxicab?

A. No.

Q. Can you describe where Joe's apartment was, relative to Father's Five?

A. Only a few blocks away.

Q. And how long did it take you to walk there?

A. A couple of minutes.

Q. And what did you do when you got to Joe's apartment?

A. We sat and socialized for a while.

Q. Can you describe the demeanor of Julie Connors that night when you saw her?

A. Yes. She was slurring her words and swaying when she walked. She was what I describe as feeling good.

Q. Relative to the other individuals who were present in the apartment, how would you describe her demeanor?

A. She looked like she had more to drink than the rest of us.

Q. Did there come a time when Joe or anyone else left the apartment?

A. Yes, Joe and Ken went out for a while.

Q. And how soon after you arrived did they go out?

A. About an hour.

Q. At what time did you arrive?

A. About 2:05.

Q. Are you sure they left together?

A. Yes.

Q. And, if you know, what was the purpose of their leaving?

A. I am not sure.

Q. Well, was there any talk about cocaine before they left?

A. Yes.

Q. How long did you stay at the apartment after they left?

A. About another hour.

Q. Had Joe or Ken come back before you left?

A. No.

Q. Did you or Julie take any drugs while you were alone after Joe and Ken left?

A. No.

Q. Did you smoke anything?

A. Yes.

Q. What did you smoke?

A. I am not sure, but I think we might have smoked a joint while they were gone.

Q. And when you left, Julie stayed?

A. Yes.

Q. Do you know why she stayed?

A. She was waiting for Joe to come back.

Q. Because she wanted cocaine?

A. Yes.

Q. Can you describe the lighting conditions in that apartment?

A. It was dim.

Q. What was the source of light?

A. I know he had a fireplace going.

Q. Do you remember talking to me in the corridor outside a few minutes ago?

A. Yes.

Q. Do you remember I asked what the light conditions were?

A. I first said dark, but when I think about it, it was more dim.

Q. And could you describe what was in the apartment in terms of furniture?

A. All I remember is a mattress in front of the fireplace.

Q. At any time have you discussed this case with Julie Connors?

A. Slightly.

Q. Did you discuss this case outside of the probable cause hearing in the municipal court?

A. A little bit.

Q. At that time, did Julie Connors ask you a question concerning this case?

A. Yes.

Q. Did she ask you whether or not the four of you took a cab?

A. Yes, she asked me that, and I told her no.

Q. Would it be fair to characterize Julie Connors as being pretty messed up that night?

MR. TUESDAY: Objection.

THE JUDGE: In that form, I will sustain the objection.

Q. Did you tell my investigator when she asked you in August that

Julie Connors was pretty messed up that night?

A. Yes, I could tell she was drinking.

Q. You say she was slurring her words?

A. Yes.

Q. And in her walk, you could tell she was stumbling around?

A. Yes.

Q. Do you dislike Julie Connors?

A. No.

Q. In fact, you are on friendly terms with her, aren't you?

A. Sort of. I don't really know her that well.

MR. CZEK: I have nothing further.

THE JUDGE: Mr. Tuesday.

MR. TUESDAY: Thank you.

THE DEFENSE FOLLOWED LYNN CLEMENTE by putting Joe's girlfriend on the stand to testify that he didn't smoke, since Tuesday had raised the possibility that the murderer had discarded a pack of Marlboro cigarettes at the scene of the murder. In fact, the calling of the girlfriend was intended to convey to the jury that Joe had normal sexual interest and didn't have to brutally rape to satisfy his sexual cravings.

Joe's mother and sister were briefly put on the stand. They were both hardworking, sympathetic, and attractive persons. Red was hopeful that the jury would at least unconsciously find it difficult to perceive such a cold-blooded murderer coming out of that environment.

The defense called several regulars from Father's Five to the witness stand to testify on the issue of Ed Lovett's reputation for not telling the truth. They described his modus operandi as one of demanding money up front for drugs and then never returning with either the drugs or the money. A bartender who had known Lovett for several years testified that he was aware of his reputation as a liar. Mary Katz not only testified as to Lovett's reputation for truth and veracity but also described meeting him the prior Saturday just subsequent to his return from Florida. She related Lovett's statement to her, retracting his original statement to the police concerning Joe's alleged admissions.

The defense's concluding witness was Julie Connors's roommate at the time of the murder, a Molly Rondo. She arrived at court with her mother. She had a sweet, girl-next-door look about her and made an excellent witness. She testified that she and Julie were listening to the six o'clock nightly news the day of the murder, when it was announced that Sasha Lewis had been killed. Julie acted alarmed and said to her, "I was with Sasha Lewis at a party. Sasha left to get drugs, and a guy followed her." Molly further testified that at no time did Julie mention to her that one of the men at the party had returned with blood on him.

Tuesday conducted no cross-examination. Red rested the defendant's case.

The judge informed the jury that the attorneys would now give closing statements. He cautioned them that final argument of counsel was not evidence, and that it was only their memory of the evidence that counted. He continued in stating that the attorneys were advocates for their respective sides and that their argument was meant only to help the jury in their review of the evidence during deliberation.

21

Closing Arguments

MR. CZEK: MR. FOREMAN AND LADIES AND GENTLEMEN OF THE JURY, final argument is that time when counsel for the respective sides have the opportunity to attempt to put the case in some perspective so that when you get in the jury room, it will be easier for you to focus on the key issues in your deliberations.

In a very real sense, the prosecutor has an advantage in final argument. I must argue first; thus, he will have an opportunity to respond to the positions I take, but I will have no chance to address the issues raised by him. So please keep that in mind when you get in the jury room and begin your deliberations.

The clerk read to you the indictment in this case. The judge is going to instruct you that the indictment is absolutely no evidence. It is simply a way of bringing the charge before this court. The defendant has no right to have his lawyer present before the grand jury, and thus there was no right of cross-examination, which is so important to the search for the truth. So, simply said, the indictment itself is not evidence and should in no way affect your deliberations.

Before I begin to discuss in detail what I consider to be the critical evidence in this case, I would briefly like to discuss three important legal concepts. Basically, we're starting from scratch when we hear the first witness. But even that statement isn't correct, because the defendant is clothed with a presumption of innocence, and that presumption remains with him until such time as his guilt has been proved beyond reasonable doubt by the district attorney. So that's the very first principle of law.

Secondly, the burden of proof is on the government. The defendant need not take the stand. He has an absolute state and federal constitutional right not to testify, and he exercised that right. And I'm sure you noticed it. You're thinking to yourself: "Well, if he is innocent, why didn't he take the stand?" However, when you're on the jury, you're bound to follow the instructions of the judge, and the judge is going to instruct you that the defendant has the absolute right not to testify, and that you are not to speculate in any way as to why he may not have taken the stand. There are many reasons why a defendant may choose not to testify and exercise his right not to do so. In fact, in light of the weak case put on by the prosecution, the defendant would be stupid to take the stand. The government is required to prove his guilt. Look at the testimony of Julie Connors and Ed Lovett. That's what their case basically rests on. Are they credible witnesses? Certainly not. They haven't proved their case at all. It's a very weak case with weak witnesses.

In any event, you heard the clerk inform you that the defendant pled not guilty to the charge, so you know his position. And you heard Gus Grazzi inform you as to what the defendant said on November 9, 1979, when interviewed by the police. And basically, his story is consistent with the testimony of the witnesses in the case.

He stated he met a girl with heavy lipstick, a Julie Connors, at Frank 'N Stein's. They went to Father's Five, found some other people, and went back to his apartment. At a certain point, he left to get drugs and later returned to his apartment.

And you noted the operating procedure of Detective Grazzi—how he destroys his notes and has a single piece of paper for forty-five minutes of conversation. So how reliable is his report in terms of the accuracy of times contained therein?

So, we have discussed the presumption of innocence and the burden of proof. Now we come to perhaps the most important principle of all, and that's the concept of reasonable doubt. What does that mean? The judge will instruct you on the technical meaning, that proof beyond a reasonable doubt means proof to a moral certainty. Mr. Tuesday is going to, I'm sure, comment on the fact that it doesn't mean proof beyond all possible doubt. The best way to get a grasp of this concept is to discuss what it isn't. Some of you may have sat on civil cases. The standard of proof in a civil case is the preponderance of the evidence. So, if you're convinced—

THE JUDGE: I don't want you to charge the jury. That's my function.

Red thought to himself, "The bastard had no need to interrupt my argument."

MR. CZEK: Your Honor, I do not intend to infringe in any way. I only wish to briefly touch on the difference between these two standards.

By the way, the judge's interruption reminds me of an important point. When I make reference to the law, I do only in an effort to put the facts in proper perspective. The judge's instruction, as to what the law is, is what counts. If there is a question as to a conflict between my statement of law and his, his statement is the statement that you take to the jury room and apply.

Now, to get back to my original point, we have in a civil case a burden of proof by a preponderance of the evidence, so that if the plaintiff convinced you by over 50 percent that he has carried his burden, you find for the plaintiff. But liberty's not at stake in a civil case. It is in a criminal case, so we have a much stronger burden. It's not a preponderance of the evidence. It's proof beyond a reasonable doubt. And I suggest to you that even if the preponderance of evidence standard were to be applied in this case, you would be required, nevertheless, to find for the defendant. They haven't even overcome that burden, let alone met the proof beyond a reasonable doubt test.

At the extreme, let's assume that one of you says, "Well, they have some evidence here. There's some pieces, but they don't quite fit together. Julie Connors is not a very good witness. Nor is Lovett, but if we really push it, maybe they just get over the 50 percent hurdle." Maybe someone will argue that line. But the immediate response is that the burden that the government must overcome in this case is one of reasonable doubt. If there is one reasonable doubt, you have to acquit. We're not talking about balancing the scales.

And before I discuss the various witnesses and the critical testimony from those witnesses, one must emphasize these important constitutional principles. Our fathers and our brothers died on the beaches of Normandy and the barren peninsula of Bataan in order to safeguard our constitutional democracy and to keep alive our Bill of Rights. But their sacrifices will be absolutely in vain if you treat these principles that the judge is going to instruct you on as mere empty words. Unless you apply them conscientiously to the facts of this case, you will not be doing your duty, and will do an injustice to all the sacrifices that have been made.

You should apply these principles the same way you would apply them if we had a Boston banker on trial, or someone from your own community, or a neighbor. Look at it this way: If your good friend or good neighbor were on trial, wouldn't you want these principles conscientiously applied to the facts? I'm sure you would, and I'm confident from observing you take seriously your responsibilities in listening to this case that you will apply these important principles, which are so critical to the conservation of our way of government to this particular defendant, Joe.

Now, let me direct myself to the testimony of the witnesses in this case. The first witness dealt with the nature of the crime, and let me say right now that the defense does not contest that this was an ugly murder and a terrible tragedy. But what purpose did all these inflammatory pictures serve? They simply brought home that point that no one is contesting. I hope you don't spend a lot of time in the jury room on that uncontested issue. And, as His Honor instructed you when some of these gory pictures came before you, you're not to let pity for the victim interfere with your examination of the critical question. And what is that? It's very simple: Has the government proved beyond a reasonable doubt that Joe committed the murder? Go directly to the testimony of the critical witnesses, Connors and Lovett, because the case rises or falls with those two.

Before I discuss their testimony in detail, let's briefly look at Jonathan Williams's testimony. How does that fit in? The government will argue that they have Sasha Lewis leaving Williams's apartment on Marlborough Street between 4:00 and 4:30. And why would that be? Because they're positioning the person that came out of that cab at a spot between Marlborough and Beacon Streets on Massachusetts Avenue as between 4:15 and 4:30. But keep in mind that Marlborough Street is a one-way street heading away from Massachusetts Avenue. Williams testified that Sasha made a telephone call before she left. All the evidence is that Sasha took cabs, particularly at night. Now, of course, there's the possibility that she didn't take a cab. But the greater probability is that certainly she took a cab and that that cab took her on Marlborough Street toward her home and away from the man left off by the cab. Now, the government's going to argue that Sasha Lewis didn't take a cab, but that's pure speculation. Let's assume, and this is only an assumption, that Joe was, in fact, in that cab. So what? What does that say? You have Sasha leaving the apartment on Marlborough Street and heading away from Massachusetts Avenue, and you have another cab stopping at the corner of Beacon Street and Massachusetts Avenue.

How can you connect them up? The only possible way to do it is through speculation. But you're not here to speculate. There's no evidence that Sasha and Joe met.

So, there's a strong possibility that Sasha took a cab directly to her home after leaving Jonathan Williams's place. Furthermore, there is evidence that the door to her apartment was open when the police arrived there, in spite of the fact she always locked it. And the evidence that there was no money at the crime scene, although she had a lot of money earlier that night, raises the distinct possibility that the motive for her death was robbery, perhaps by someone who awaited her at her apartment.

You had the testimony of the cab driver, Sidney Goldberg, relative to the waybill submitted in evidence. It had two men being picked up at Joe's place. But is there any time on that waybill when these gentlemen were supposedly picked up? And there's no identification of Joe Grady being in that cab. Furthermore, the two individuals are described as sober and gentlemanly. So the prosecution has this theory that Grady was at his apartment at 4:00, but then we have Julie Connors saying he was gone for a while. And how do they handle that inconsistency? You can come up with all kinds of speculative theories as to what happened, but you can't rely on those. For you must only convict on proof beyond a reasonable doubt, and the government simply doesn't have it.

So, once again, even assuming for the sake of argument that Joe was in that cab, it doesn't get the government anywhere. It simply puts Joe and Sasha in the same general vicinity.

And then there is the critical question of time of death. The medical examiner wouldn't give a straight answer on it. He works for the state and comes up now with a time of death at trial that contradicts the pre-4:00 a.m. time of death he gave over the phone to Detective Lou Levitt shortly after the murder. Now, the prosecution's theory is that the medical examiner's statement to Lou that death occurred approximately between 1:30 and no later than 4:00 a.m.

doesn't mean what it says. But "no later" would have absolutely no place on that document if the "approximately" referred to more than the 1:30 time. You don't say approximately 1:30 and no later than 4:00 if the 4:00 is "approximately." No later than 4:00 is no later than 4:00. Do not forget that his call to Lou came after he had taken into account the other factor in determining time of death, which is the state of rigor mortis. So which is more accurate, and on which should you depend more: his statement shortly after the murder, or his testimony here, where he knows the theory of the government's case? He works for the state, and he comes in and now pushes the time of death forward so that it is consistent with the state's theory of Joe Grady as the murderer.

Enough of Jonathan Williams. Let's discuss Richard Raymond. A couple of days before the murder, he pulls up the blouse of Sasha Lewis, exposing her breasts. Right after the murder, he calls up Donna Cressey and says, "Leave my name out of this." We have his testimony of the incident in the bar relative to the man who had broken in Sasha's door. Don't these factors raise a reasonable doubt in your mind as to whether Joe Grady is the murderer?

Now, let me discuss Julie Connors and Ed Lovett, because when you come right down to it, the government's case rises or falls on the testimony of these two witnesses. How should we analyze the testimony of Julie Connors? How are you going to handle her? I suggest you approach her this way: Put the issue of hypnosis aside initially, and look at her in terms of how well her credibility stands up, apart from the application of the expert testimony as to the effect of hypnosis. The way I see it, there are seven major basic problems with her testimony, each of which raises a reasonable doubt as to whether she's a credible witness. Number one is the question of her sobriety that night. She starts drinking in the Back Bay Lounge. She says, "Oh, I just had a couple of drinks." Then she goes to Frank 'N Stein's alone for a couple more drinks. But she claims she is sober when she goes to the party at Joe's place. But what does Lynn say?

Lynn says Julie was slurring her speech. And she adds, "Julie was wobbling about. She was unsteady on her feet."

So, we have Julie Connors who, while not being absolutely drunk, certainly appears to be very close to it. And what about her statement under hypnosis as to what she was drinking in December when Joe came into Father's Five? According to her, she had drunk fourteen strong gin and tonics. I suggest that the evidence indicates we have an alcoholic here, apart from any other problems she may have had. And that fact alone should raise in your mind real problems as to how reliable her testimony is on the issue of what happened in the wee hours of that fateful morning.

Let's get to the second major problem with her testimony— drugs. She said she was a regular smoker of marijuana and she was into pills. She admitted she may have smoked marijuana the afternoon before the murder. And Lynn testified that they may have smoked a reefer in the apartment that evening. She conceded she became a heroin addict after the date of this alleged murder. She also testified that she was a regular user of cocaine before the twenty-ninth day of October. Note in particular her statement that when you shoot cocaine, you sometimes got blood on your arm. Factor that testimony into your analysis.

But we have many other major problems with this witness, Julie Connors. What about the lighting in Joe's apartment that night? What did Lynn say? That it was dim and that the only light was from the fireplace. So you have a serious question of lighting and the ability of someone who was even sober and not on drugs to accurately perceive, remember, and describe what he or she observed that night.

Then we have the question of the contact lenses. Did she have them in or not the night of the murder? But you remember the transcripts of the hypnotic session: "I'm seeing a movie. It's Robert Redford. I can't see without my contact lenses." Did Detective Ripley at any time interrupt and say, "Wait a minute. I'll get your contact lenses?" Wouldn't that have been the normal thing to do if, in fact, she was referring to not having contacts in during the hypnosis? You also have Detective Ripley stating that a witness under hypnosis has his or her eyes closed. And Ripley conceded Julie had her eyes closed, so she wouldn't have any use at all for contact lenses. Her argument is: "I didn't have time to put them in." But you heard the testimony of Detective Grazzi, that after her initial statement on February 1, before hypnosis, she was given time to go home and freshen up. She certainly had plenty of time to put them in.

The point here is that there's a reasonable doubt right there as to the defendant's guilt. You can't rule out that Julie Connors didn't have contact lenses in the night of the murder. You don't have to come to an absolute conclusion as to whether she did or not. But if you can't say for certain that she did, then the government has a real problem. And maybe that explains why her statements are so inconsistent. If, in fact, she didn't have those lenses in, then it's clear that she didn't see very well. In combination with the drinking, drugs, and dim lighting, she's not going to see much of anything and be able to, with any accuracy, relate what she's seen.

Then we get to the fifth major problem. If, in fact, Joe had come back with blood all over him, is Julie not going to ask any questions and then make love to him? Does that make sense? The judge will instruct you to use your common sense too. You're supposed to analyze the evidence in light of your own experiences and your basic common sense.

The sixth major problem is as follows: We have the testimony of Molly Rondo, Julie's roommate. Julie testified, "I told Molly the day of the murder that I saw blood on Joe." We call in Molly and she absolutely denies mention of any blood. And what else did she say? She says, "Julie said that she was with Sasha Lewis that night, and Sasha left to get drugs." But Julie had testified she was not out with Sasha that night. Isn't that the absolute crushing blow to the government's case? Are you good people going to give one iota of credibility to Julie Connors after hearing that testimony? I suggest there's just absolutely no way you can, if in good faith you're looking closely at these witnesses and analyzing their credibility.

The last major problem to keep in mind is the inconsistencies in the testimony of Julie Connors. She says, "We took a taxi," under hypnosis. Every other witness says no taxi. And here she now agrees she took a taxi but only after discussing the question with Lynn before a pretrial hearing. She said under hypnosis: "Three people went to Joe's apartment." The other evidence is that four people went. She said in her statement under hypnosis that the defendant was wearing a blue sweater, but now she has him wearing a T-shirt. She has Joe wearing blue and white sneakers, and when asked whether she's sure, she says, "Well, he was wearing jeans, so I assumed he was wearing sneakers." She's confabulated. She's filling in those spaces where there is a memory gap. She's making assumptions. But did she tell Detective Ripley that she only assumed that? No. She stated it as a fact.

So, we have these several different inconsistencies that in themselves are very disturbing. Ladies and gentlemen, let me move on. I hope I've given you some basis for focusing your discussion in regard to the credibility of Julie Connors. Let's turn to Ed Lovett now.

Before I get to him, let me briefly discuss the significance of hypnosis. I reemphasize that you don't necessarily even have to get to the issue of hypnosis, for there are ample grounds apart from the influence of hypnosis for you to conclude that Julie Connors isn't a credible witness. But then, if you need icing on the cake, so to speak, analyze the testimony of the expert witness. Note his demeanor. Look at his background. Dr. Ox testified that once the witness has been put under hypnosis, irrevocable damage has been done, for the witness's memory has been polluted, and his testimony thus is not necessarily reliable. Hypnosis is a very suggestive process. It lowers critical judgment. Once the witness has been hypnotized, he can't separate out his memory before the induction from the end product. It's all one memory now, including the confabulations and the filling in.

There are other problems with the hypnosis. There was no tape recording of the pre-hypnotic phase, where there is often suggestiveness unwittingly conveyed to the witness. Detective Ripley conceded he had no intent of even tape-recording the post-hypnotic period after the person has come out of hypnosis, even though Dr. Ox pointed out the danger of suggestiveness there too. And there is the transcript that's not complete. And isn't that disturbing? How credible is the government's position that there was only one minute left on the tape when the plug was "accidentally pulled?" You heard what Dr. Ox said relative to Ripley's hypnotic technique immediately prior to the sudden ending of the tape. When he got Miss Connors to focus on the glass of ice in front of her, that suggests he was beginning to launch into a whole new area and that, in Dr. Ox's opinion, it was highly unlikely that he was coming to a close.

Let us now move to a discussion of the testimony of Ed Lovett. Do we have a credible witness, one who wasn't impeached and on whom we can rely? I see five major problems with Lovett's testimony. First, you have the fact that he gave this statement, in which he alleges that Joe made certain admissions, when he's under arrest in the police station on a serious charge, to wit: extortion. Now, how reliable is a statement when one gives it under those conditions? That's the question you must pose. And note he didn't mention anything at that time about the disparaging statement that Joe allegedly made in Father's Five concerning Sasha Lewis. And then you have the fact that he has pending cases in several different courts. He testified that it was his understanding that these courts would be told about his testimony in this case before disposing of his cases. And we have Detective Grazzi finally admitting that the Boston Police took Lovett around after he made his statement against Joe to clear up defaults at the various courts. That's problem area number two. In this respect, note also that Lovett referred to Detective Grazzi as "Gus" and described him as a "nice guy." What does that say about how the cops are treating Lovett?

Look at the reputation testimony relative to Lovett. And why is that important? Because in determining whether you're going to believe someone, or how much credibility you will give his testimony, it is important to know the reputation of the person. And what did we hear as to Lovett's reputation in the community where he basically functioned? On direct examination, he told you he was employed, but when cross-examined, he reluctantly conceded he had not worked for the circus. So, it wasn't correct of him to say that he was presently employed. In any event, we don't have a businessman, where we can go to his business community and establish his reputation. And who knows where he lived?

So what do you do? You go to the place where he hung out, and Father's Five was that place. And what's his reputation there? You heard the witnesses testifying as to his reputation.

The fourth problem is the $200 check. Lovett thought he would get the money. But Joe takes it all. Lovett is angry with Joe. Right there you have a motive explaining Lovett's testimony.

And then we get to the last problem—the testimony of Mary Katz. In fact, Ed Lovett testified that he told Katz that he lied when he said Joe made those admissions and that he was willing to pay the price. He claims now that he made such a retraction only because he was "afraid of those girls." Well, he wasn't afraid to go into Father's Five that night, was he? You think he would have been, but apparently he wasn't. We have corroboration from Mary Katz as to the making of that statement.

So, once again, will you believe Lovett farther than you can kick him? Would you convict your own worst enemy on the testimony of Lovett and Connors?

However, let's assume, just for argument, that you do believe Lovett. Then let us look at the alleged statement made by the defendant to him. So Lovett is in the bar with his friend Joe, and Joe says, "That girl is an asshole. She wouldn't go out with me." Well, how often do a couple of guys in a bar make comments like that? Use your common sense. How many times has one guy said to another guy, "That girl is an asshole," or words to that effect? Does that make him out to be a murderer? Does it follow that because Joe said Sasha Lewis is an asshole, if he even said it, then he's the murderer? So, that statement doesn't improve the government's case even if you believe it was made.

What about the alleged statements of Joe in the car? Everyone knew that Sasha Lewis had been murdered. How many times have you heard one guy say to another, when he's mad, "I'm going to kill you, Mack. I'm going to do a number on you"? There was wide coverage of this murder. People knew about it. And then what's the next question? It's a leading question from Lovett. He says, "I bet you killed Sasha Lewis." And Joe allegedly responds, "Yeah, I did." Bragging among two guys. Does it mean that he actually killed Sasha Lewis? I suggest that even if, for some strange reason, you believe Lovett, and believe that Joe made those statements, it doesn't necessarily follow at all that he is the murderer. In any event, isn't it strange that Lovett didn't ask for details if in fact Joe made the statements? Wouldn't it be normal to ask for details at that point, if in fact Joe had made the statement?

So then we get to the testimony of the chemists. If you haven't enough at this point to acquit, and to acquit quickly, this testimony should absolutely resolve the issue. It's not contested that the defendant has type AB blood and was a secretor. There is evidence of seminal fluid in the material that the medical examiner obtained by swab from the anus. However, the medical examiner now claims he didn't take the material from the anus, but rather from the perineum, which is the area between the vagina and the anus. But what did he say in his original report as to where he obtained the sample and what did he write on the sample jar? "Material from anus." Thus, the evidence seems to be overwhelming that the sample came from the anus. And what does that tell us? Simply that Joe could not have deposited the semen in the victim's anus since he is a type AB secretor, and no type AB blood was found in the semen.

You heard the defense expert's testimony that there was a substantial amount of semen. Mr. Tuesday made a big point of the fact that the defense expert examined a different portion of the material. But I hope you weren't misled by that. Sure, he examined a different portion, but it was the same material. Thus, one must conclude that argument is a red herring. In any event, our expert had enough material to clearly determine that it was semen and to determine the blood type therein.

Now, there's testimony from the state chemist: "I can only conclude the defendant was not the depositor, if you assume there was only one depositor." But what was said by the defense expert, William Wise, a man who specializes in the area, who has impressive credentials, and who has written many articles on the subject? He said, "It doesn't matter whether there are two or three depositors. If any of them had an AB blood type, you would find evidence of the B." That makes sense. It's a very simple idea. If you're a secretor, you leave traces of your blood type, provided there's an ample amount of semen. And even if there are two or three people contributing, the B is still going to be there if the depositor had an AB blood type.

So, there you have it. If that does not create a reasonable doubt as to the guilt of Joe, I don't know what would, particularly in light of all the other problems the government has with their own witnesses. And, of course, the burden's on the government, as I said before. They didn't even carry their burden with their own witnesses; and then, on top of that, we have the testimony of the defense chemist, which exculpates the defendant.

In conclusion, I have every confidence you will freely discuss this case and candidly express your views to each other. But in the final analysis, there's no passing the buck. Each one of you in your own heart and mind must come to your own determination on the facts and apply the law as laid down by the judge.

Wouldn't it be terrible if you made a mistake? If the judge makes a mistake on an issue of law, it can be appealed. But if you make a mistake on the facts, that's it. It's final, and nothing can be done about it. What if, three months from now, in the middle of the night, you wake up and say, "Oh. I think I made a mistake." It's too late to correct it, and a terrible injustice will have occurred.

The issue is clear. The government has not proved, as is its burden, the guilt of Joe beyond a reasonable doubt. Their witnesses are weak. Julie Connors is not credible. Ed Lovett is not credible. And the testimony of the defense chemist, in and of itself, creates a reasonable doubt.

I am confident that, in the highest traditions of this Commonwealth, you will return the only verdict consistent with the evidence—the only verdict possible if you conscientiously apply the law to the facts, and that is a verdict of not guilty.

THE JUDGE: Thank you, Mr. Czek.

MR. TUESDAY: May I proceed, Your Honor?

THE JUDGE: Yes.

MR. TUESDAY: May it please the court and ladies and gentlemen of the jury, before I go into the facts of the case in an attempt to persuade you that the Commonwealth has proven its case beyond a reasonable doubt, I would like at this time to thank His Honor for providing the Commonwealth with a fair trial in this particular case. I would also like to commend my brother for fighting vigorously for his client's rights. But most of all, I would like to thank each and every member of the jury for listening very attentively during this long and sometimes difficult trial, in that we had to work Saturdays and had to go beyond the time limits that we usually sit as jurors in Suffolk County. I commend you for giving both the Commonwealth and the defendant a fair trial.

Red Czek leaned over to his young assistant and remarked, "Tuesday is going too far with this flattery. It will get him nowhere. I see the jury is turned off. The bastard is also implying Joe is guilty, but that I deserve a medal for representing him anyway. I should have objected. Damn him."

My brother's closing argument suggests to you the greatest conspiracy since Watergate. He argues that Detective Grazzi has destroyed notes because he wanted to hide something in this particular case. He tells you the medical examiner, Dr. Richmond, a man who has performed more than eight thousand autopsies in the Commonwealth of Massachusetts, lied on the stand. He claims the police hypnotist in this case destroyed a portion of the tape of the hypnotic session in order to hide evidence from you. According to Mr. Czek, everyone in this case has conspired. It's a giant conspiracy perpetrated by the Commonwealth of Massachusetts to accuse Joe Grady of the murder of Sasha Lewis.

There's an old saying among older lawyers in this Commonwealth. It goes something like this: "When the law is against you, you argue the facts; when the facts are against you, you argue the law; but when the law and the facts are both against you, you make a lot of noise." And that's exactly what Red Czek has done in this case. He has smoke-screened the key issues.

MR. CZEK: Objection.

THE JUDGE: Sustained.

MR. TUESDAY: The defense wants you to believe that Richard Raymond is the murderer in this particular case, because he pulled up Sasha Lewis's blouse approximately a week prior to her death, exposing her breasts. But are you buying that? I hope not.

Now, let me make an observation, because I don't want to usurp His Honor's function. He gets paid to make rulings in this case. He gets paid to give you the law, and I'm not about to tread upon his function but lightly. What "beyond a reasonable doubt" does not mean is that the Commonwealth must prove its case to a mathematical certainty. Nor does the Commonwealth have to prove its case beyond all doubt, because if it were held to such a heavy burden, there would be very few, if any, convictions in the Commonwealth of Massachusetts in criminal cases.

I told you at the outset, when I rose before you in my opening statement, that there would not be witnesses who would come in and testify that they observed Joe Grady take a blunt instrument and crush the skull of Sasha Lewis eight times. I never promised you that. I told you it would be like a puzzle, and each witness would add to a piece of that puzzle, and that after that puzzle was completed, you would see the face of Joe Grady as the murderer of Sasha Lewis. And I suggest to you that the Commonwealth has achieved its burden of persuading you beyond a reasonable doubt that Joe Grady is that person.

Now, Mr. Foreman and ladies and gentlemen of the jury, there is no greater right that a human being enjoys than the right to life. There is no greater wrong than to deprive a person of his or her existence. It's the ultimate wrong. No state can function and exist if it does not protect its citizens and punish those who illegally take a human life. Whether you're an individual of bad character, or whether you're a person who has contributed a great deal to our society as an outstanding citizen, in the eyes of the law, there is no distinction as to one's right to life.

Of course, a person should not be convicted unless the Commonwealth proves beyond a reasonable doubt that person's guilt. I ask you to use your common sense, as I know you will, when you go upstairs to deliberate. Because if you went upstairs only looking for a doubt, then the lawless people in our society would come to think that conviction would be very remote and that life would be very cheap today. I know that when you deliberate, you will use your common sense and everyday life experiences in deciding this particular case.

What do you think the real purpose was of calling Mrs. Grady and the defendant's sister? Sure, they're nice people. Was it so important for the defense to put on the stand Mrs. Grady, the mother, and his sister just to testify that Joe does not smoke Marlboros or doesn't smoke at all, or was there another specific purpose, another reason for calling Mrs. Grady and the sister to testify?

MR. CZEK: Objection, Your Honor.

THE JUDGE: I'll allow it. I assume he's going to suggest to the jury that it's for them to decide.

MR. TUESDAY: We had testimony from Dr. Richmond, the medical examiner, one of the so-called conspirators in this case, in an attempt to convict Mr. Grady. He gave you, based upon his numerous years of experience as the medical examiner, his opinion as to the approximate time of death. He said he did certain temperature taking. He observed rigor mortis in the body, and based upon his experience and knowledge, he formed an opinion as to the approximate time that Sasha Lewis met her death. He testified that it was some hours—I believe five and a half to eight hours—prior to eleven o'clock when he took certain temperatures of the liver. And if you take that statement that the medical examiner gave to you, the five and a half to eight hours, you have a period of time from, I suggest to you, 3:30 in the morning until 7:00, when the death could have occurred. And I ask you, when you go out and deliberate, to keep that time frame in mind.

Did the medical examiner, Dr. Richmond, appear to be an honest person, or was he evading questions, as Mr. Czek wants you to believe? Does the medical examiner have a stake in the outcome of this particular case? Is he conspiring with me to change the time of his opinion as to the time of death? I leave that for you to decide, ladies and gentlemen of the jury. Ask yourselves whether Dr. Richmond is also a part of this great conspiracy that my brother believes is being perpetrated, to try to trick and persuade you that Joe Grady is the killer of Sasha Lewis.

MR. CZEK: Objection, Your Honor.

THE JUDGE: I think the reference to conspiracy has been overdone already, and I would suggest, Mr. Tuesday, you go on to something else.

MR. TUESDAY: Let me now discuss Julie Connors. Miss Connors testified as to what she recalls occurring on the evening of October 29 and the early morning hours of October 30, 1979. She made statements to Detective Grazzi, and she made a statement under hypnosis.

Ask yourselves whether or not you're going to say the exact same thing on so many different occasions when one is asked certain questions concerning a particular thing. Are you going to be that consistent? Are you going to be that accurate as to what you tell a different person on different occasions? Was Miss Connors wrong when she said she went to Joe Grady's apartment? Was she wrong when she told you that Joe left the apartment after being there for some time? Sure, Julie Connors may have been inconsistent on some things, but as to the most important part of her testimony—in this case her own statement relative to the time that Mr. Grady absented himself from his own apartment and the fact that when he returned he had blood on him—she was consistent about that. For what purpose in the whole wide world would Miss Connors want to come in and testify falsely under oath against Joe Grady?

What axe did Miss Connors have to grind against this defendant, such that she would state that she observed blood on Mr. Grady when he returned if it weren't true? Why would she make up the fact that when she saw Joe Grady return to the apartment, his eyes were bloodshot, he was slightly sweating, he was tired, and his pants were ripped, when they weren't when he left? She indicated to you where the blood was located: on his arms, neck, and shirt. She told you that she used heroin and that she smoked marijuana and drank. She placed her life in front of you.

Let me now discuss Mr. Ed Lovett, the fellow who testified wearing a Jethro Tull shirt, dungarees, and work boots. He told you that he was a friend of Mr. Grady for approximately five years and that they socialized frequently together. Mr. Czek wants you to believe that one of the reasons that Ed Lovett is perjuring himself in this case is because of the fight over $200. Did Mr. Lovett come in and perjure himself because of a $200 dispute? He also wants you to believe that Mr. Lovett is testifying because of the pending criminal cases against him and his fear that he must testify to avoid jail. He's denied that any promises, rewards, or inducements have been made to him. I concede that Mr. Lovett is not the most upstanding citizen you have seen in the Commonwealth of Massachusetts in your life experience, but it's a different world out there, ladies and gentlemen of the jury. Ed Lovett wasn't arrested for a rape, murder, or assault with the intent to murder. He testified he had some motor vehicle violations, as well as a breaking and entering case pending. He also told you that there was a pending case charging an attempt to extort money from a person who had paid him to destroy his motor vehicle, the same motor vehicle that he was in with Mr. Grady when the incriminating statement was made by Mr. Grady. What else did Mr. Lovett tell you? He testified that seven to ten days prior to the murder of Sasha Lewis that man said (*indicating the defendant*) that she was "a fucking cunt who wouldn't go out with me." Lovett also told you that while they were in that red Mustang, Grady said that he wanted to drive the car. Lovett refused. So Grady said: "Pull the car over or I'll pull a Sasha Lewis on you." Lovett responded: "You killed her, didn't you?" And what did Grady say? "Yeah, so what? I'm getting out of here. They're going to hang me on the nineteenth anyway." Lovett conceded he was "no angel," but after hearing what his good friend Grady had said, he felt obligated to contact the police.

Now, you heard from other witnesses on this case, and I know it has been a long day, because after I sit down, you have approximately one hour and fifteen minutes after recess to hear from Justice Regan as to the law. So, I'll try to pick up the pace and go through some of these other witnesses.

Contrary to the opinion of Mr. Czek, the case does not rise or fall only upon the testimony of Miss Connors and Mr. Lovett. There are other pieces of the puzzle that I suggest to you. What about Sidney Goldberg, the taxi driver, who tells you that he received a call to go to 486 Beacon Street, where he went, and that he picked up two persons and took them over to 31 Peterborough Street? They went up the stairs, and only one came down after being up there a minute or two, and he drove him back to the corner of Massachusetts Avenue and Beacon Street. And what did Mr. Goldberg testify to as to the approximate time he dropped off the man we suggest was Grady? About 4:15. And isn't it coincidental that that's the approximate time that Mr. Williams indicates that Sasha Lewis left his apartment? Is this but another coincidence, that he lived in the same approximate area where the body was found?

Is it another coincidence that Joe Grady worked in the area as a construction worker, and that he was working in the building next to the building where Sasha Lewis was murdered?

Is it a coincidence that two to three days after the finding of Sasha Lewis's body, he was walking out with a shirt rolled up with blood all over it? Mr. Grady appeared slightly surprised when observed by Mr. Brown, and without Mr. Brown's asking him where he got the blood on his shirt, Mr. Grady volunteered: "I was in a fight with three guys."

And is it a coincidence that Julie Connors saw blood on his neck, blood on his arms, blood on his shirt, bloodshot eyes, and that he appeared tired? Who's kidding whom? And was it just another coincidence that Grady was kidding when he said that he killed Sasha Lewis?

My brother, Mr. Czek, in his closing argument, has made much ado about all the constitutional rights that Grady has. But Sasha Lewis had certain rights too. But this defendant took away two most precious rights that any human being has.

As he made the statement, he whirled around and pointed at the defendant.

Mr. Czek: Objection, Your Honor.

The judge ignored Red.

Mr. Tuesday: The right to life and the right to make peace with her Maker. She was deprived of both by this animal.

Mr. Czek: Objection!

Red bounced out of his seat as he screamed his objection.

The Judge: Sustained.

Mr. Tuesday: It's very easy to want to give a break to somebody. It's not easy being jurors to do our duty when we must pass judgment upon our fellow man. But if you go upstairs to deliberate, and because either you liked Joe Grady's mother or his sister, you make your decision based upon some sympathy toward them, then you endorse lawlessness. Since you're the voice of Suffolk County, if you endorse lawlessness, then you endorse a lawless society. I have every confidence you will not do that in rendering your verdict.

The Judge: Thank you, Mr. Tuesday.

22

Jury Deliberations
and Verdict

THE JUDGE CHOSE A FOREPERSON AND INSTRUCTED THE JURY THAT HIS
vote counted no more than that of the other jurors, and that his role
was to direct the discussions and see that everyone had a chance to
give his or her opinion. He reminded them that a verdict of guilt
or innocence must be unanimous. The clerk then put a slip with
each juror's name, except for the foreman's, into the traditional
small wooden barrel. There would be sixteen jurors seated, but four
would be alternates. They would be necessary because of sickness,
a death in the family, or any other valid reason. He spun the barrel
and pulled out, one at a time, a slip with the name of a juror.
The last four selected did not show it but naturally were greatly
disappointed to have sat through the whole trial but not be a part

279

of the deliberating jury. Each juror was given a copy of the judge's instructions, and the foreperson was given a copy of the verdict form. The judge instructed jurors not to indicate how numerically divided they were if they submitted questions to the judge during deliberations. The jurors were then sent out to deliberate.

The foreperson asked for a straw ballot to see where the jury stood in spite of the judge's suggestion that they not do so until they had discussed the issues for a while and everyone who wished to enter the discussions did so. The judge did not want the jurors to harden their position early, such that it would later make it more difficult for them to listen to opposing arguments.

The straw vote was eleven to one for conviction. The only hold-out was an older woman who argued that hypnosis was junk science and that blood type eliminated the defendant as the killer. Most of the others pointed out the nature of the crime, the statement the defendant made to the cops, the failure to exclude the defendant as the depositor of the semen, since the semen sample that excluded him did not come from the rectum, and the testimony of Julie Connors that revealed blood on the body of the defendant shortly after the murder.

One juror stated: "Why would he be a defendant if he were not guilty?" The rest of the jurors did not speak up to remind the juror that there was such a thing as the "presumption of innocence" and "proof beyond a reasonable doubt." Another juror chimed in, "Fuck the Constitution. He is guilty as hell. The defense lawyer is full of shit."

The lone holdout realized she would have to explain her position very well if she was to convince the others that there was such a thing as the burden of proof beyond a reasonable doubt. Another juror in a business suit entered the discussion: "Why didn't he testify if he was so innocent?" The lone holdout juror responded that the judge had told them not to consider his failure to testify or use it in any way in their deliberations. Another juror piped in, "Oh, hell, we do what we want. We do not have to account to anyone for what we do." The holdout continued to argue that the whole case rested on the credibility of Julie Connors and Ed Lovett: "How can we have confidence in a verdict based on the hypnosis of Connors and the long criminal record and bias of Lovett?"

The foreperson called for another straw vote. The jury split was now six to six. The original holdout continued to express her case for acquittal: "How can we ignore Grazzi's destruction of his notes?" She pressed her fellow jurors who still wanted a conviction by repeating the three constitutional principles that were supposed to be applied to their consideration of facts: presumed innocent until the government proves beyond a reasonable doubt the guilt of the defendant. She felt she now had the six holdouts on the run. She knew that Julie Connors was the key to the government's case. She continued: "How credible can she be when you combine these facts with the unreliability of the hypnosis?"

The animated discussions continued for some time. Finally, there was only one holdout for guilt. He stubbornly held to his position, stating, "We'll be here until hell freezes over, because I am not going to vote not guilty." He had not given up trying to convince the others of Joe's guilt.

The rest of the jury would not have a hung jury, if they could help it. They continued to hammer away at the juror's theory of guilt. The youngest juror, a student, spoke for the first time: "Do you really believe a person can remember better under hypnosis? Look at the defendant's expert, Dr. Ox. Who did the government have as its expert? No one except the police detective conducting the hypnosis. How unbiased could he be, when his job depended on the reliability of the science of hypnosis?"

While the jury deliberated, Red and Susie could do nothing but wait nervously for the verdict. As they sat in the corridor, every time a clerk or court officer passed by, Red would ask: "Is there a verdict?"

He was conflicted. In a way, he wanted a verdict quickly, because he knew that a quick verdict was usually a defense verdict. On the other hand, he feared a verdict of guilty, and did not want the court officer to come out to tell them there was a verdict. He actually wished for a question from the jury, because that would put off the dreaded decision. The anxiety increased, as a question could reveal what way the jury was leaning.

If they came back with a request that the concept of "reasonable doubt" be defined, the defense could be hopeful of a favorable verdict. However, if the jury asked to have the definition of premeditation or malice on the murder charge be given again, Red would be concerned about a possible conviction.

As Red was heading toward the men's room, a court officer emerged from the jury room and headed toward the exit, followed by the jurors. He wondered what that was all about, as he had never seen that before. He asked the clerk, who was sitting at his place in the courtroom. The clerk did not know the answer but surmised they might be going out for a smoke.

Red knew that all the jurors could not be smokers, so he decided to find out. He left the building and soon found the jurors spread out in the courthouse garden, talking among themselves under the watchful eyes of the court officer. Red tried to determine who was talking to whom, in an effort to determine which jurors were leaning toward a defense verdict and vice versa. He looked for the youngest juror, who he believed was pro-defendant, so to speak, to determine who might be of the same view in the deliberations. He was conversing with an older female, but Red did not know which way she was leaning.

He had mixed feelings about his observations. The young, somewhat quirky juror was not speaking with the middle-aged man who sat in seat twelve, next to the young man. Red had observed during the trial that they were both looking at him and Joe several times. None of the other jurors made similar eye contact. But Red detected a slight smile from the young man.

The jury reached no verdict on the first day of deliberations, without even asking questions of the judge to clarify the instructions. Red ran into some jurors as he was waiting in line to pay for his parking ticket. One juror was behind him, and Red momentarily thought he should maybe move aside and let the juror go ahead of him. But he thought better of it, as it would look like he was pandering to the juror, and he realized this juror might relay the incident to the other jurors, who might then be critical of him. He knew that in a close case, jurors might unconsciously factor into their decision-making their impression of defense counsel.

On the second day of deliberations, the jury came back with a question: "Could we have the statute that defines murder read to us?" The judge apologized to the jury and stated that in his opinion they would be confused if he read the statute, because it used archaic language that did not track with the language used in the jury instructions.

Shortly thereafter, the jurors came back with another question: "Should we consider the typos in the verdict form in our deliberations?" The judge had to be very careful in giving his answer so as not to offend the jury, as the question was so ridiculous. One can never know what a jury is thinking, and they sometimes ask the strangest questions.

Later in the day, the jury returned with yet another question: "What would happen if they could not agree on the charge?" The answer, of course, was that there would be a hung jury, since the jury must be unanimous as to guilt or innocence. The judge sent the jury back with an instruction to continue deliberations. He did not tell them that a hung jury would mean a mistrial and the case would have to be tried again. Red chose not to object to the judge's handling of the question, as he felt the answer would perhaps put pressure on the jury to reach a hasty verdict. For a hung jury was better than a guilty verdict if you could not get an acquittal.

Red, from long experience, knew that it was impossible to tell what a jury was going to do. Sometimes when he talked to a jury after the verdict, he found out their decision was based on the most inexplicable reasons. So although Red was buoyed by the last question, he did his best to control his optimism.

From time to time, Red visited Joe in the lockup to bring him up to date on what was happening. He was surprised that Joe seemed so calm. He knew Joe had complete trust in him, but he cautioned Joe that one can never tell what a jury would do.

Time marched on. The third day of deliberations was almost complete. It was sixteen hours of deliberation without a verdict, not even a question nor shouting in the jury room. Sometimes during deliberations, jurors' raised voices in argument can be heard, but not with this jury. Red was becoming increasingly concerned and nervous. All day the possibility ran through his head that there would be a hung jury, and then the ordeal of a new trial, where the prosecutor would know the defense case and probably have the advantage. But on the other hand, maybe the transcript at the first trial would provide inconsistencies that could be used to impeach the prosecution witnesses. The other possibility was a conviction, with Joe spending the rest of his life in prison without any chance of parole.

The jury, on the fourth day of deliberations, sent a note to the judge informing him that they were deadlocked. He then instructed them to continue deliberating: "No other jury would be better able to decide this case than you. Listen carefully to the views of those who do not agree with you as to the correct verdict. But you should not change your position just to reach a unanimous verdict if, after further deliberations, you have a conscientious belief in your position."

Shortly thereafter, Red observed a court officer approach the clerk with a piece of paper that appeared to be another note from the jury. The clerk went straight for the door to the judge's chambers. When he returned momentarily, Red sensed that the jury had reached a verdict. He inquired of the clerk if there was a verdict. The response was a "yes." Red's nervousness, already extreme, increased, as he now knew that the moment of truth had arrived. Seasoned counsel can often tell before the verdict is read aloud what it will be by observing the facial expressions of the jurors as they file in. If they all look solemn and/or look away from the defendant, a verdict of guilty is probable. But if any of the jurors cast a glance at the defendant, that could be a good sign for the defendant.

Red could not resist glancing at the jurors. One of them, the young guy who would occasionally peek at Joe during the trial, did quickly survey the general area where Red and Joe were sitting, so Joe's hopes were buoyed.

The court officer took the verdict slip from the foreman and handed it to the clerk, who in turn handed it to the judge. He examined the slip to see that it was procedurally correct, that answers had been given to all the questions posed, and that no ambiguity existed and then handed it back to the clerk so he could return it to the foreman for reading, without indicating by his expression what the verdict was. The clerk addressed the foreperson and asked: "As to the count of murder, does the jury find the defendant innocent or guilty?" The foreperson responded: "Not guilty."

Relief and elation best describe Red's immediate reaction. He placed his hand on Joe's shoulder and with a smile whispered, "Congratulations."

Joe responded, "I told you I was innocent."

EPILOGUE

HYPNOSIS ON TRIAL: ANATOMY OF A MURDER CASE IS A FICTIONALIZED account of the 1979 murder of twenty-four-year-old Susan Marcia Rose, in Boston. I was the defense attorney in the 1981 murder trial that resulted in an acquittal.

In August 2023, as I was nearing completion of this book, a sixty-eight-year-old former convict named John Michael Irmer walked into an FBI field office in Portland, Oregon, and told agents he wanted to confess to the murder of a young woman, her name to him unknown, decades earlier, in Boston. Authorities took a DNA sample from Irmer, which proved to match DNA samples recovered from the crime scene in the murder of Susan Marcia Rose. Boston Suffolk County District Attorney Kevin Hayden stated, "This was a brutal, ice-blooded murder made worse by the fact that a person was charged and tried—and fortunately found not guilty—while the real murderer remained silent until now."

Acknowledgments

The Massachusetts Bay Transportation Authority, which runs the commuter train service in the greater Boston area, deserves a hearty thanks for its contribution to this book. The MBTA normally gets knocked around quite a bit by complaining commuters. However, most of this book was written on the commuter run from Thoreau's Concord and my home to my Boston waterfront law office. Because of the demands of a busy law practice, the book could not have been written without the forty-five minutes' writing time in the morning and evening that the train service provided.

Thanks also to Trisha Thompson, Allison Gillis, and Susan Turner at Small Batch Books for their help in editing, designing, and publishing this novel.

<small>STEPHEN BAYLIS HRONES</small> received his bachelor of arts from Harvard College in 1964 and his law degree from the University of Michigan Law School in 1968. He was a Fulbright scholar in Paris from 1968 to 1969. He has spent his career specializing in criminal law, police misconduct, and military law, including defending U.S. soldiers before American military tribunals in West Germany as a civilian attorney. He has taught at several schools, including Suffolk University Law School; Southern Federal University in Rostov-on-Don, Russia; and Northeastern University School of Law. He has been a television network commentator on ABC, NBC, CNN, Fox, and MSNBC, among others, and has written extensively on criminal law. His books include *How to Try a Criminal Case* (Prentice-Hall, 1982) and *Criminal Practice Handbook* (Lexis Law Pub, 1999).

Hrones has received many accolades throughout his career, including being honored by the National Lawyers Guild in 2009 for protecting the constitutional rights of the poor. He attributes his success to his passion for seeking justice for minorities who have been poorly represented and is proud to have obtained freedom for four innocent men who had wrongfully spent many years in prison. This is his first novel.

www.ingramcontent.com/pod-product-compliance
Lightning Source LLC
Chambersburg PA
CBHW030347020726
47493CB00003B/729